The setting was too intimate. The booth at the
[H]est Hotel way too small. Finus sat too close.
C[as]andra squeezed her thighs together. She smiled
a[...]able at David and Lydia, who both looked
a[...]n. She glanced at the man beside her.
H[...] a rare mood, almost giddy. Tonight he'd
a[...] star[t]ed the Reverend Doctor's bow tie, dark suit,
s[...] shirt. His black leather clad thigh grazed
l[...] against hers.

[...]n of the cloth has no business wearing leath-
e[r]

[...]oing *to hell for my thoughts.*

Except on Sunday

Regena Bryant

Genesis Press, Inc.

INDIGO LOVE STORIES

An imprint of Genesis Press, Inc.
Publishing Company

Genesis Press, Inc.
P.O. Box 101
Columbus, MS 39703

ISBN-13: 978-1-58571-443-8
ISBN-10: 1-58571-443-7
Manufactured in the United States of America

First Edition

Visit us at www.genesis-press.com
or call at 1-888-Indigo-1-4-0

Dedication

To D'Andre in exchange

Acknowledgements

I'd like to thank my immediate family, Paul, Kalen, Micah, and Nicole for giving me the space to finish this book.

Deborah Schumaker at Genesis Press for the opportunity and the gift of Sidney.

Sidney Rickman for the eagle-eyed edits and wonderful guidance.

And my happy family and friends everywhere.

To God be the Glory.

Chapter 1

"Girl, comb your hair and put on some clothes. I just met two fine brothers and they invited us to lunch."

Cassandra glanced up from a mystery novel as her sister, Yolanda, burst into the master bedroom of the summer cottage they shared. "We've been here less than twenty-four hours and you've already met a man. Amazing!"

"No, I met *two* men, and they're waiting. The short one's yours," Yolanda chattered as she pulled a tennis skort and pink T-shirt out of her sister's suitcase. "Put this on. They're waiting on the porch. Come on, get up, let's go!"

"Okay, okay." Cassandra stood up and gazed in a mirror.

"Yes, put on some makeup," Yolanda instructed.

Cassandra grimaced.

"Let's go, okay?"

Cassandra had come to Michiana to relax, not chase men. Now she would have to spend her first afternoon entertaining a short man so Yolanda could flirt with his tall friend. 'The Short One' was what people called her, even though she was five foot seven. Yolanda stood six feet tall and had the looks of a model. Compared to Yolanda, Cassandra was just average-looking. Brown skin, brown eyes, nose a little wide, but she did have pretty hair. Cassandra tugged at the elastic band that held her hair captive. She frowned as her hair fluttered down to rest on her shoulders. Unfortunately, the stress of an unfaithful man and career demands had thinned her hair a bit over the past three years, one of the many aftershocks from that lying cheat she'd almost married. It was a constant reminder to be careful.

"Here, put on these shoes and hurry up!"

She shook her head at the strappy fuchsia four-inch wedge-heel sandals Yolanda held out. "I'm not wearing those hooker shoes. I'll wear the sandals you made me buy last week."

Yolanda attempted to make her fashionable, but she rarely took the advice. They were both educators, but Yolanda, an art teacher, took a broad brushstroke of artistic license with her dress.

They stood for a second at the front door and inspected each other. Cassandra shook her head again at Yolanda; tank top, no bra, and daisy dukes. *Oh my!*

"Good, you look nice," Yolanda said. "Relax. Remember, we're here to have fun." She gave Cassandra a gentle shove. As soon as they stepped onto the porch the men stood.

"Hi, I'm Will and this is Doc."

She looked Will up and down as he spoke. Yolanda was right. The man was fine. He was just over six feet tall with a cinnamon-brown complexion. Success and determination oozed from his clean-shaven face. His Exchange khaki shorts revealed a pair of thick and pretty brown legs, and a Calvin Klein T-shirt rippled over his muscular chest.

She extended her hand to Will. "No last names?"

The shorter man stuck out his chest. "No, you can just call me Doc."

Will shook his head in shame. "My boy here has rules for his vacation. For two weeks, he tries to divorce himself from certain realities, like his full name."

"Interesting choice of words—divorce. You two aren't married, are you?" Cassandra asked.

Doc cast a sideways glance at Will. "Just like a sista to focus on the word *divorce*."

Doc had a distinguished appearance. He stood just under six feet tall and had a slimmer frame than Will. His complexion reminded Cassandra of Godiva chocolate. His face featured the same determined jaw line as Will. They both could have just stepped from the pages of *GQ* magazine.

"No, ma'am. Not divorced, not married, not gay. And you may rest assured that we are not wanted by any city, state or local authorities," Will said.

"Excuse me, I am not wanted. I can't totally vouch for you, Cuz." Doc sported a wicked grin.

"Okay, and we're cousins," Will added with an equally wicked gleam in his eye.

Yolanda stepped forward. "Then we're just Yolanda and Cassandra. But you can call me Yogi."

As Will's gaze traveled over Yolanda's body, an appreciative half-grin split his lips.

"We're going to walk to a diner in the village, if that's okay with you two. It's not far." Doc stepped off the porch and strolled away.

Yolanda returned Will's appreciative gaze. "We're ready, let's go."

Will offered Cassandra a stunning two-dimpled smile and his arm.

"I don't have any rules, do you?" Yolanda asked in a flirtatious voice as they strolled down the parkway.

"No ma'am. No rules, no regrets."

As they followed Doc down a tree-lined street, Cassandra focused on the juxtaposition of neat cottages and mini-mansions.

Will slowed. "I should explain to you both the rest of Doc's vacation rules." He took a deep breath. "No last names, no discussion of background, jobs, where you went to school, what church you belong to, and definitely no 'who do you know'. These rules are important because without them we're sure to find some connection, according to the six degrees of separation theory." He gave both sisters another sexy, deep-dimpled grin and picked up the pace.

Cassandra watched Doc's broad back. *What kind of person takes the time to make vacation rules?* Well, as far as she was concerned, it was fine. She didn't like the initial sharing of personal information that came with meeting new people anyway.

When Will roared in laughter, she was sure her sister had said something racy. She turned her head toward a couple waving at them from a porch swing. Doc slowed his pace, waved at the couple, and never looked back toward her. Her shoulders stiffened. This wasn't going to be fun.

They found a table in the corner of a '60s-style diner complete with a checkerboard floor and jukebox. The sisters sat opposite each other in retro chrome and vinyl chairs at a Formica table as the cousins stood by the jukebox.

Cassandra cast a hard-eyed stare at her sister. "Yogi, I don't know."

"Come on, I like Will. Doc seems nice."

Cassandra rolled her eyes.

"Look, we're in a public place, and you know I can make one phone call and find out exactly who they are."

"I just think we should be careful," Cassandra whispered as the cousins closed in on the table.

Will sat next to Cassandra. "This place is famous for its clam strips, so we ordered those to start."

A familiar syncopated beat filled the diner. Yogi bounced up and down in her chair. "That's my song," she cried.

"Girl, what you know about Evelyn Champagne King?" Will said as he rose to his feet. "You're too young to know how to do the washing machine."

Yolanda shook her head and popped her fingers to the beat.

"Well, come on, then."

"Excuse me." Doc hopped up and walked toward an older couple at the opposite end of the diner.

Cassandra rested her elbows on the table and sighed. *Do I look that boring?* She watched Will and her baby sister burn up the dance floor. She smiled and waved. Yolanda was having fun. Doc was a bit of an odd duck, but she decided to make an effort. She pushed back a bit from the table and gave a half smile as Doc approached. Without success she racked her brain for something to say that would not violate his rules. They sat silently and stared at the other couple on the dance floor until the food arrived.

"Hold up, ole boy, you're going to hurt yourself." Doc laughed as his cousin sat down and drank half a glass of water without taking a breath.

"So what kind of music do you like?" Cassandra blurted out.

Doc flashed a perfect smile and broke his silence. They shared the experience of coming of age in the '80s. Roaring over Prince's butt-out jeans and lamenting the loss of Phyllis Hyman.

When the summer song from 1984 thumped out of the jukebox, Doc stood and offered her his hand. "Would you like to dance?"

Soon the four of them were laughing and dancing the freak, spank, and bump on the checkerboard diner floor.

As the afternoon waned, Will and Yolanda made plans for the rest of the evening. Cassandra kicked her sister under the table.

Yolanda stood up and gave her the let's-go-to-the-bathroom head toss. "Excuse us."

"Look," Yolanda rounded on her as soon as the washroom door closed. "Go ahead and admit you're having fun." Yolanda nudged her. "Girl, Doc can dance."

Cassandra bowed her head and giggled. "You are so nasty."

"The man's got some sexy moves. What's your problem?"

Cassandra rolled her eyes.

Yolanda narrowed her eyes and stuck out her chin the way she had when they were little girls. "I didn't tell you earlier, but their house is next door to ours. At least we know where they live."

Cassandra crossed her arms over her chest. "That doesn't mean anything. They could be renters, like us."

Yolanda's eyes begged. "Come on, we only have a few days of freedom and I really like Will."

Cassandra studied her baby sister's face. She knew the pain and disappointment that lay behind her bright smile and expertly applied makeup. "All right, just be careful."

When they returned to the table Doc was gone. "We have a late tee-time," Will explained as he led them to the diner's door.

Outside, Doc interrupted a conversation with a couple of young women to wave them onward. "Go ahead, Will, I'll catch up."

Cassandra followed the new 'couple' across the village green. Yolanda had tried for years to get a rental in the resort community of Michiana, Indiana, the hot spot for Chicago's urban elite. She'd jumped at the opportunity when their sixty-nine-year-old sorority

7

sister, Lucy Baker, announced she was not up to the challenge of opening her summer home this season. Michiana was similar to the Inkwell on Martha's Vineyard, where African-American families had carved out a little hamlet of their own.

In addition to the charms of an eclectic mix of artist studios, antique shops, and novelty stores, there was also an active marina and a small strip of Indiana dunes steps from the Baker cottage.

Doc caught up with them as the street turned residential. Several times during lunch he had left the table to greet people as they came into the diner. Now he was stepping onto porches and speaking to people. From a distance she noticed that the people, especially the older ones, seemed to revere him. An elderly lady Doc was speaking with on a plant and flower-filled porch waved. Cassandra smiled and waved back.

He's rude, but seems well-respected.

Doc rejoined them.

Yolanda dropped back and let the guys walk ahead. "Will is going boating with Doc tomorrow and he wants us to go with them."

Cassandra stopped and looked ahead at the mysterious cousins who had stopped to chat with a couple of gray-haired ladies. "Are you crazy? No. It's one thing to go for a walk or bike ride, but it's something else entirely to go out into the middle of Lake Michigan with two people we don't really know. We don't even know their full names."

"Then don't let me go alone."

He gets an awful lot of hugs and kisses from little old ladies to be a villain.

She let her guard down. A bit.

❦

Cassandra sighed and stretched in a deck chair aboard Doc's boat, the W2. Doc described his vessel as a mini yacht, but in her estimation they were sailing on a full-fledged yacht. As she shivered in the cool lake breeze and reached for the thick cotton beach towel at her feet, she spied a bit of Chicago's famous skyline.

Yolanda was stretched out in the sun, sleeping like a contented cat, worn out from a swim with Will. Cassandra was too shy to wear a bathing suit in front of two men she barely knew, not with her hips, so while Will and Yogi swam, Doc gave her a crash course in boating. It took a lot of effort to captain a boat, but he made it look easy. Today he was approachable, charming, and friendly, even nice.

Her mind warned her not to fall asleep, but her eyes were heavy. The book on her lap felt like a brick. When it slid to the highly polished deck, she closed her eyes behind her sunglasses. She detected the sounds of dishwashing clatter and conversation from the galley. The cousins had gone below to clean up after the gourmet lunch they'd served. Maybe it was the resonance of their voices or the stillness of the lake or the lack of real cleaning up they had to do, but she heard their conversation clearly.

"As you well know, not my type." She recognized the timbre of Doc's voice. "The sister is fine in an artistic sort of way. But you know where I am. No temptation."

She shifted in the chaise lounge, wary of falling asleep. No way would she fall asleep on a boat in the middle of the lake with two men she'd met only yesterday.

"Man, Cassandra's a nice lady. Bookish, yes, but she has intelligent conversation." Will's voice had a nice quality. Given her professional voice training she couldn't help wondering if either of them could sing. Cassandra sighed, too content to reel at Will's description of her. It would be rude to listen any more, but…

"True that, and I've been your wingman with less benefit to me. At least she *is* interesting to talk to. But I think we would agree she's no DAMM girl."

Both men laughed at Doc's comment. Cassandra snorted and shifted so she could hear better.

"We still sticking to that, cuz?"

"Seems to me you've based your whole life on that. You're the one in the entertainment industry, and I have never seen you with anything less than a full DAMM."

"That's right, man, because only a DAMM girl…" Will exclaimed.

"Can make you say DAMN, *GIRL,*" the cousins sang in unison.

She sat up, her brain engaged. *"Damn girls" must be their rating system for women. That lying cheat Greg always said there were only two types of women.* A blush of anger burned her cheeks. His betrayal still hurt. *I can only imagine which type a "damn girl" is.* Cassandra took a deep, cleansing breath. *Will's in entertainment. Wonder what Doc does?*

"But that's me. I thought your profession might have matured you." Will's tone turned serious.

"Actually, it has, and I have been wanting to speak to you about how you're living. You need to slow down." Doc's cadence sounded authoritative.

"Is this a personal or professional observation?"

"I'm on vacation, so purely personal. No, I can never really go on vacation. That's both my personal and professional assessment. We need to talk."

"Okay, you're the boss, but just hold it a few days because *I* can go on vacation, and she's damn good enough for the next few days."

By Friday, Cassandra was tired of them all: Will's flirtatious charms, Yolanda's constant begging for her to hang out with them, and Doc's funny ways. One minute he would be as charming and funny as Will and then, in the blink of an eye, he'd turn moody and withdrawn. She was grateful for what she'd overheard on the boat. For some reason hearing that conversation helped her relax around the cousins. She could care less if she didn't measure up to their female standard. If she'd learned anything in the past three years it was what kind of girl she was. She might not be a "damn girl" but she was not totally undesirable, either. What were women in the middle called? *Normal.*

She wasn't the kind of girl that gave it up easily, like her sister. Yolanda's nature had left her with two children and no husband. She longed to be a mother, but planned to have the husband first. When the right man came along, she'd get involved again. But now she was too focused on the upcoming school year and her new job.

Cassandra sat on the patio of the Baker cottage, anxious to read the Easy Rawlins mystery she'd checked out of the library. Her peaceful days were numbered. Next week her mother, Phyllis, and Yolanda's children would arrive for a two-week stay. Fourteen-year-old Jalen and six-year-old Yasmine hadn't had a proper vacation in years. She looked forward to the children coming.

The back door banged as Yolanda arrived on the patio to interrupt her much-anticipated afternoon reading and nap. "Cassandra, the boys have invited us for a picnic and bonfire. You game?"

"No, I don't think so. I'd rather sit here and read this book than spend another minute talking to Doc while you giggle and neck with Will."

"Neck? Girl, get a vocabulary. It's summer break and I'm free from my kids for a few more days. Chill that. Will is fine and I am ready."

"Ready for what? I know you wouldn't sleep with a man when you don't even know his last name."

Yolanda put her hand on her hip and pointed her freshly polished blood red fingernail towards her. She twisted her hip and cocked her head to the left. "You really have to learn to live, just give in to the moment. Go with the flow."

Cassandra shot straight up. "I just can't believe that you are considering sleeping with him." She took a deep breath. "You're going to do what you want anyway, doesn't matter what I say. But you should be more careful. Think about your children." She lay back. "You remember what I told you about their conversation on the boat. We're not even their type."

"*You're* not their type, but you are a faithful wingman. Come on, go with us."

"No, I'm your children's aunt and I sure as hell won't aid in the making of another child."

"Whatever, Sister Polly Pure."

That hurt. Yolanda knew the full circumstances surrounding her broken engagement. Cassandra buried her head in her book. Somewhere between meeting Easy Rawlins and the end of the first chapter she nodded off.

A voice registered in her ear and a waft of masculine cologne drifted to her brain. It took a moment to focus.

"Whatcha reading?"

She looked up to see Doc standing over her, smiling. He was freshly shaven and smelling good. Cassandra shifted in the chair. Damn.

"Walter Mosley, an Easy Rawlins mystery," he answered his own question. "That's good stuff. Did you read *Devil in a Blue Dress*? It's the first in the series."

"No," she answered slowly. She struggled to sit upright in the chaise lounge.

Doc extended a hand to assist. "Have you seen Will?"

"No. Why don't you ask Yo-Yo?" Cassandra's less than flattering nickname for her sister came out of her mouth before she could stop it.

"I don't think *Yo-Yo's* here. I rang first at the front door, and when there was no answer I came around to the back. My guess, she's with Will."

She didn't like the smirk on Doc's face when he called her sister Yo-Yo. Her lips pursed. "My Lord."

Doc's eyebrow shot up. "I hoped to find Will here. I want to sail this afternoon."

"Go alone." She was ready to be alone again with her book. She'd already fallen in literary love with Easy Rawlins.

"No. Rule number one, I never sail alone."

"Don't you mean rule number two?" She reopened her book.

Doc sat down in the chair opposite her and closed his eyes for a moment. "Come with me."

"No, thank you. I plan to sit right here, read this book, and relax."

"You can relax on the boat. There's no better place. Cool lake breezes, calm water. Come on. Go sailing with me."

Cassandra looked closely at her summer neighbor. His expression said he wasn't used to being told no.

"I have to go back to work tomorrow, and I really want to get the boat out today. You can read on the boat. We can even have a book discussion. I've read all of Mosley's books."

Wonder what kind of work he has to get back to on a weekend? Cassandra swung her feet onto the brick patio and hesitated. For some reason she believed his promise not to bother her while she read, and she had enjoyed her earlier outing on his boat. And Yogi had encouraged her to go with the flow. "Okay, just let me change shoes and grab a bag."

True to his word, once they reached the boat, Doc only disturbed her to offer a cold beverage, snack, or pillow. She watched him as he worked, calibrating instruments and polishing brass fittings. He reminded her of the guys in her old neighborhood polishing and primping their cars. Instead of reading she turned over in her mind what little she knew about him. He was a handsome man and when he wanted to be, he was nice. And judging from his hobbies and clothes he had some money. It was hard not to speculate about his identity, especially since he'd worked so hard to keep it a secret.

Right before sunset he pulled the boat into the dock. "Let's go get something to eat. I did promise you a book discussion."

"That's not necessary."

"Now, Miss Cassandra, I insist. I want to know what you think about my man Easy. What's your pleasure? Steak, lobster, both? I know every good spot around here." He grinned and extended his hand to assist her from the reclining deck chair where she'd spent the afternoon doing more watching than reading.

"Actually I'm dying to have a really good cheeseburger."

"Then you're in luck. I know where we can get the best burger around, but…" He hesitated. "We'll need to go in the car, if you are comfortable with that."

She paused. *He's perceptive.* "Why not."

Cassandra followed Doc up the path to the cottage he shared with his cousin. Since Cassandra and Yogi had not been invited to spend any time at their house, they speculated it was also off limits, per Doc's vacation rules. Yolanda delighted in teasing Cassandra with all sorts of wild speculations about the cousins since there never seemed to be any lights on at their house.

She could see now that the property the cousins shared held two houses. The larger house, a two-story colonial with lots of windows, was hidden from the street by a forest of trees and a long drive.

"I'll get my car." Doc walked towards the smaller structure on the property. Cassandra tried not to be nosy as she waited on the expansive brick patio that separated the main house from the garage. Her eyes widened as she took in the patio furnishings. They were more expensive than anything she had in her living room.

She started at the roar of a car pulling out of the garage. A midnight blue Porsche Boxster drew to a stop beside her. Doc hopped out and assisted her with the low step into the vehicle. She chose not to complain about his speed as he raced through the small resort community and onto a state highway, where he increased the speed. He slowed down only when waved past the security gate at the Michiana Golf and Yacht Club.

Once inside the private club, the captain helped them don navy club blazers before seating them. Cassandra cast a self-conscious glance around the private dining room and then exhaled in relief. Most of the diners also wore club jackets over their casual summer clothes.

As soon as they were seated, Doc's cell phone rang. He excused himself to take the call, then returned with a deep scowl. Out of respect for his vacation rules, she looked down at her plate. This was going to be a long meal.

"That was Will."

She looked up and took a sip of water.

"He took your sister shopping in Chicago. Don't expect to see them until tomorrow." He gazed past her shoulder and waved at someone at another table. He turned his eye on her for a second. "That said, let's enjoy our dinner. What do you think about Mr. Mosley's book?"

Her eyes darted from side to side. "I'm enjoying it so far."

His expression lightened. "You like Easy. Most women do."

She snickered a little too loudly, then leaned back and nodded. Easy Rawlins was just her type of literary hero: strong, solid, sexy, a little dangerous. But in real life she wanted honest, safe, and reliable. She took stock of her dinner companion. She'd never trust a man who wouldn't tell her his Christian or family name.

Chapter 2

The Reverend Doctor Finus Gideon Gates paced the corridor in front of his bishop's office. He paused at the heavy oak door and ran his hand across the raised grain in remembrance. His father had once occupied this office. Finus sighed and examined his watch again. Ten minutes past four. The bishop was running late, again.

He took another stroll down the hall lined with awards, certificates, and memories. He prayed that the meeting would go smoothly. Too often, his weekly meetings with Bishop Sutton required him to address items published in the local African-American gossip rag, the *Black Pages*, or to account for some bit of internal church gossip. It was a shame that he could not compliment, smile at, or be seen in the presence of a lady without it spawning a rumor.

They were a peculiar people. He chuckled at the variation of the church motto that he and Will had come up with in high school. "A particular people for a peculiar time" was the official motto for his church, the Baptist Methodist Assembly. Established in the 1920s by three African-American physicians in New England, the Assembly had grown into a national denomination. The church that Finus loved was meant to be a close and supportive fellowship, but sometimes…

"Sometimes," he muttered as he turned around at the old oak door. Sometimes the closeness of the church offered him no comfort. Growing up, everything he did was reported to his parents. As a young adult, every time he was seen somewhere he shouldn't be, that got back to them, too. Now they watched because many in the church thought he should marry. Too many well-meaning women were working overtime to help him marry their daughter, sister, friend, niece, or even themselves.

Finus drew in a deep breath and his mind wandered back to his vacation. *Man, it was nice to just hang out with a lady and not feel any of that pressure.*

But what if people were already gossiping about his vacation with Will? Why was he what if-ing? Things had been going well. He'd been very careful not to look in the direction of any woman for well over a year.

The hearty laughter of Rev. David Broadnaux interrupted his thoughts. The door to the bishop's office swung open and David sauntered out. Finus glanced at his watch; four-fifteen.

He strode toward the bishop's door. "How'd you fare, David?"

"Don't worry, Finus, he's in a good mood. But this isn't a day for long-winded conversations. He's ready to start his vacation." David's voice filled the hall. "And, he's handing out the work. Glad I got broad shoulders. The bishop just took away all my vacation relaxation."

"I see you made it back safely. How did Lady Broadnaux enjoy her vacation?"

"Rev, those two weeks in 'Bama were just the thing for her. It was good to be home for a minute. I'll tell Lydia you asked about her. *He* said we betta not keep him waiting, so you better go head on in." David motioned toward the inner sanctum. "And we heard you out here pacing. Man, you are far too uptight."

Finus bristled and shook David's hand before passing into the familiar office.

"Come on in, son. Take a seat, but don't get too comfortable." Fred Sutton's booming voice greeted him at the threshold.

Finus followed the instructions of the man who had succeeded his father. He crossed the large office and sat in a wing-back chair across from the antique oak inlaid desk that once belonged to his grandfather.

"Let me just finish this note, then I'll be right with you."

The bishop's large hand moved rapidly across a note pad. Fred was famous for his memory, but Finus knew this acclaim came from the copious notes he kept.

Hope those aren't for or about me.

Fred looked up. "I saved the best and easiest appointment for last today. And thankfully I've got nothing for you except these assignments."

Finus exhaled. He reached up to unknot his signature bow tie.

Bishop Sutton held up his large hands. "Whoa, now, before you go getting comfortable, let me give you your assignments. Yes, they are heavy, since I won't see you for over a month."

"I can't believe you'll be away for a whole month. Is Inez ready to go?"

"Ready? She's been packed for two weeks. She needs this vacation. In fact she told me if we didn't go on this second honeymoon, I would be going on my second divorce."

Finus leaned back in the chair. "You know Inez isn't going anywhere."

"I didn't think Constance would leave me, and yet on the eve of my elevation she did. If I don't get out of here soon, Inez just might. She really got more than she bargained for when she married me."

Finus nodded. Time and circumstance moved so swiftly he often forgot that at fifty-five Inez was still effectively a new bride.

"These past three years have been hard on us. So much so that we're going to take a page out of the Gates family playbook and go incognito. For the next two weeks, at least, we're just going to be Fred and Inez, a big-boned middle-aged couple from Chicago."

"In-cog-negro, as Mama used to say."

Fred stood and stretched his long legs. "Do you think we'll get away with it?"

"Well, sir, Mama used to say it got harder to do after Daddy became bishop. Yet even now I'm grateful she insisted on those two weeks away from everything every year. Some of my happiest memories were those vacations when we'd go away to the lake and just be."

Finus's tone grew wistful as he remembered summer vacations with his now-deceased parents.

"I'm willing to try, for Inez."

"It might just work. We hung out with the ladies that rented Lucy Baker's place for two weeks without revealing our names. Well, I didn't reveal mine." Finus chuckled.

"Lucy Baker rented to non-Assembly members?"

"Don't know. No last names or background when you are in-cog-negro. You'll want to remember that. But I don't believe they are members since they didn't know me."

"Oh yes, everyone in the Assembly knows our famous favorite son," Bishop Sutton teased.

Finus stiffened and shifted in his chair. "I didn't mean it like that."

"Relax, but that does remind me of one other thing." The older man sounded weary. "Let me make this quick. First, I trust you were strong enough not to fall into any of your old patterns with your cousin."

Finus gripped the chair's padded arms.

"Just checking, you know I had to ask. Just as you know I'm glad you spent your vacation at the lake, and that Will was with you. You've stayed away long enough." Fred cleared his throat. "By the way, Inez wanted me to ask if you tended your mother's garden."

"Now she knows I was not going to do that." As the conversation turned personal, he tugged again at the end of his bowtie.

"I'm just the messenger."

Finus's hand dropped back into his lap. "Yes, sir."

"Listen for your assignments and do not interrupt me again." Bishop Sutton walked toward his desk and picked up a folder. "Next Saturday I'll ask you to attend the ladies fashion show luncheon at College Station."

Finus scowled.

"Then I'm sending you back to the lake to run the chapel while Ford takes his break. I trust, since you'll be alone, that you'll reach out for help if you need it." He glanced over the top of his glasses.

"You know I won't truly be alone. Surely you are in cahoots with certain members at the Chapel and have already set up a watch care. Which is why you are disappointed to learn Baker rented out her cottage. Lucy Baker was probably at the top of your list to watch out for me." Finus sighed. He appreciated Fred's concern, but he was not sixteen years old. "I know my limitations. Don't worry about me. I'll be fine, and you know I'll be watched like a hawk. Or shall I get that dog?"

"Weren't you preaching just last month about the value of having a church family that watches out for one another?" Fred chuckled. "But I digress." He lumbered over and handed Finus the assignment folder.

Finus studied the list of meetings and administrative tasks that he would attend to on the bishop's behalf over the next month. A ladies fashion show and a few meetings were a small price to pay for another month at his beloved lake house. Running the chapel was a fluff assignment, and being under the watch care of the chapel's membership wouldn't be so bad. He would eat well, and he could see Cassandra again.

"I know you're wondering why I gave the Cathedral over to Broadnaux instead of you."

Finus looked up.

"I need for you to spend more time relaxing. The pace you keep is too great, and it's no secret you're a tad too intense." Bishop Sutton reached behind his desk, picked up his briefcase, and headed toward the door. "And you've got a lot of nerve pacing outside of a sitting bishop's door."

Finus reached up and unknotted his bow tie.

"I want you well rested for the project you'll undertake this fall. If you have some more to say, come over to the house for dinner. I'm getting out of here. And you would do well to tend your mother's garden. You might find it relaxing." Fred held his hand up to silence Finus. The bishop always had to have the last word.

While he was in no position to keep score, Finus figured Fred owed him one for attending today's poorly produced ladies fashion show/luncheon. The overabundance of single and semi-single churchwomen who attended the function ensured he did not have one moment of peace from the time he entered the banquet hall until he sped away in his beloved Boxster. He turned onto his street in Michiana and glowered at the number of cars lining the street. This many cars only meant noise. He needed a good night's sleep. Tomorrow was Sunday. He barreled around his drive to the garage. When he stepped out into the steamy summer evening, the noise he expected greeted him: loud music and louder talking from the Baker cottage next door. His prayer for a peaceful evening would go unanswered.

He stood for a few minutes on his expansive brick patio and watched the fiery reds and oranges of the setting sun as he listened to the classic R&B music that invaded his space from next door. His stomach stirred as hickory smoke teased his nose.

Finus walked around to the front of his house to clear out his mailbox. Just that quick someone had parked a car at the end of his drive. He shrugged. The car didn't block him in. No need to make a fuss. Here he was taking something in stride without a witness to testify to his generous nature. The smell of smoked meat spoke again. He had been invited to what Cassandra said would be a family party. He looked up at the mellowing sky and remembered the great conversation they'd had at the yacht club. They'd talked about politics, public education, and Easy Rawlins without violating his vacation rules. She really was a kind lady, but he wouldn't go over tonight. It wasn't worth an encounter with her sister. He was too tired and hungry to deal with any questions from Yolanda about Will. Then he saw the sign over Cassandra's door: *Congratulations Dr. Cassandra Brownley*. That and the scent of barbeque changed his mind.

Cassandra stood in the back door of the Baker cottage and observed her guest. He must have arrived while she was out getting more ice, and now he'd been drawn into a game of dominos with her uncles. If she knew the man better she might warn him to watch his wallet. Maybe that wasn't necessary. Her uncles had promised good behavior during her celebration.

"Pi-yow," Finus cried as he stood up and laid down a double. "Ha-ha, you brothers thought you were going to take me to school. Well, I'm going to take you all to church right here, right now."

She hurried on to the patio to save Doc. He didn't know what he was getting into, talking trash with her uncles. They were some true Chicago old-schoolers.

"Hi, Doc, how long have you been here?"

He cast a side glance to greet her and kept one eye on the table. "Hello, Cassandra, or should I address you as Doctor? M.D.?"

"No, I just completed a doctorate in education. I hope you don't mind my parking in your drive. I had to run out for some more ice and I lost my spot."

He excused himself from the game. "No problem, and congratulations! I think now would be a good time to introduce myself. I am the Reverend Doctor Finus Gideon Gates."

Cassandra took a small step back. "You're a reverend. I was close. I told Yolanda that I thought you might be a monk. I'm glad you came. Can I get you anything, Reverend?"

"Now, don't go getting all formal on me now. Please continue to call me Doc. You see, this is why

I did not fully introduce myself when we met. I hope you didn't think I was too rude for not giving you my full name. It's just that people tend to act funny when they learn I'm a reverend. As I recall, you said there would be some good barbeque tonight. I'm starving."

"I did, and you're in for a treat because my people can cook. Sit back down and I'll go fix you a plate."

She hurried to the kitchen and began loading two plates with the traditional family barbeque fare: hickory-smoked ribs drenched in thick, grill-browned red sauce; collard greens, dark green and perfectly cooked so they still had some bite to them; spaghetti covered with cheese and more meat than sauce; and of course homemade mustard potato salad. She sensed someone behind her and turned her head.

"It's a little hot and smoky for me on the patio. Can we find somewhere to eat inside?" Doc asked.

"Of course. Let's try the living room."

They settled into a quiet spot in the living room and he dove right into his food. "This is good," he murmured between bites. "Now that my vacation is over you can ask me anything, but first tell me about yourself."

She twirled her fork around the spaghetti on her plate. Was this the same person who two weeks ago imposed the 'no exchange of personal information' rule? She lifted the forkful of noodles to her mouth. As she chewed slowly she caught an expectant expression on Doc's face. *I'll just give him the résumé.* "I taught social studies for the Chicago Public Schools for ten years, and in the fall I'll start as a principal in a suburban district, at Westmore High."

"My parents live in that district." He paused and wiped his mouth. "Well, lived. They were assigned to the area to build a church for our denomination, the Baptist Methodist Assembly."

Cassandra's face twitched.

"What's that look for?"

"You're BMA?"

"Yes, ma'am, third generation. My maternal grandmother was an early member and my father served the church as a bishop. You really can ask me any questions you want to about our church or myself."

"I was just wondering…" Cassandra looked down at her plate. She wanted to pick the right words. How'd this moody man turn out to be a minister? Why had she always been warned to stay away from the BMA? She'd heard that they had some strange practices and a very selective membership. Cassandra looked up and her eyes settled on a patch of barbeque sauce that stained the cuff of Finus' crisp white shirt. "I don't think I know many BMA members."

"How well do you know the Bakers?" He took a sip of sweet tea. "Cassandra, do you know how Lucy Baker is getting along after the death of her husband?" His tone conveyed real concern and a warm pastoral compassion.

"I'm not sure. You should ask Yolanda, she's closer to the Bakers than I am. I almost forgot the Bakers were BMA."

Finus forked up another mouthful of greens, so she asked another question.

"I've always heard there are strict guidelines for membership in the BMA."

"None other than accepting Christ."

"Okay, then is it true that you have to be wealthy to join? Or that the church dictates where BMA members can live? Or that members can only marry within the church?"

He set his fork down and shook his head. "That's a lot of questions. And the answer to all of them is no. You and your family are welcome to join us at our Chapel by the Lake in the morning. It's just two blocks up the road. I'm sure you've seen it."

" 'San, girl. Where are you?"

Cassandra jumped at the sound of her mother's voice; or was it her mother towering behind her that startled her?

"Doc—I'm sorry, Rev. Gates. This is my mother, Phyllis Brownley."

Phyllis was an older, more modestly-dressed version of Yolanda.

He rose to shake her hand.

An uncomfortable silence filled the room as Phyllis gave him a slow once-over.

"Doc lives around the corner. He and his cousin showed Yogi and me around."

Phyllis cut her eyes at him. "Gates. I thought your name was Gideon."

"Gideon is my maternal family name. I am Finus Gideon Gates."

Cassandra's neck whipped from him to her mother.

"I see." Phyllis turned to her daughter. "Aunt Gloria is ready to go, and she insists that the family pray before she leaves. Everyone's gathered outside on the patio." Phyllis turned back toward Finus to finish her slow-eyed assessment. "And since we don't have a minister in the family, maybe Reverend Gates could lead us in prayer?"

Finus cocked his head to the side. "No, ma'am. I would not turn down an opportunity to go before the Lord, but it sounds like your elder is prepared. I would be honored to stand with your family."

Unease filled Cassandra's stomach. Phyllis, through Yolanda, knew something she didn't. They were definitely going to include her in their girl talk tonight.

Finus broke the silence. "After you." He deferred to the ladies to lead the way out to the patio for prayer.

An hour later Cassandra went through the house with an industrial-size black trash bag while Yogi and Phyllis hit the kitchen. She needed a few minutes to figure out how she was going to work her way into the running dialogue between her mother and sister.

Their mother was the type who wanted to be friends with her children. They called her Phyllis, and the grandchildren were banned from any form of grandma. Yogi and Phyllis talked about everything. She always felt like the ugly stepsister when they got together.

Cassandra had vowed to never again share the intimate details of her relationships with anyone after sharing them with Yolanda, who'd passed them on to Phyllis. She didn't know what hurt her more, Gregory's indiscretions or her mother calling her a blind fool for missing all of the clues. She paused for a moment at the kitchen door and listened to her mother and sister cackle and gossip about their family members.

When she entered the kitchen, Yolanda started right in. "So do you know his name now?"

She modulated her voice to hide the anger that roiled in her stomach. "How long have you known, and why would you tell Phyllis and not me?"

Yolanda waved her off. "Chile, I knew who he was the day after we met. You forget I called Lucinda Baker."

"You ain't right. Why didn't you tell me?"

"No, 'San, you ain't right. I wouldn't tell you nothing, either," Phyllis chimed in. "Miss Don't Talk to Me, I Moved to the Suburbs, Stay Out of My Business." Phyllis never missed an opportunity to remind Cassandra that she was displeased with her decisions over the past three years. In the aftermath of her broken engagement, Cassandra had enrolled in a doctoral program, changed jobs, and moved to the suburbs. What she called healing, Phyllis dubbed shutting the family out.

Yolanda jumped in before an argument started. "Get off her, Phyllis." She turned to her sister. "What do you want to know about the good reverend, girl? 'Cause I've got the full four-one-one."

"First, why you didn't tell me? Did you all know the deal and the joke was on me?" That uncomfortable feeling closed in on her again as their mother glared at her across the room.

"No, it wasn't like that. But it was cute to watch you two. What do you think Will and I laughed so much about? Doc being so careful not to reveal anything about himself, you being so careful not to ask." Yolanda stepped away from the sink of dishes. "By the way, Will wanted me to thank you for going along with everything. He said Doc is kinda funny and it's not good to upset him. If I had busted him out, like I wanted to, they probably wouldn't have spent any more time with us. Will made it clear his whole purpose in coming from L.A., where he's a big time entertainment lawyer, was to make sure Doc enjoyed his vacation. I didn't tell you for selfish reasons."

Cassandra's fingers tightened around the top of the trash bag. "I hope you all enjoyed your laughs at my expense."

"It's not like that. Doc didn't know. Will didn't tell him. I told you, Will said he was funny like that. But now you know his name, wanna know who he is?"

Cassandra shrugged.

"Aw, 'San, don't be like that. You might want to sit down and get a piece of cake because Lucinda gave me a full rundown on the Reverend Finus Gates."

Cassandra sat down at the small kitchen table covered with foil-wrapped bowls and reached for the pound cake. Yolanda pulled a quart of ice cream from the freezer and Phyllis set out three bowls, spoons, and a knife.

"I want to hear this, too," Phyllis said as she sat down. "What kind of preacher is he, not wanting to pray and wearing a Rolex?"

"Oh, God, he's not one of those prosperity preachers, is he?" Cassandra wished her mom wasn't sitting there. Phyllis had given Doc a thorough once-over. She herself hadn't noticed his watch.

"No, he's BMA. The BMA doesn't have to preach prosperity. That stuff only works on poor folks like us, but Doc does have more money than God."

"Yolanda, really," Cassandra exclaimed.

"Watch your mouth," their mother admonished.

"Okay, but the boy's got more money than Carter's got pills. According to Lucinda, his family owns lots of property in the city and his mother was some kind of stock market genius. He's an only child and both his parents are gone, so with the real estate, insurance, and stock portfolio, he's loaded." Yolanda plopped down on a kitchen chair. "In addition to the lake house and the Porsche, there's also a mansion in the suburbs, out near your house, I think."

Cassandra cut a slice of pound cake and passed the knife to her mother.

"Anyway, he escorted Dianne Madison in her debutante debut and dated Lucinda in college." Dianne Madison was the most beautiful girl in their sorority and Lucinda Baker was just vivacious. "He likes beautiful women, mainly models, so I'm much more his speed. If I hadn't already slept with his cousin, I'd

be all up in his face. But I do have some standards."
Yolanda stopped to take a breath. "You can have 'im."

"I don't want him."

Yolanda waved her hands palms up. "As the kids
say, whatever. Oh, and Will explained the whole
'damn girl' thing. It's their code. It means only danc-
ers, artists, models and musicians need apply."

Cassandra pushed her bowl back and stood. She
didn't need to hear any more because even if she did
like him, it didn't matter. She didn't qualify. "I'm tired,
I'm going to bed."

Her mother's voice followed her out of the kitchen.
"See, there you go running away right when the conversation is about to get good."

The Chapel by the Lake was a small whitewashed
county church. It wasn't ornate or prestigious looking.
In fact, it looked a little run-down. The pews were covered in a worn cottage blue fabric and the altar cloths
looked as if they could use a little starch and repair.

*There's nothing different here, just another black
church.* Cassandra glanced up into the pulpit but
couldn't see Finus. Her view was obstructed by an
overly large lectern.

The Chapel conducted a simple service, but they
didn't leave out any of the usual African-American
church traditions. As much as she hated to, she stood
up when the visitors were recognized. When asked,
she quickly stated her name and sat down.

"I've noticed that she's kind of shy, Church," Finus started before she could get comfortable again. "Stand up again, 'San."

Her mouth twisted that he took the liberty of calling her by her family nickname.

"This is newly minted Dr. Cassandra Brownley, and some of you will take pleasure in knowing that, this fall, Dr. Brownley will join the administrative staff of Westmore High School. The congregation at Garden Cathedral has been praying for some diversity on the staff of that school and, lo and behold, look who turns up as my summer neighbor. Dr. Brownley and her family are spending the month at the Bakers' cottage. Let us make sure they feel welcome as we continue in prayer for the Baker family." Again he spoke with a warm, compassionate tone.

The service continued with the congregation's recitation of the twelve tenets of the BMA. The church truths seemed like a lot of rigid common sense, simple to understand, complex to live out.

After Rev. Gates made some brief announcements and read a message from the Bishops' Council, he preached the shortest sermon Cassandra had ever heard. It was all about the importance of family celebrating each other's accomplishments, with a crack on her uncles for cheating at dominos. He actually called them some slick, still-Jheri-curl-wearing brothers. He caught her eye after he made that remark and she shrugged her shoulders and smiled broadly. His sermon ended with what sounded like actual instructions for how to live until the next service.

Different, but not so strange.

The closing hymn, "God Be with You", was familiar, so she sang along with the congregation. But during the benediction she stood on unfamiliar ground again as the congregation recited the assembly's motto: "A particular people for a peculiar time."

On the last day of her vacation Cassandra sat on Finus's patio and waited while he completed some yard work in the garden beyond the hedge wall. She'd offered to help, but he'd insisted that she relax with a glass of lemonade.

She couldn't sit still. This might be the last time she saw him, and she wanted to spend the time talking, not listening to him mutter from behind a hedge.

"I'm bringing you a glass of lemonade, it's hot out here." She walked around the six-foot hedge to join him in the garden. The small English garden suffered from what looked like several years of neglect. Remnants of morning glory and pink perennials spilled out of their beds. A climbing rose bush and another trailing vine competed for the remainder of the space.

"You know, there's more than a day's work out here. If you're not careful, that rose bush will be moving into your house soon," she advised.

Finus groaned. "Thanks for the lemonade. Could you just set it over there?" He pointed toward a pair of chairs under a willow tree. She sat down and quietly observed as he surveyed the garden. He was a little overdressed for gardening in a short-sleeved dress shirt and bow tie.

"I thought you were over here pulling weeds."

"In my own way, I am. And now I'm done."

He sidled toward her and closed his PDA. As he crossed the short distance, she noticed something unsteady in his gait.

He plopped down and stared at his feet. "Sorry we couldn't go out on the boat today, but I needed to get this done. This would not have been a good day for boating anyway."

The last day she might spend with him was like the first. She couldn't think of anything intelligent to say. Maybe all her words were exhausted. They had spent many late nights on the patio debating politics and education. He was knowledgeable on a wide range of subjects and had opinions on everything. But he wasn't annoying about it.

She took a glance at Doc. He didn't look happy. When he was in a good mood Rev. Doc, as the children called him, was just a big kid. He'd taught Jalen to navigate his boat and spent one evening chasing fireflies with Yasmine. *If I were looking for a man, or better yet, if a man like him would look my way… No, I'm not ready to even think about that. Besides, I'm not his damn type.*

Finus couldn't keep still. He took a sip of his lemonade and spilled half of it. He stood up abruptly and shook his left leg. "Cassandra…"

"Yes?"

"Never mind," he mumbled. He shoved his hands into his pockets, sat down, then popped back up. "Well, my friend, you may sit here as long as you like but I've got to go."

"I'm sorry. I forgot you're working. Guess it's time to for me to go."

His face twisted. "I said you could sit here as long as you liked. It's time for me to meet Rev. Ford and turn the Chapel back over to him." He studied his watch. "I'm late, so I'll say goodbye now. I'm to return to the city tonight. So, Miss Cassandra, it's been my pleasure. Please give my best regards to your family." Finus smiled politely, accepted her goodbyes, gave a little bow, and shuffled up the garden path.

He should have walked the three blocks to the Chapel's parish house. He should have asked for Cassandra's help. During the three-block drive he decided not to return to the city tonight as planned. Finus sat in the car for at least twenty minutes trying to steady his hand. The last person that needed to know he wasn't feeling well was Alice Ford. One of his father's last official acts was to assign this small parish to Cecil Ford. Cecil hated politics and loved the disconnection of living full time at the lake. Alice, however, resented being out of the Chicago church loop, so she found other networks to give and receive information. With slow, deliberate movements, Finus slipped out of the Boxster and rang the doorbell of the parish house.

For a woman who'd just returned from two weeks in Europe, Alice was up to speed on all the gossip. During dinner, she asked Finus to confirm the reports about the marginal success of the College Station ladies fashion show and asked a lot of questions about the Brownley family.

Alice rose to clear the dinner table. "Maybe I should stop by in the morning with a pound cake."

Finus's leg shook under the table. Frustrated by Alice's determination to gather gossip and the inability to control his movements, he rocked back and forth. "No, that won't be necessary. The family's gone and Cassandra is leaving in the morning."

"I was hoping to meet her."

He cut his eyes at Alice and attempted to lift his empty plate.

Alice gently moved his shaking hand aside and picked up his plate. "If you gentlemen will excuse me, I know you have things to discuss. I'll go prepare the guest room for you, Finus, and then I have to call my sister-in-law before it gets too late. Finus, you remember my sister-in-law is Ellen Whitney, a trustee at the Cathedral."

Of course he knew Ellen Whitney. He also knew the news he wasn't feeling well would precede him to the city.

Chapter 3

Exhausted after a long day at work, Cassandra flopped into her favorite chair and cast a satisfied glance around her den. It had taken her two years, but she finally had it decorated. She sank further down in the crowning touch, a couple-sized overstuffed easy chair. She loved the soft, dusty rose fabric and delicate floral print, even if Phyllis said it was too pink and frilly.

The first day of school had gone well and she had a ton of work spread out on the ottoman next to her feet. *Better get to it soon or I'm gonna fall asleep in this chair.* She didn't bother to check the caller ID when she reached to pick up the chirping phone. Yolanda was the only person who called anyway, her or Phyllis.

"Hello."

"Dr. Cassandra Brownley?"

She thought she recognized the voice. "Yes?"

"Hello, Cassandra, it's Finus Gates."

"Doc. How are you?" She hoped her voice didn't reveal her total surprise.

"Fine, fine, thank you. It has been a while. I wasn't sure you would remember me."

"Doc, you know you're quite an unforgettable character." *Why's he calling me?* They'd had a great time this summer but she'd assumed their friendship wouldn't continue beyond a casual 'hi' at a social event, which wasn't likely since she rarely went out.

"If you're talking about my antics at the lake, then that must have been my brother." Finus paused while they both laughed. "Cassandra, I'm calling for two reasons."

"Oh?"

"There's an opportunity at our church that I would like to recommend you for."

"Recommend me?"

"Yes. I told you about our project to open a high school program for African-American students in the suburban areas. We're finding that a lot of our youth are not thriving in the suburban schools, for reasons I'm sure you are well aware of."

"Yes, it's one of the reasons I was hired."

"Exactly. It's the transfer from the urban to suburban, culture and class."

"Yes, I'm aware of all of the issues. Remember my dissertation topic? We talked about the problems."

"Yes, we had some interesting conversations. I was impressed with your knowledge. Anyway, our church is in the final stages of chartering a high school and we are budgeted to hire an educational consultant from Houston. But I think we might do better with a local person. My bishop agrees, and I want to recommend you."

"I'm flattered, but I'm not a consultant. I've only been an administrator for a few years."

"The fresh perspective we need. The consultant from Houston seems a little, shall I say, set in his ways."

She sat up in the chair and the conversation flowed, an easy conversation about school administration, education, and the state of urban youth.

"Oh, God, it's almost midnight! Doc, I've got to be at school early."

"Hey, watch out, Thou shall not," he gently warned.

"Don't start preaching, Reverend, or we'll never get off this phone. I really have to say goodnight."

"Goodnight, Cassandra. I'm sorry to keep you up so late. I'll set up the interview with our board, if you agree."

"Sure, that sounds fine, Doc. Goodnight."

"Wait there was one more thing. I saw Yolanda at the Pan-Greek picnic. Were you there?"

"I left early."

"And I came late. Too bad. You could have met Cherie. She came back with me from our annual conference and spent a week before she returned to L.A." Finus had shared with her over the summer how helpful his cousins Will and Cherie had been to him since the loss of his parents. Will, Cherie, and their mother, Jo, were his closest relatives.

"I'm sorry to have missed her. Now I really have to say goodnight."

Cassandra paced nervously outside a conference room in the basement of the Garden Cathedral. It was her second trip to a BMA church and she was duly impressed by the grandeur of this building. Well, what she had seen. When she arrived for the interview Finus had rushed her through a side door and down a flight of stairs so fast that if a fire broke out she wouldn't know how to exit the building. Finus had told her she had a few minutes to catch her breath before he called her into the meeting. While she waited, she pondered his moodiness. She was sorry he'd picked her up this morning. His surly attitude made her more nervous. The only words he'd voiced this morning outside a mumbled greeting were to complain about the difficulty of finding her house. Over the summer she'd noticed he had uneven moods, but this morning—whew. She sat down on a simple wooden chair to wait. The door opened and a pleasant-faced lady ushered her into the meeting.

"You may be seated," Finus said and pointed to a chair at the near end of the conference table.

"I prefer to stand."

There were seven other people in the oak-paneled conference room. They all appeared to be well-seasoned professionals. It was clear the large man at the head of the table was the bishop. The conference room contained all of the usual equipment: a pod phone for conference calls, a computer with a docking station, and a drop-down screen for presentations. The walls were lined with awards, certificates, and pictures of distinguished gray-haired men.

She stood through the introduction of the school development committee and while she gave her opening statements. She always reverted to her voice training when she was nervous. It always helped her in unfamiliar situations and gave her something to do with her hands besides fidget.

It was a challenging interview. These were experienced professionals and their quest for quality came through in their questions. "I've prepared an executive summary of my dissertation and have copies of it in its entirety for anyone who would like to review the document."

"I'd like a copy," said Finus. It was the only request for her full dissertation.

Finus watched Cassandra closely, noting the way she stood and held her hands. It reminded him of something, but he couldn't think past the dark spot in his brain. He rubbed his temple and prayed his headache would dissipate. He didn't want to spoil their planned lunch.

His headache had started last night and reached a peak as he tried to locate her house this morning. His year-old GPS system already needed updating. Then she'd tested his patience by going back into her house while he put her box of materials in the trunk. He was already running late and feeling unsteady. But when she re-emerged not a minute later, Grace Kelly-style with a scarf and big sunglasses and apologized for forgetting he drove a convertible, she made him smile. Finus jumped, turned, and tried not to scowl at Bishop Sutton for nudging him.

"Additionally, I have prepared a list of personal and professional references if you would like to receive them at this time," Cassandra continued.

"Yes, we would," Rev. Gates responded as the spokesperson for the group. As her references went around the table, one of the committee members spoke up.

"I'm Gladys Herbert. One of your references is Dr. Reginald Herbert. He's my nephew."

"Yes, Dr. Herbert and I attended City College together and I've worked with him on many of his community health education projects, most recently the HIV/AIDS awareness days sponsored by the Westside Health Center."

"That's good to know. I'm sure you don't remember, but I think I met you at a wedding where you sang."

Cassandra nodded in agreement.

Finus cast a hard glare in Gladys's direction. She looked over her glasses at him, shot him that mother's look, and kept talking. He caught Cassandra's smile out of the corner of his eye. He scowled and looked down at his paperwork.

"You have a beautiful voice. It's nice to see you have accomplished so much." Mrs. Herbert nodded to Finus that she was ready to yield the floor.

He went immediately for the opening. "Final statement, Dr. Brownley."

She shifted her footing. "I am certainly interested in this opportunity to see how my theories would work in practice, but at the same time I'm new in my position with Westmore and I would have to discuss any additional responsibilities with my principal."

"If that is all, Dr. Brownley, please excuse us to conclude our meeting."

Cassandra sat outside of the conference room and tried to figure him out. The Reverend Doctor Finus Gates had been cold, impersonal, and exacting throughout the interview. He'd fidgeted and seemed to struggle to pay attention as she presented her credentials. He didn't even show emotion as he spoke about how his mother had provided the endowment to build the school in her will. He hesitated only slightly when he explained for her benefit that initially the school was to be named in honor of his father, Wallace Gates, but his father had approved the use of church land for the building only on the condition that it be named for Finus's mother.

Another hour passed before the committee members filed out of the conference room. In turn they all stopped to shake her hand.

"It was nice seeing you again, dear." Gladys Herbert extended her hand. "Your presentation was polished and professional, very impressive."

"Thank you."

"And whatever became of that young man who was with you at the wedding? Did he become the civil rights attorney he planned on being? Did the two of you marry? I can't tell these days with the way you girls keep your maiden names and not everyone wears a ring."

"Gregory became an attorney, but I believe his practice is mostly corporate. We didn't marry," Cassandra said, for the first time without regret.

"Oh, well. Anyway, nice to see you again. Have a good day."

Finus stepped into place as soon as Gladys Hebert moved. "Dr. Brownley, may I formally present Bishop Frederick Sutton."

She extended her hand and received a warm, two-handed shake from Bishop Sutton. He was a big bear of a man and had cast a stern and imposing presence during the meeting. Close-up, she could tell he was a gentle giant.

"I'm impressed, Dr. Brownley. I was just telling Rev. Gates here that it must have been Providence that placed you in the house next to his this summer," Bishop Sutton said with a huge grin. "I also understand that in addition to your new job you also have a home in our area."

"Yes, sir, in Somerset."

"Have you found a church in the area?"

"No, sir, I'm still attending my home church in the city."

"Well then, let me extend to you an invitation to worship with us anytime you don't feel like making the drive to the city. I'm sure Rev. Gates filled you in on our denomination. We're just like everybody else, Bible study on Wednesday and two services on Sunday."

"Yes, thank you, Bishop Sutton."

"No, thank you, Dr. Brownley, for your time this morning. Finus, I'll speak with you later. I've got to pick Ms. Inez up and make it to the Northside by one p.m. for that fashion show." Bishop Sutton patted Finus on the back and went off down the hall.

"Shall we?" Finus motioned for her to follow the others.

Back in the Boxster, she hoped his mood would lighten now that the interview was over. *Maybe I should suggest we go to the Patio and have a cheeseburger and fries.*

Silently, Finus signaled and drove at breakneck speed to the area around the mall. He didn't speak until he decelerated on the exit ramp.

"Do you like Braxton's?"

"Yes." She'd never been able to afford Braxton's.

Thankfully they were seated quickly. The waiter seemed to know him so their orders were promptly taken. He ordered coffee and the special of the day. She ordered water and a bowl of lobster bisque. Best to eat light.

"Do you drink much coffee during the day?" she asked, wondering if coffee accounted for his nervous movements.

"Sometimes. I find that caffeine helps elevate my mood." Finus's reply was snappy and he had a sour face. They had little conversation during lunch. This was so different from earlier meals they'd shared.

She held back the hundred questions she wanted to ask him about his mother and the initial plans for the school, thinking that he might be preoccupied with the big undertaking.

"Do you care for dessert?"

She shook her head no.

"Are you sure? They have the best key lime pie here. I'm going to have a slice to go if you can't be tempted to join me," Finus said in the friendliest voice that had come from him all day.

She scrutinized his face. As much as she wanted to try the flourless chocolate cake, she declined. His hand shook slightly while he settled the bill. She decided that while the coffee seemed to elevate his mood it definitely made him jittery.

When they arrived at her house she expected him to get out of the car and open the door for her as he had over the summer. But he seemed disinclined to move after he wished her a good weekend. She opened the passenger door and got out of the Boxster by herself. She turned around at her front door to see him race out of her drive. He drove so fast she didn't have time to wave.

Chapter 4

On the third Sunday of September, Finus sped toward the Garden Cathedral. He glanced over at Cassandra and offered a weak smile.

"I can't afford to be late," he complained. "Bishop Sutton often rewards the late man by calling him to preach."

When they arrived he ushered her through a side door of the church and directed her toward the sanctuary. "Make yourself at home. I'll see you after service." He disappeared and Cassandra stood unnoticed in the vestibule. Missed notes from the choir as they warmed up greeted her as she entered the sanctuary. The ushers were gathered around the back pews assigning stations for the day, and a small group of congregants knelt before the altar.

She sat towards the back and observed. The fragrance of fresh flowers and wood oil filled the air. High above the outer walls were twelve brightly colored stained glass windows, each depicting a tenet of the church. The pews were covered in rich purple velvet and the dais filled with lush, fresh floral arrangements. She marveled at the beauty and grandeur of the sanctuary.

She snapped to attention when the organ heralded the eleven o'clock hour. A procession of robed choir members and clergy proclaimed the call to worship. By eleven ten, visitors were acknowledged with the traditional invitation to stand and introduce themselves. Cassandra stood and shifted her feet as she waited to be recognized. Her hands turned over and over since it was obvious she would be the last visitor addressed.

"May I present to the congregation Dr. Cassandra Brownley. Dr. Brownley is the new associate vice principal at Westmore High," Finus started.

Oh, aah, amen, and a round of applause greeted her.

"Dr. Brownley will also serve as our educational consultant on the Gates school project. I will give a formal introduction of Dr. Brownley when we share the school progress report. But for now, Dr. Brownley, please come and be seated in the patch. Let us make all of our visitors feel at home."

In a flash an usher stood at the end of the pew and extended a white gloved hand to escort her to the front row. Now she remembered Finus had asked her to sit in one of the three rows up front. He called it the patch, three rows reserved for church mothers, ministers' wives, and the bishop's special guest.

"My, my, how lovely my garden grows," Bishop Sutton said before addressing the congregation. He made some brief comments regarding reports from the convention, and then continued with the order of worship. "Our congregational prayer will be led this Sunday by the Reverend Gates."

He was elegant, eloquent, and inspiring. She opened her eyes to sneak a peek at Finus while he prayed. He looked in his element as he stood before the congregation in his liturgical robes. She wondered who she looked at. Yes, it's the same man, but today he's different. The Reverend Doctor Gates is presiding. This isn't Doc from the lake.

After prayer, the service continued with announcements and other general church business, which included the Gates school report. She stood, turning her hands over again while Finus made some brief comments about her credentials.

He paused for a moment and looked down at his notes. "Well, this is interesting. Church, it says here that Dr. Brownley is a classically trained soprano with a five-octave range." He looked over at the choir director who was staring excitedly at her. "Isn't that rare?" He turned back to the prepared dossier. "It also says Dr. Brownley has sung before presidents, the Queen of England, and the Pope."

The congregation *um*-ed and *ah*-ed again.

He motioned from the pulpit for her to sit down. "We did not know that!"

She took her seat and remembered the back and forth she'd had with Janet Jones, his secretary. It had taken Janet three calls to get something personal out of her. She had shared her vocal accomplishments only after Janet, quoting Finus, said the biographical sketch was impressive but bland.

She was grateful God had blessed her with such a voice. It had paid for her education and provided her the opportunity to see the world, but that was all behind her now. She glanced at the senior choir as they rose to offer their A selection. As the choir struggled through an old standard, she smiled at Gladys Herbert in the soprano section.

The man ordained to bring the message was the Reverend David Broadnaux. He preached a powerful, down-home sermon on trust. She wrote down the scriptural references and some of the down-home anecdotes he used. Trust. She knew a few things about broken trust.

As soon as benediction was spoken, the ladies in the patch closed in on her.

"Please come again, dear." *Nice.*

"Are you the lady he met at the lake?" *Nosey.*

"God bless you for the work you are doing at that school. Lord knows they need somebody like you." *Very nice.*

Cassandra glanced at the doors where the clergy stood shaking hands with the congregants as they passed out of the sanctuary. The line to shake Finus's hand was populated by what seemed to be every woman under forty in the building. Yolanda had been right about one thing. The women dressed. Yolanda had advised her to take it up a notch this morning. Cassandra smoothed down the skirt of the simple straight brown suit she wore. She hadn't seen so many peplums, kick pleats, ruffles, silks, and animal prints in one place at the same time in years. Her home church had a relaxed dress code and only the church mothers wore hats and pearls on Sunday morning.

It was clear the Assemblywomen, young and old, still followed the African-American tradition of dressing to the nines for church. There were some sharp sisters hoping to catch Finus's eye. She looked ruefully down at her skirt. It didn't matter since in some respects he was now her boss.

She turned around to answer a gentle pat on her shoulder. "Hi, I'm Lydia Broadnaux. Did you enjoy the service?"

"Yes, I did."

"I hope you're a patient person. It will be a while before they're ready to leave," Lydia continued.

"I'm sorry?"

"Excuse me. I just thought maybe you came with Rev. Gates."

"I did."

"He's something, isn't he?"

"Yes, he is." She flushed and clasped her hands together.

"David and I, my husband is Rev. Broadnaux, we're just in awe of him. I've never met anyone like him. We're simple people from a small town in Alabama and not used to being around such an esteemed group."

Lydia had wide amber eyes that sparkled as she spoke. The well-cut navy boucle-suit she wore didn't match her unsophisticated air.

"Dr. Brownley, did you enjoy the service?"

She turned slowly. Behind her stood the man himself, resplendent in his liturgical robes, definitely a Reverend Doctor.

"Yes, Rev. Gates, it was very nice."

Finus reached around her to kiss Lydia on the cheek. "Good morning, Lydia."

"Good afternoon, Finus. No, excuse me, Rev. Gates."

"Lydia, it's always Finus for you."

"I wanted to say the right thing since you were being so formal," Lydia said.

Finus grinned. "You have such a sweet soul."

"It was nice chatting with you, Dr. Brownley."

"No, Mrs. Broadnaux, it's Cassandra, please."

"Thank you, and I'm Lydia. I hope to see you again very soon."

Finus turned to scan the emptying sanctuary. A few of the older ladies scattered amongst the pews turned their attention towards them.

He folded his arms in a regal stance and gave the women a princely nod.

Cassandra's eyebrow shot up.

"Cassandra, it's going to be a little while before I can leave. Bishop Sutton has requested to see the clergy in conference."

"Okay, then I'll just have to sit and wait." She'd never attended church with a minister before and had not anticipated the possibility of Finus having to take care of business after the service.

"Are you sure? I can—"

"Do I have a choice? You're my ride."

"Exactly." He turned on his heel and strolled confidently through a door behind the pulpit.

She left the emptying sanctuary and took a seat in the church lobby. There were still a few people about.

She met several parents with students at Westmore. She chatted briefly with Gladys Herbert after she hung up her robe. She waved goodbye to the counting team after they finished their task and left the building. She was still waiting when the ushers finished their meeting and left their office.

While she waited, she recalled her weekend. On Friday night Finus had called to congratulate her and to make sure she'd received the box of documents he'd sent to her house. He'd asked if he could stop by Saturday night because there were a few documents that needed her immediate review. Their phone call had lasted until after midnight, and he was again the personality that she'd enjoyed so much over the summer.

Finus was very talkative over the phone on Friday night as he shared more details about his life. Curiously, he referred to himself by different names as he described the different facets of his life. Dr. Gates held a BMA-endowed chair of religious history at Moody Bible Institute. Finus Gates looked over the real estate business his mother left him. And Rev. Gates, well, he did not yet hold the office of pastor, so he was at the disposal of the bishop.

Without bragging, he'd told her about the attention that he received from Assembly women. He described it as being hunted by a streak of tigers. She recognized Doc's humor when he told her how he'd used the school project to help him escape from a Friday night singles meeting at the Cathedral.

On Saturday night, as promised, he'd stopped by with the documents. But they didn't work. Just after he arrived, Yolanda, on her way to answer a booty call, dropped her children off without coming inside. Finus greeted the children by ordering a pizza. Then they'd all watched a movie. When he left shortly after midnight he informed her, in his don't-say-no way, to be ready at ten-fifteen in the morning. He would personally escort her to church. So, here she sat waiting for the Right Reverend Doctor Gates to come out of his conference.

"Excuse me, miss. Are you waiting for a ride home or something?" An elderly gentleman in a paper-bag-brown suit similar to hers stood before her.

"No, I'm waiting for Rev. Gates."

"Well, miss," the gentleman began, "all of the clergy are in conference and I need to lock the building. They all leave through another entrance, so I suggest that you go ahead on home."

Before she could open her mouth, Finus strolled out of the main sanctuary. Even without his liturgical robe he cast a regal presence.

"Cassandra, I'm sorry. I didn't expect to take that long."

"Rev. Gates?"

"Good afternoon, Deacon Jones. Ready to lock up?" He winked.

"Reverend, I didn't know the young lady was a guest of yours."

"Yes, Deacon, this is Dr. Brownley, our educational consultant for the Gates school. You must have been downstairs during that part of the service."

An embarrassed flush crossed the deacon's face. "Nice to meet you, ma'am."

"We'll leave you to lock up. Cassandra, you've been invited to dinner at the bishop's residence." He had offered to take her to Sullivan's, a black-owned banquet hall popular with the after-church crowd. Sullivan's was famous for its sumptuous soul food buffet served with a side order of contemporary gospel music.

She shrugged her shoulders and gathered her handbag. "Dinner at Bishop Sutton's house sounds fine."

"Excellent," he exclaimed as he stiffly extended his arm and pointed her toward the outer doors.

Deacon Jones walked ahead of them and opened the remaining unlocked door. Before they were two steps away the deadbolt lock clanged.

"We are going to the last house that we lived in as a family," Finus said while driving along the side streets to the bishop's official residence. His tone seemed to be slightly more relaxed.

"Another boyhood home?"

"Not really. Mother built this house while Dad was building the Cathedral. She said she needed something to do. Anyway, I lived there for a while when I was in grad school. Inez is kind enough to let me keep my old room. You did meet Inez Sutton this morning?"

Cassandra nodded.

"Good! After Mom passed, Fred and Inez moved in. They took care of Dad in his final year, and, when Dad passed, he gave the house to the church and gave me to the Suttons. I think the church got the better of the deal." He chuckled.

"With the plan for you to live in the house again when you become bishop?"

"You know, Cassandra, I don't know. Yes, I have thought about it, becoming a bishop, but I don't know if it will ever happen. I can't even get a church to pastor."

"Why not?"

"Fred says I'm not ready. He says I 'ain't fit.' "

Cassandra laughed. "I can't imagine the learned Bishop Sutton using the word *ain't*."

"Yes, he said it, just like that. Says it all the time! You'll have to remember that Fred is from Alabama and he likes to pepper his speech with his Southern charms."

She relaxed into the butter leather seats of his Boxster. This was the Doc she knew from the lake. "I'm sure he just means it to encourage you."

"That's an interesting way to put it. I'll try to remember that. Fred and Inez have been good to me, a second set of parents." He slowed down just a tad as they entered a residential zone and his tone changed. "You mentioned Friday that you thought Fred's standards were 'rather restricting.' I wanted to share with you that I don't mind. I know he has my best interest at heart, and it's one of the church's tenets to graciously submit to authority," he sermonized as he turned onto a private, tree-lined street.

The house that Wilma Gates built was a modern, box-like structure with lots of windows and steel. It looked cold and out of place nestled against a backdrop of old-growth forest.

"Surprised, aren't you?" Finus parked in the circular drive, which was already lined with six other luxury automobiles. All clergy at the bishop's call were welcome at dinner.

"Yes. Your mother must have been an amazing woman."

"That would be one way to describe her."

After they entered the house and exchanged hellos he gave her the standard visitor's tour. The glass and steel structure that seemed cold on the outside was warm and inviting inside.

The mansion was filled with mahogany woodwork and art that should have been in a museum of African-American history. He showed her original writings of the BMA founders, yellowed and preserved under glass. There were original oil paintings from Crite and Tanner. He insisted she use the first floor powder room to freshen up. It held a mirror that had once hung in the Vatican. He played down the significance of the piece, saying that it had been in a bathroom at the Vatican, too. But she was impressed.

The final stop on the tour was the solarium, a great hall with ten-foot windows overlooking the forest preserve behind the house. "There are often occasions when a hundred or more members need to be entertained, and, in her later years, Mom insisted on doing that at home."

In the midst of this huge steel house filled with art and history, she sensed the warmth of a family's home.

"Welcome, welcome, I'm glad you chose to come." Fred Sutton greeted her with a bear hug. "What do you think about this house? Did Doc give you the nickel tour?"

"Yes, it's very impressive. I was just telling Rev. Gates that his mother must have been an amazing woman."

"Yes, that Wilma was something else. But what's with this Rev. Gates stuff?" Fred socked Finus playfully in the arm. "Loosen up and at least invite the lady to call you by your Christian name."

"I don't know what's gotten into her today. She usually calls me Doc. Are you ready? Can we eat?" Dinner was not served until Bishop Sutton blessed the table.

They joined the others in a grand dining hall with a table set for twenty. During dinner, there were many questions from Inez Sutton, Lydia Broadnaux, and the other wives. Their questions were nosey but not obnoxious, just the general inquiries people make when they're getting acquainted. But every answer attracted more interest. As more questions emerged about how she met Finus and their shared vacation by the lake, the more the huge dining room seemed to shrink. It felt like she was in a confessional booth.

Finus and David Broadnaux altered the course of the conversation with jokes. She couldn't tell if that was intentional, but the focus shifted. Finus had a perfect foil for his antics in David. David was a big, fine man with a heavy Southern accent and good comedic timing.

After dinner the ladies took their desserts into the sunroom while the men retired to the den to watch football. Shortly after six she ventured into the male den to ask Finus to take her home. In saying her good-byes, she reminded Bishop Sutton that Monday was her biggest workday. "I'm sure there will be some new discipline case on my desk as a result of something that happened over the weekend."

They sped through the early autumn evening.

"I had a lovely day. It's nice to get a glimpse into the life of the clergy. You're an interesting group."

Finus didn't answer.

Cassandra seethed and sank into her seat. *How is it possible that his mood could shift so suddenly?*

"You did well," Finus said after he decelerated off the highway. "By the way, I never talk when I'm driving on the highway."

Cassandra didn't reply, her nose bent out of shape by yet another rule.

"You did very well at church and dinner," he repeated in a ministerial tone.

"Was today another interview?"

"No, it's just that the last person I brought to church caused much drama. Even with Deacon Jones you didn't make a fuss about being my guest."

"Well, there was no reason for drama, and everyone was so nice. Although I see what you mean by the attention you get. Do you realize that it was mainly young ladies in line to receive your greeting after service?"

"Yeah, Rev. Gates got it like that."

"Well, Rev. Gates, better be careful with that."

The Boxster closed in on her house.

"I really am enjoying getting to know you better. Not many women are secure enough to develop a friendship with a man," he said as he came to a stop in her driveway. He hopped out of the car and walked around to help her out of his vehicle.

"No, most sisters couldn't do it." He leaned against the door and flashed her one of his wicked grins. "So, Dr. Brownley, any time you care to attend the services at the Cathedral I'm happy to escort you."

"I don't know. It's been a long day. I'll let you know."

She watched from the porch as he returned to his car and sped away, driving entirely too fast.

During the next week, she pondered Doc's compliment. She wondered if she was secure enough to develop a friendship with a man like Finus Gates.

Chapter 5

To pass the half hour between the school board and senior choir rehearsal, Gladys Herbert sat in the quiet of the cathedral's sanctuary on the pew where she and Wilma used to sit and dish.

"I'm very impressed with her work." Gladys caught herself when she realized she spoke aloud to her deceased pew mate. "You're still with us," she whispered and looked around the sanctuary. Wilma's influence was alive in the sanctuary, from the color of the pews to the beauty of the stained glass windows that she had commissioned.

A month into the project and things seemed to be going well. Gladys even managed to persuade Finus to hold the meetings on Thursday so she could participate in her two favorite activities and make only one trip.

"Which, as you know was no easy task."

Things seem to be going well, until this afternoon. As well as Gladys knew Finus, she hadn't been able to read his expression today. She couldn't tell if he was happy with Dr. Brownley's work, if he regretted bringing her to the committee's attention, or if something else was going on.

"Wonder what you would make of the current spate of rumors about Finus and Cassandra. She seems like such a serious-minded girl. You'd like her."

Gladys had been one of Wilma's most faithful friends. When Finus was three she was his first Sunday school teacher, and later taught him high school English. She proofread every paper he wrote, including his dissertation. Her service on the school committee was in tribute to Wilma.

Gladys laughed out loud. "Oh, chile, the time you spent in prayer over his choices in women."

Finus's penchant for beautiful women was well-known throughout the Assembly. "Those last two were something."

The model was beautiful. Though part Asian, she identified herself as black. The week before his ordination, she spoke of an intimate relationship with Finus in an interview with *Black Pages*. That had created a stir, but Fred ordained him anyway.

Then came the model/actress who went by only one name. She wore an inappropriately short multi-animal-skin skirt with a tight animal-skin jacket to Sunday service, an outfit too *haute couture* for the traditionally well-dressed crowd at the cathedral. She crowned her outfit with an English top hat draped in black tulle, featuring a two-foot tiger-striped ostrich feather. The ensemble made her eight feet tall. Fred slyly thanked her for dusting the light fixtures. Her outfit prompted a profusion of animal prints in the Assembly. For the past year, women wearing every kind of animal print, natural and unnatural, had pursued poor Finus.

One-name's acting, however, ruled the day. Her act took place during the sleepy middle of Finus's sermon. She stood, extended her long arm to the ceiling, and folded her body into a perfect S. She jerked, then held herself erect, all eight feet, and let out a whoop. She looked and sounded like a whooping crane. A mortified Finus moved to close his sermon. That was the last lady he'd brought to church. There had been rumors of others, but none he'd brought to church until now.

"I don't like what I heard at the missionary circle meeting last week." The gossips had placed Finus at Cassandra's house every Friday and Saturday night for the past month. "The rumor is Finus is not the only man she's seeing." Gladys grew silent in acknowledgement that Wilma wasn't sitting next to her today. She reached into her handbag and pulled out a Kleenex. She didn't like gossip, especially some of the mess spouted by many Assembly members. And if she didn't pull it together the talk would be about her.

"There's Gladys in her same old seat."

She turned around at Ellen Whitney's voice. She silently vowed to listen out for anything that might affect her old friend's son because, in spite of himself, she loved Finus.

It didn't take long after rehearsal for the talk to start.

An alto section member started, "Many of the ladies wonder if the privileged prince is done being the Assembly's biggest playboy. Dorothy Jones told me he took Dr. Brownley to dinner at the bishop's house."

"His new lady friend seems like a sensible woman. Maybe he's finally ready to set a proper example," Mother Pierce suggested.

Ellen Whitney chimed in. "The relationship seems to be enduring. I've known about it since the summer."

Mother Pierce rose to leave. "It's too soon to tell."

"It's been a while since he's brought anyone to church. Is he dating? Last I heard he wasn't," a tenor with a marriageable daughter asked. "You know, I doubt he's seeing that lady in the plain brown wrapper. That isn't his usual type. Remember the last two he brought through here?"

The talking trio laughed.

Gladys entered the discussion only to end the talk about Finus. "Ladies, we must remember one of our church tenets is to respect leadership, and we shouldn't speak about a member of the clergy in such a fashion. Now I know most of you have watched Finus grow up, and we've been discussing his antics for years, but we need to remember that he's Rev. Gates now."

Cassandra sat on her bed on the first Saturday in October painting her toenails. This ritual reminded her of the problem with Greg. When they first became engaged she had to be polished, dried, and ready to go out by six p.m. However, as their wedding date drew nearer, she could paint her nails at midnight and be in no danger of his coming in before they dried. Now every dateless Saturday night she painted her nails and chatted with her toes. She looked over at the emerald green display on her alarm clock; eight-thirty. "Here we are again, girls." She wiggled her toes. "Waiting for a man."

While her nails dried she reflected on all the things she'd learned in the past month. Like why the district gave the newest principal discipline as a first assignment. It tested the mettle. Her toughest decision had been to expel an African-American male athlete, a star basketball player. Now she was at odds with the seven other African-American staff members.

Her thoughts drifted to the Gates school and Finus. The project was progressing swiftly under his leadership. Finus insisted the Gates school exceed all state and district standards. He would ask the same question seven times or seek seven sources of information before he settled an issue. He'd taught her that seven was the biblical number of completion. His process was tedious, but she could already see results from his methodology.

She couldn't put her finger on it, but there was something about him. Someone had called him by at least three tag names recently, and the more time she spent working with him, the more she understood the reason. The man had three distinct personas.

Big Brother Bow Tie was an appropriate moniker. Finus was an impeccably dressed man with designer suits and hand-tailored shirts. He wore fancy cuff links and topped off his personal style with his signature bow ties. Fastidious Finus was also a fitting description because he was precise, methodical, and picky to the *n*th degree. Dr. Jekyll-Rev. Hyde was also appropriate. Finus's mood could change at the drop of a dime.

The name she used most when she spoke to him was Doc. Doc was kind, funny, open, and compassionate, all the good things he'd been over the summer. Her intuition warned her there was something he wasn't telling her. He had moods, and at times he was so fidgety that he couldn't sit still. Despite the fact she was not some 'damn girl', she was attracted to him.

She'd seen a lot of him since their first committee meeting. He took her out for dinner to celebrate her new jobs and the conversation about the near ninety percent drop-out rate in the Chicago public schools was so good he continued it by calling her as soon as he got home.

Since then, they talked almost every night. Their conversations always began with the school project and drifted to other topics, like politics and social and cultural issues.

At precisely nine-thirty the doorbell rang. She bolted down the stairs. She'd waited all day for this late night working session, but wondered and worried as she hurried towards the door. What kind of mood he would be in? Had she done enough research into standardized testing?

She looked through the peephole and paused to behold the Reverend Doctor Finus Gates resplendent in a charcoal grey suit, crisp, tailored white shirt, and dark maroon paisley print bow tie. She fumbled in her haste to open the door.

"Good evening, Cassandra. Are you prepared to discuss testing standards?" Finus swept past and she inhaled his familiar fragrance, a manly blend of Oriental spices with just a hint of something sweet. She trailed him to the den. They settled into their usual chairs around her wrought iron bistro table.

By his greeting, she knew to be on her toes. Fastidious Finus was in the house. He started right in and did not relent for over an hour as he sought to understand the implications of the current trend towards standardized testing as a way to measure school performance.

"I'm satisfied. I have enough information to make a decision, and I don't wish to work on any additional topics tonight. Please excuse me while I call my car service."

Whew, he could blow a cold wind. She waited while he completed his call. "Has something happened to your car?"

"No, sometimes I don't drive. My driver should arrive in a few minutes. It's a bit stuffy in here. I'll wait on the porch." He rose, gathered his briefcase, and started for the door. Cassandra followed, inhaling deeply. *You're a bit stuffy, but Lord, you smell so good.*

"Cassandra, may I ask a favor of you?" Finus began while they waited on her porch. "Would you attend a benefit with me next Saturday evening?" He continued without waiting for an answer. "It's a fashion show and dinner dance, and the proceeds are being donated to the Gates school. You might think of it as one of your duties as our educational consultant." He stopped to take a breath of the crisp autumn night air.

"Personally, it would help me if you would come as my guest. There are far too many single, desperate women at these functions."

She held her breath for a second. He hadn't asked her for a date.

"It helps if I don't show up alone. Cherie used to attend these kinds of functions with me before she moved back to L.A."

"Sure, if it will help." *No, not a date. A reality check. He wants to use me to ward off the tigers?* Too bad. She had a serious schoolgirl crush on him, and standing here in the harvest moonlight wasn't helping.

He muttered something.

"I'm sorry, Doc, what was that?"

"I was asking that you be ready at one-thirty tomorrow afternoon." Fastidious Finus was always precise.

"Sure."

"Fine, fine, and since we're going to Evanston, I'll take you to an African restaurant, after."

She'd almost forgotten she'd agreed to go hear him preach tomorrow. "Won't there be a church dinner after the service?"

"Yes, but I don't usually have the opportunity to eat at these functions. And we won't stay long."

"Why, because of the tigers?"

Finus smiled for the first time all night. "Yeah, that too."

❦

In the weeks following the fashion show Finus invited her to attend several other church events, mainly events put on by the numerous auxiliaries of the Assembly. Finus grumbled about having to attend these events, but afterward he'd take her out to dine on international cuisine.

"I never knew I liked Greek food," Cassandra said as dessert was served at the Isle of Greece restaurant.

He pushed back from the table. "I'm glad you enjoyed it, and I hope you like the vasilopita. It's a traditional dessert, and they say if you find a coin in your cake it will bring you luck."

The waiter, dressed in a traditional foustanela skirt, presented the rounded yellow cake. He took a bite.

"Hey, I found a coin." He feigned surprise. "Let's see if I have any luck with what I want to ask you."

She looked up from her cake plate.

"Cassandra, would you consider appearing as a guest soloist at our upcoming youth revival?"

She stared at the table cloth to hide her disappointment. "I don't think I'll be able to do that. I don't make many singing commitments anymore. Not with my schedule."

"Girl, if I had your gift, you couldn't keep me from singing."

"I'm grateful for my gift, but I also have my responsibilities. It takes so much to perform, with the rehearsals and such. My plate is really full. And I'm sure you have a fine singing voice."

He leaned forward. "No, I can't sing a note. Haven't you noticed? I don't sing during service. I understand you're busy, but this would be singing with our youth choir. The youth choir master is a particular friend of mine. He's been bugging me to ask you. Besides, this is a special program for the young people. It would give you the opportunity to meet some of the potential students for the Gates school. Also, there's someone else I really want you to meet."

Her jaw tightened. She recognized his people-don't-say-no-to-me tone, the same tone he'd used that day at the lake when he convinced her to go sailing with him. *Oh God, who's left to meet? He must have introduced me to hundreds of people over the past month.* She reached for the check folio the waiter set on the table between them just to have something to do. "I'm sorry I can't, but I will take care of this."

"No, ma'am, and please don't offer to pay again."

Cassandra opened the check folio and inspected the bill. It was a little more than she'd expected. When she looked up, Finus was scowling. "Have I violated one of your many rules?"

He stretched out his hand for the bill. "No, but you are attempting to violate one of our church's tenets."

"Are you trying to tell me it's a BMA tenet for the man to always pay?"

"No, it's the proper place doctrine you're trying to overstep. I invited you to church tonight and to dinner and I would not be in my proper place if I did not pay for our meal. Now hand over that check before I find myself in hot water with the bishop."

She held on to the bill and scanned the restaurant while he frowned. They were not the only African-

American diners, so there could be other Assembly members in the restaurant.

"Fred holds his clergy to a very high standard, and I would be in deep trouble if I allowed you to pay that check. You never need to pull out your wallet when you're with me. I also need to tell you that you need not touch a door, and you should expect that I will always help you with your chair or coat. It's the manner in which you deserve to be treated, anyway."

He sounded so resolute that she handed him the folio. "All right, thank you for dinner and for the way you always treat me so nicely. I was going to give the compliment to your mother, but I see it's due to the bishop."

Finus laughed. "No, ma'am, the compliment should be given to my mother. Hers was a stricter standard than Fred's. Who do you think influenced him?"

Cassandra raised her water glass to the memory of Finus's mother. "For raising a true gentleman."

It was true. He'd been a perfect gentleman, except for the day of the interview. She pushed the vasilopita around on her plate. When her fork struck a gold coin, an old sermon point ran through her mind. *I don't need luck, I need to pray.*

Two weeks later Cassandra sat in her den and glanced at her watch. It was already ten-thirty. "I don't know if I'll make it tomorrow night. It's been a very hard week." She should have been in bed, but she'd stayed up late because he said he'd call.

"You've got to come. The young people have worked so hard. They'll be in complete charge and we've planned a special service. There will even be a special presentation on the school. Everybody is looking forward to meeting you."

In the last few days she'd translated 'meeting somebody else' into 'meeting someone special.' *Well, I really can't blame her. If my man were talking to another woman so much I'd demand to meet her, too. Might as well get this over with.* "Okay, what time should I be there?"

"You should have received the program in the mail." He sounded angry. "I asked Janet to send it several days ago."

"Well, hold on, it may be here in this pile. I haven't gotten to my mail yet." Finus had called just as she walked in the door, at ten p.m. A fight after the varsity football game had extended her day and caused her to miss a hair appointment, the real reason she didn't want to attend the revival. She ambled over to the bistro table and picked up the mail.

"I can't offer to pick you up, and the service starts at seven sharp. And just so you know, the Assembly does not operate on CP time," he chatted as she shuffled through bills and ad circulars.

"Okay, I've got it." She ran her fingers across the fine grain of the envelope from his office. She opened the letter and fingered the fineness of the paper, then read over the program.

"I have the details here; District Wide Youth Night, first Friday in November. This should be very inspiring for the young people. I'll be at the Cathedral at six forty-five."

"A sister that knows Lombardi time. I'm impressed."

"No, a person who knows how to keep a job." They continued to talk about their respective weeks and the challenges she faced as the school disciplinarian until her second line beeped. Cassandra cradled the phone in the crook of her neck so she could check her watch. Eleven-thirty. They had been on the phone for over an hour.

"Who could possibly be calling at this hour? Doc, I better get this. I'll make every effort to be on time." She switched the phone over.

" 'San, it's me. Sorry to call so late, but I just got home from a sorority committee meeting. There's something I need to tell you. "

"You called me at this time of night to gossip?"

"I knew you'd be up talking to Doc. Sure there's nothing there?"

"Yogi, I'm working for him. Anyway, he just reminded me that he has someone he wants me to meet tomorrow night."

"Uh-huh. Are you sure it's a woman? Because that's not what I heard tonight. Sorors say he's dating you. Did Shay hook your hair up?"

"No, I missed the appointment."

"Ugh, it's late and I'm not going there. So listen up, I got to tell you what I learned tonight about Doc."

"Yolanda, I'm really not interested."

Yolanda forged ahead. "You know every single woman in that Assembly and the city just about is after him."

Cassandra sighed.

"I went out to dinner with some sorors in the Assembly and they were all up in your business. They knew everywhere you've been in the past month. The BMA is not happy about an outsider coming in and taking their most eligible. I told them you were just working for him."

"Yolanda." Anger burned in her ears. She held the phone away from her ear and counted to ten. "Yogi, you know it's not like that."

"I know, but that's not the word running though the Assembly. I just wanted to warn you."

"Warn me about what?"

"About Doc. You know he can be moody, but the word is that he can also be downright mean. I don't know what he did to Lucinda, but the Bakers are clearly mad at him."

Cassandra took a cleansing breath. Yolanda was only trying to look out for her. And he had already snapped at her a time or two. "Okay, Yo." She softened her tone. "It's been a long day and I'm tired. Goodnight."

"Goodnight, but you call Shay and reschedule that hair appointment. If you're going to that service tomorrow it will help if you're looking your best."

She hung up and hurried through her bedtime rituals. She rushed to get into bed only to roll over twice trying to fall asleep. Just as she dozed off the phone rang.

"Hello?"

"Cassandra, it's me. I just wanted to check to see if everything was all right."

"Yeah, Doc. Why?"

"Late night phone calls are usually bad news."

"No. It was just Yogi."

"Okay. Goodnight, Cassandra." His voice was warm and soothing.

She hung up and wrapped herself in the warmth of his concern. She rolled over and snatched her blanket up to her shoulders. *You know damn well that was pastoral concern, not personal*, her inner voice warned.

Chapter 6

At 6:47 p.m., Cassandra settled into a second row pew at the Garden Cathedral. Scanning the crowd, she didn't see anyone who might stick out as a 'damn girl'. She shrugged. As the rat-a-tat-tat of a marching band filled the sanctuary, her focus shifted outward. The congregation rose and clapped in time to the spirited beat of the processional. Finus had warned her tonight's service would be different, but he hadn't told her how different. A drum line replaced the traditional BMA organ herald.

Bishop Sutton and Inez led the processional in grand style. They were followed by the guest preacher who was dressed in a bold gold silk suit. The line continued with several other ministers and their wives. At the rear, David and Lydia Broadnaux hustled to the beat. At last, the stately Reverend Doctor Gates marched in alongside an absolutely stunning woman.

The procession slowed and the drummers took up positions in front of the altar. Cassandra positioned herself to take full account of the woman on Finus's arm. She was exactly what Cassandra envisioned a 'damn girl' would be: tall, slender, light skinned, beautiful. Her makeup was flawlessly applied and her salon-fresh shoulder-length bob sat perfectly still on her shoulders as she matched Finus's stately stroll down the center aisle. She wore a stylish giraffe-print suit with just the right accents of chunky amber-colored jewelry. Everything about her was perfect. As they passed, Cassandra noted the expensive giraffe-skin shoes the lady wore on her perfect small feet.

Lydia settled into the pew next to her and nudged her. Cassandra mumbled a greeting. Her attention was focused on the great care Finus took to seat his lady in the front pew, next to Inez Sutton.

Inez leaned over from the first pew. "Cassandra, did Finus invite you to the steak fry at the house tonight?"

"No," she said. A lump formed in her throat. She swallowed hard and looked down at her feet. If she looked up she would see all too clearly the back of Finus's lady, with her perfect posture, perched on the front row. She pulled the program out of the hymnal holder in front of her. Tonight's preacher had an inspiring story.

Rev. Isaac Reynolds had grown up in south central LA. He'd overcome the crime, drugs, gangs, and social ills to become a BMA minister. The bio said he'd practically raised himself when his mother fell to crack. She glanced up at the preacher for the hour. Isaac Reynolds was thirtyish, tall, and light skinned, with good, curly hair. His vitae boasted academic credentials and 'a whoop that could set an Anglican church to dancing.' When she glanced over at Finus, he was smiling broadly at his lady. She lowered her head and reviewed the order of service.

The drum major tapped for attention and the youth choir performed a gospel standard with a hip-hop flair. The piece was very well done, and Cassandra stood with the entire congregation to applaud the young choirmaster who'd arranged the piece.

As the applause died down Finus stood, whispered to the guest preacher, and took his place behind the lectern. With a wide, bright smile he congratulated the choir and the youth department. Cassandra looked down at her size nine feet and decided to leave as soon as the service ended.

"Miss Iva Peyton will now lead us in the recitation of the twelve tenets of our beloved denomination," he announced. "Miss Peyton is one of the tireless leaders of our youth department. As she makes her way to the podium, let us give her appreciation for her efforts and the example she is setting for our youth, in particular the young ladies of this congregation."

Iva Peyton rose from the place where Finus had so carefully placed her to pose at the small lectern to the left of the preacher's desk in the pulpit. In addition to her beauty, Iva Peyton was an excellent speaker and led the recitation perfectly. When she finished, Miss Peyton smiled warmly at Finus and stepped gracefully back to her seat.

Cassandra sat though the choir's B selection and devised ways to get out of the building without having to meet Finus's perfect girlfriend. She ran a hand across her arm. The supple softness of her chocolate brown suede jacket slowed her pulse. The cream batik-print wrap dress she'd borrowed from Yolanda flowed across the top of her brown wedge-heeled boots. She looked good tonight, but she didn't measure up. Damn.

During the offertory prayer she peeked up into the pulpit to steal a look at Finus. Isaac Reynolds caught her eye and returned what looked like a hungry gaze. Her head bowed and bobbled. Her hands folded into her singer's stance and she spent the remainder of the service focused on her fingers.

As soon as Bishop Sutton pronounced the benediction she said goodbye to Lydia and made a beeline for the door.

"Good evening, Dr. Brownley."

She stopped at the sanctuary exit and turned to face Finus. *How'd he get through all of these people?* Most people were slow to leave or were headed to shake the hand of the preacher of the hour. Isaac Reynolds had just preached one for the ages.

"Hello, Finus."

"How are you this evening? You look very nice, but I notice you also look like something is bothering you. I had to use the ushers' corridor or I would have missed you. Is everything all right?"

She shook her head and melted to the soft tones of his concern.

Finus frowned. "Then you were planning to leave without speaking to me?" He paused. "I want you to come to dinner with us, have an opportunity to talk with Isaac. Maybe you can get him to sign those books for you."

"You've been with him all week and you haven't asked him to autograph those books? What have you been doing?"

He gave her his wicked little grin. She knew he hadn't done what she asked. Rev. Reynolds had recently published his autobiography, and she'd asked Doc to get several copies autographed for some students at Westmore.

He turned and looked around the sanctuary. The back pews had cleared. "Won't you stay long enough to meet Rev. Reynolds? Sit with me for just a minute."

"No, thank you, and I'll pass on dinner. It's been a long week."

"A moment of your time, Dr. Brownley." He placed his hand on the small of her back and guided her toward the back pew.

In spite of the place a thrill shot up her spine.

A few minutes turned into half an hour. Assembly members with this or that to say to Finus interrupted constantly. Cassandra's brow furrowed as Isaac Reynolds walked towards the back pew.

"Well, fine job, Rev. Reynolds." Finus rose to extend his hand to the visiting preacher, who now stood in the aisle next to the back pew. "May I present my friend, Dr. Cassandra Brownley?"

Isaac Reynolds moved into the second to the last row with an outstretched hand. He gave her a long, slow full view and the same wolfish look. "Yes, my pleasure."

"Hey, man, keep her here for me. There's someone else I want her to meet." Finus turned to Cassandra. "Wait for me," he ordered.

She tried to withdraw her hand from Isaac's grasp.

He held on. "Did you enjoy the preaching?"

Why is he fishing for a compliment from me when he's already received a hundred? She pulled again and freed her hand from his grasp.

She watched Finus's back as he walked toward the choir loft and his perfect lady.

"I understand you have the voice of an angel. How did they let you out of heaven?"

She shook her curls. "I'm sure there are Assembly members wishing to speak to you. Nice meeting you."

"Perhaps, but I am under direct orders from my host to keep you here. And I'm known to do exactly what I'm told, sometimes." His eyebrow rose suggestively. "Might I invite you to have dinner with me at Bishop Sutton's house?" Isaac's voice had a smooth, silky quality. She looked around for Finus. He was on his way back with Iva Peyton.

"Cassandra, you know your sorority sister Iva Peyton. Rev. Reynolds, this is Miss Iva Peyton." The damn perfect lady politely executed the greeting protocol with a perfectly manicured hand.

"Iva, try to convince Cassandra to come to dinner with us. I'll be right back, don't leave." Finus waved a finger at Cassandra and took off again. She was stuck between the proverbial rock and a hard place.

"It's nice to finally meet you, Soror Brownley. I've heard so much about you, and I just haven't had the opportunity to speak to you when you've worshiped with us."

Cassandra wrapped her hands into her singer's pose in her lap. "Thank you. I wasn't aware you attended… "

"You haven't answered my question," Isaac Reynolds said in a tone not to be ignored. Roughness seeped through the fabric of his silk suit.

"No, thank you. I'm tired and will be going home," she said flatly.

Rev. Reynolds reached out and covered her hands with his. "If you are tired, you can ride with us. Finus is driving his Mercedes tonight, and I could help you retrieve your car later."

"No, thank you," came out a little louder than she intended as she extracted her hands from under his.

Iva smirked. "If you're tired you probably should go home. Better safe than sorry."

Cassandra looked around to see where Finus has gotten to; he'd just have to be angry with her for leaving. She had to get out of there. She got up and tilted her head as if preparing to sing. "Goodnight."

She drove home sad, lonely, and angry. Sad because Finus had no interest in her. Lonely because he wasn't coming over this weekend to work. The nasty looks from Isaac Reynolds she could shake off. But Iva's snide remark burned in her ears and angered her.

As a favor to his fellow prelate, Bishop Sutton had assigned Finus as host for his revival preacher. While he played host to Isaac, Finus had the opportunity to observe tiger prowls when he wasn't the quarry. In the western district Rev. Reynolds received the type of attention Assembly women in Chicago showered on Finus. Unlike himself, Isaac didn't ignore them.

On his national speaking tour Isaac was encouraged to change his tune. The bishops hoped Finus could help polish some of Reynolds's rougher edges. He had just turned thirty and, on his bishop's advice, Isaac was looking for a wife.

Reynolds received dozens of invitations for coffee, cake, and chicken, and to maintain appearances Finus accompanied him. Isaac charmed, flirted and impressed church mothers, all the while maintaining one mantra: "I'll know it when I see it."

"That's it, right there." Isaac nudged him as they sat in the pulpit towards the end of the choir's A selection. Finus didn't have time to look; he knew Isaac was doing his usual scan for open faces, those people among the congregants who give encouragement to a speaker with their expressions. He rose to make the evening announcements. The services continued and he didn't have time to follow up.

Finus descended from the pulpit immediately following the services. He had to get to Cassandra. She looked nervous or ill. But he wasn't quick enough. Before he reached the second pew she was gone. If Lydia hadn't pointed him towards the entry doors, he would have missed her. The only way he was able to intercept her in the crowded Cathedral was through the ushers' passage. Though he'd sat with her for half an hour, she wouldn't tell him what was bothering her. Now, two hours later, he was tired of answering questions about her.

During the steak fry there were too many questions about Cassandra. He couldn't decide if he was annoyed with his friends or Cassandra. She had left tonight after he specifically asked her to stay.

"Stop glowering in that corner and come help me in the kitchen." Inez tapped him on the shoulder and he followed her into the kitchen.

Inez opened the door to the freezer. "Isaac's sure asking a lot of questions about Cassandra."

"I introduced them. Introduced her to a good brother and she doesn't follow up." Finus spoke to the steel door and tried to joke off what was really bothering him. He missed her, but at the same time was glad she wasn't there. He moved over to the breakfast nook and stared out the window.

The conversation in the car had started out complimentary. Isaac said he liked Cassandra's soft and pretty look. He pointed out that she was not what he expected from Finus's description. Isaac went on to talk about how he liked the cut of her dress and the bounce of her hair as she enjoyed the choir's singing or nodded in agreement with a sermon point. Isaac continued by sharing his observation that wearing boots put a certain sway in a woman's hips. His conversation turned crude when he outlined how he'd like to make Cassandra's hips move. He even told Finus that he was hoping to see Cassandra's nice dress crumpled on the floor and her bouncy hair lying limp from sweat on his pillow before the sun rose. Finus's hands balled into fists.

Inez stationed herself in front of him with two gallons of ice cream. "Excuse me. I was just asking."

"Inez, I continue to tell you all that Cassandra and I are just friends," he snapped.

"Take these into the hall for me, please."

He returned to the hall, set out the ice cream, and tried to adjust his attitude. He joked with the Broadnauxes until Cassandra's name came up.

"Isaac couldn't stop looking at her. For a minute there I thought he was looking at you." David nudged his wife.

"He was looking at Cassandra?" Finus asked.

"Gates, I told him she was your girl. And he said you said she was just a friend. Then he said no man keeps a friend that fine. Then I told him not to go there because you're the bishop's son. But Reynolds said you *were* a bishop's son, past tense."

Finus crossed his arms over his chest. "How many times tonight do I have to say it? Cassandra and I are just friends."

"Well, that's good to know."

His head jerked around. He hadn't realized Iva Peyton had joined their tête-à-tête.

"Will you all excuse me?" He stalked past Fred just in time to get the nod to join the bishop in his study. When Fred was tired and ready for his guests to go home, he'd retreat to his study with one or two family members until the house cleared.

Finus sat behind the desk staring at the computer screen. Isaac was also tapped to spend some quality time in the study, and all he could do was glower as Isaac spent the better part of the hour inquiring about the plans for the Gates school and Cassandra.

"I'd like to come back as soon as next week and do a public book signing to benefit the school and possibly see Dr. Brownley. From what I've gleaned, I'm convinced she is just the type of woman I'm looking for. Pretty, educated, shy, and quiet." Isaac spoke expectantly.

Finus rose from behind the desk where he saw, but did not read, his email. "That reminds me that I have an assignment," he purposely interrupted. "Cassandra wanted to have some books signed for the African-American Student Council at her school. Tell you what, I'll go get them out of the car, you sign them here, and we'll drop them by her house on the way back to the city."

"Good looking out. I wanted to get another look at her." Isaac reached into his breast pocket and pulled out a pen.

"No, my brother, it's past midnight. We'll drop those books on her porch. You should know that you never disturb a lady at this hour."

"Man, many women, even some in this city, would accept my call at any hour."

"Maybe, but Cassandra's a lady and I would not risk my friendship with her by disturbing her at this hour. I'll be right back." Finus looked down his nose at his houseguest.

"I looked out tonight and wondered for a moment who that was sitting in my patch. I did a double take when I realized it was Dr. Brownley. Do you have a problem with Reynolds wanting to approach her?" Finus stopped cold in his tracks. Fred wasn't known for saying much once he retired to his study.

"I think he already has," Finus said more to Isaac than Fred. Isaac clicked open his fountain pen.

"Some men see weeds, others wild flowers," Fred mused.

At one a.m. Finus delivered a box of books to Cassandra's porch. Her house was dark and an electric company truck was parked in front. When he returned to the car Isaac made no attempt to hide the fact that he was keying her address into his PDA. Finus punched the steering wheel and floored the accelerator.

Chapter 7

Cassandra passed the weekend engaged in her usual tasks, running errands and babysitting. On Sunday morning she made an overdue visit to her home church.

Late in the afternoon, after a huge family dinner, the Brownley women gathered around the kitchen table. The conversation turned straight to men.

"What are you getting out of the friendship?" Her mother sat down in the worn kitchen chair.

Cassandra's stomach clinched. "A much needed education. I can't believe the way women throw themselves at Finus." She leaned forward. "I thought you'd be glad to see me going out. It's been three years." *She can't argue with that.*

"Looks to me like you're getting the short end of the stick, and possibly five pounds; you're looking a little chunky today."

Cassandra twisted her lip.

Phyllis stood up to start the dishes. "Meeting any eligible men?"

Yolanda hooted. "No, the question is, will any men approach you when you're with him. I hear the BMA is very respectful of their clergy, something about a creed or code."

Cassandra pulled at her collar. "Finus always introduces me. In fact I met his girlfriend Friday night. Yogi, do you know Iva Peyton?"

"Yeah. Ooh, I can't believe how desperate some women are. She isn't his woman. She's one of the sorors I had dinner with the other night. She was the main one asking questions about you. Lucinda told me you should watch out for her, she wants him bad. I heard she even moved here to chase him. Talk about tigers, now that's a cat."

Cassandra shook her head. "She never said a word about knowing you."

" 'San, answer my question. What are you getting out of this? I can't put my finger on why, but I don't like him."

"Whatever, Phyl." Yolanda started to clear the table and bumped her sister's shoulder. "Now come on, those Assembly women are convinced there's something going on. And are you sure that there's no interest there?" Yolanda held her hand up to stop her cries of protest. "That's one rich man. I know you're not a gold digger, and I guess I'm not a good one because I saw him first. Doc's nice looking, but his cousin Will is *fineeee*." Yogi swished toward the sink to help with the dishes.

"Yes, I'm sure. He sees me only as a friend and if I had any thoughts otherwise I got that straight Friday night." Friday night's affairs tumbled out of her mouth.

"You're talking about that preacher I saw in the *Black Pages*. They had a feature on him and his book." Phyllis was an avid reader of the weekly free African-

American community news and gossip paper. "Are you sitting here telling me that you dismissed him because you didn't like the way he looked at you?" Her mother bowed her head and shook it.

Yolanda threw her hands up in surprise. "Wait, I saw that article, too. Phyllis, if that man had looked my way, I wouldn't be sitting here with you today!" Yolanda strutted around the table, then back to the sink to high-five their mom.

" 'San, you get real. What's a man supposed to do? You didn't like how he looked at you? And you couldn't deal with whatever Gregory wanted to do to you. Girl, if you knew how to respond to a man maybe you could keep one."

Cassandra sat quietly for a second with her hands folded in her lap. *That does it.* Without another word she packed a plate of leftovers and went home.

Cassandra reluctantly rose from her easy chair. It was the first Thursday evening since September that she'd gotten home before seven. She needed this evening's mental break. Finus usually took her out for dinner after the school project meetings to continue the discussion, but this evening he had another engagement. She hadn't planned to think about anything important until she went to work in the morning, but the day's mail had brought a task she needed to attend to.

She'd decided early on not to make a habit of calling Finus. And after seeing the "tigers," she'd made it a point to avoid any impression of pursuing him. For the briefest moment Friday night, when they sat in that back pew, he showed such concern she thought there might be a chance. Then he introduced Isaac and Iva. She lumbered over to the bistro table to search for his card. When she found it she turned it over and dialed the number he'd scrawled on the back.

"Hi, Finus, it's Cassandra."

"To what do I owe this pleasure? I think this is the first time you've called."

"I'm sorry to disturb you. Are you still at the church?"

"Yes, I'm in the office. I have a meeting with Iva Peyton, then I'm assigned to drive Ms. Inez home from choir rehearsal."

Cassandra felt a check in her spirit and drew in a cleansing breath. "I won't hold you. I just received payment for my consulting, and I have a question."

He laughed. "What, not enough?"

"No, it's more than enough. I can't believe I'm being paid this much money for my advice."

"Cassandra, your wise counsel is well worth the cost. Indeed, the whole board is impressed with what you have done so far."

"That's nice, but—"

"No buts. Learn to accept a sincere compliment."

"The but was for something else." It was fun to talk to Finus when he was in a good mood. "Why is this check from you?"

"Oh, that. Yeah, well, um, technically it's not from me. Uh, actually it is from me."

She'd never heard him hem or haw before. *How charming.*

"Let me explain. You know the money to start the school comes from my family. I'm in the process of establishing a foundation to channel that kind of contribution. When the legal work is finalized, you will be paid by the Gideon-Gates Foundation. But in the meantime the checks you receive come from an account my attorney set up for expenses associated with the school's start-up."

"I can't take your money."

"You are not taking any money. You're earning it, and, like I said, the money was earmarked to pay for consulting. You are actually saving me money in travel expenses."

"So let me understand. Your family is able to finance the building of a school?"

"No, ma'am, we've contributed enough to start it. The church is contributing the land, and ultimately the school will be supported by tuitions. You've seen the budget. My family is just funding the endowment."

"And you can afford to do this?"

"Yes—how should I say this—my parents left me well-prepared financially."

"Finus, are you really a millionaire?" *Uh-oh, shouldn't have said that. He'll think I gossip about him.*

"Does that matter?"

"No, because it's certainly none of my business. I'm sorry if I was out of line."

"Okay, let's leave it and let me ask you about your wallet. What are you going to do with the money you're earning as our consultant?"

"I don't know, pay some bills, give some to Phyllis. There's enough here to, well, I've been thinking about going in with Yogi on a vacation home."

"That all sounds good. But why don't you take some of it and buy yourself a new dress and go to the NAACP awards dinner dance with me?"

She sucked in her lower lip. "Sorry, I can't."

"What? Can't buy a new dress or can't go to the dinner?"

"I can't go to the dinner with you. I have a date."

"I see. Dr. Brownley has a date."

She didn't care for his teasing. "It's possible."

"With whom?" he asked.

"Actually, it's someone I met recently, your frat brother, Whit."

"Oh, no, Cassandra, you can't go out with James Whitney." His tone was filled with disdain.

"What's wrong with Whit?"

"I'd rather see you with anyone besides that brother."

She rocked back. "Oh, like that nasty Isaac Reynolds?" This was the second time she'd let something that she had not intended to say fly out of her mouth. Her hurt feelings from Friday night reemerged.

"Call Whit and cancel," he demanded.

She stretched. "No, I won't."

"You should trust me on this. I know Whit. He's not a righteous brother."

Her faced burned from his pastoral scorn. "Well, Finus Gates, that's your opinion. But I will take your advice and buy a new dress. I've got to go. Goodnight."

❦

Even though Inez Sutton couldn't carry a tune in a silver bucket, Gladys was glad she'd joined the senior choir. Inez had missed the last few rehearsals because of the bishop's schedule, so Gladys filled her in on the talk.

Inez shared her concerns about the after-rehearsal discussions of the senior choir, and had made it a point to be here tonight. Gladys was confident that together they could dissuade the choir members from discussing Finus tonight.

Inez frowned at Gladys when the discussion turned to Finus. For a choir that never traveled with the preachers, they knew everywhere Finus had been in the past month and that Cassandra Brownley had gone with him. The BMA truly was a denomination made up of friends and family. Such-and-so's cousin at Evanston met Cassandra at their annual fashion show. Mother Pierce's good friend at the College Station church sat with her when Finus preached there last week.

"I think she seems to be a nice lady, maybe a little shy."

"But what about the electric company's truck parked in front of her house at least three times a week?"

Gladys and Inez exchanged weary looks. There was more to come. The most faithful gossips kept a story circulated about the meeting between Iva Peyton and Cassandra at the youth revival.

"I heard if Rev. Reynolds hadn't been there to keep the peace one of those ladies would have snatched the other bald-headed. And I'm not saying which one."

Gladys patted Inez's arm. Inez was itching to speak, and they both knew if she did her words would be repeated and turned over a hundred times.

"Now, ladies." Inez couldn't hold her piece. Everyone turned toward her. When the bishop's wife spoke, all ears listened. "Dr. Brownley and Iva Peyton did not argue at the revival."

Ellen Whitney jumped in. "Inez is right. Rev. Gates and Dr. Brownley are just friends. In fact, Dr. Brownley will be sitting at my table this weekend at the NAACP awards celebration with my Jimmy. And we think she's just the type of girl who would be good for our Jimmy."

Inez closed her hymnal and whispered to Gladys, "I'm going to give Finus an earful on the way home."

Chapter 8

Cassandra was startled each time her phone rang on Saturday. She refused to take any calls from James Whitney. When the phone rang again just after nine-thirty she glanced at the display. F.G. GATES. She lifted the receiver. "Hello."

"Hello, my friend. I looked for you at the dinner tonight." His tone conveyed a good mood.

She tensed. "Did you see Whit?"

"Wasn't looking for him. Where were you?"

"I'll tell you, but you have to promise not to gloat."

"Okay, okay."

She took a deep breath. "Your frat brother must have mistaken me for a loon. He called me long after midnight last night, saying, 'Baby, I'm on my way over.' And you and I both know men don't come over after midnight to talk. I don't know who he thought he was talking to, so I hung up. Ten minutes later my doorbell rang."

He inhaled sharply. "You didn't answer?"

Her chest heaved. "Of course not, but that's not the end of it." *Why am I telling him this?* "He was either drunk last night or he's crazy because he had the nerve to ring my bell again this evening. Like I'd go anywhere with him now."

"What did he say this evening?"

"He didn't say anything, to me. I didn't answer the door, must have been washing my hair." She looked at her reflection in the dark glass of her patio door. She'd spent a lot of time and good money in the salon to sit at home tonight.

"Good girl!"

"And?" She held her breath and waited for his comment.

"And what? You said I couldn't gloat. I know it's late, but can I? Can I come by?"

"Well, I don't know, Yolanda's kids are here."

"Oh."

Contemporary gospel music played in the background. *Where is he? The dinner dance should be in full swing.*

"Tell you what, I'll be there in less than an hour and I'll bring you something to cheer you up. You sound a little disappointed."

When her doorbell rang she checked the peephole and paused. Again he stood on her doorstep in sartorial splendor. Tonight he wore a navy pinstriped suit with a red-and-navy striped bow tie. As he entered her house, she inhaled. *Does he always have to look so good and smell so right?* Her knees buckled.

He held up the huge bag from the Cheesecake Factory. "I brought cheesecake."

She followed him into the den, where he settled himself in her double chair. She cut her eyes at him.

That Finus always took the best seat for himself. She set the cheesecake on the bistro table and took a seat at the end of the sofa.

"The dinner dance was a nice event. I did some networking and politicking. I think the board might issue a proclamation in support of our school."

She beamed and sucked in her lip. "That's wonderful."

Cassandra turned her head toward the kitchen at the sound of her garage door opening. The children ran past the den on their way to the back door.

"Whoa, Jalen, Yasmine. Stop. You need to speak to Rev. Doc."

While the children spoke she rose. "Excuse us, Doc."

Cassandra made it to the doorway of her kitchen as soon as the back door opened. "You know to take those boots off before you walk across my kitchen floor." She spun around. Finus stood behind her with his coat on his arm. She cocked her head to one side. "This is my brother James. We all call him Brown."

He reached his arm around her to shake her brother's hand. "Nice to meet you."

Brown nodded. "Same here. 'San, I stopped by to crash. I'm on the back end of sixteen hours. I didn't know Yogi's kids were here or that you had company." Brown and his duty radio often slept on her sofa during his overnight shifts as an electric company trouble man.

She studied the grime on Brown's uniform; he'd had a tough night. "Don't worry about it. Go crash in the den. We'll go into the living room. The kids are on their way back upstairs so you won't be disturbed." She glanced down at the children.

Jalen dragged his feet across the kitchen. "Can we have cake, too, Aunt 'San?"

"No, it's too late for you to eat sweets. Take Yasmine upstairs and get in bed."

"I knew it. You just want us to go to sleep so that you and him can go into the bedroom," Jalen challenged.

Finus looked down at his shoes.

"These are Yolanda's children," she said.

Finus looked up and offered a smile. "Let me take this one, while you put Princess Yasmine to bed."

She didn't know what Finus said or promised but when she returned to the living room, Jalen apologized and went immediately upstairs.

They sat in companionable quiet for a minute. She took a few bites of the cheesecake, then remembered her mother's words. She dropped the fork in her lap. "Can you explain to me how men think? I mean Whit, and I talked over the phone a few times, but what made him think I would hop straight into bed with him?"

Finus put down his fork and stared at her for a moment. "Your hair looks nice. Did you do it yourself?"

Cassandra shook her head. "No."

He pointed his fork at her and grinned. "I'm not going to defend all the good brothers because another knucklehead messed up. I don't know what's wrong with James. His parents are real good people. I am, however, grateful you found out about him so quickly."

"Well, I've been fooled before so I try to catch on fast." Gregory's face flashed in her mind's eye.

"Just don't settle," he cautioned.

"And don't you cross the line," she returned.

"What line?"

"You know, the color line. I'm guessing you would be a prime target for the white girls. Handsome, successful, and rich. I'm surprised you don't have a streak of white tigers on your tail."

"I can spot a gold digger a mile away, a white tiger or otherwise. And I'd never cross the color line."

She picked up her cup and leaned back into a sofa cushion. "Why not?"

"Two reasons. Number one, could you imagine what would happen if I brought a white woman up in the Assembly?"

"I'd like to be a fly on the wall." She leaned forward. "No, I take that back. I'd lead the attack. Now what's your second reason?"

"I would never disrespect my mother or aunts in that fashion. Mother would have considered it the highest form of disrespect."

"Your mother raised you right."

"What about you? Ever date a white boy?"

The smile on her face broadened. This was her friend Doc, suit jacket off, bow tie loosened. "A few years ago my answer would have been a resounding no, but as I've aged, and my prospects have become more limited, I'd consider it. If he was a decent man. And he wanted to date me for the right reasons."

"You don't want to be a white boy's chocolate fantasy?"

"Reverend Gates!" Her tone shot up an octave. "You are so bad. No, I'm not interested in giving anybody a taste of the forbidden fruit."

He laughed and forked up a bite of his cheesecake, then frowned after he glanced at his watch. "Look at the time, I better go. Cassandra Brownley doesn't talk to men after midnight."

She stood up and jutted out her chin. "That's right. It's time for you to go anyway, because I'm going to church in the morning."

Finus rubbed his palms in glee. "Good, what service are you attending?"

"I'm not going to the Garden. I'm going to Northside Baptist. I've visited there a couple of times. It's a nice church."

"I know the pastor; Paul Means is a good man." His brow creased. "Are you ruling out joining the Assembly?"

"I like the Assembly. But I need to find a church home out here. I'm depending on the Lord to lead me to the right one."

"I'll escort you."

She crossed her arms over her chest. "Don't you have to work tomorrow?"

"Not necessarily. I'm not officially on staff and Fred doesn't mind if I visit around because I know where I belong. What time does service start?"

"I didn't invite you to come with me."

Finus flashed one of his wicked grins as he stood. "That's the problem with black women. Decent man trying to take them to church, and…"

"Okay, okay!" She raised her hands in surrender. "Eleven o'clock, but it's too much for you to drive all the way back out here in the morning."

"Who said I was going home tonight?"

Huh?

"I'll pick you up at ten-thirty. Don't make me late like you do for the Cathedral. By the way, are the children going with us?"

She smiled softly. *He's too thoughtful.* "No, their mother will be here. Guess my house is the family hotel tonight."

He turned toward the front door. "I think that's nice, Cassandra."

While he put on his coat, Yolanda waltzed in. The three of them stood in the entry foyer and chatted.

James Brownley's voice boomed as he entered the living room. He walked up and hugged his baby sister. "Didn't expect to see you until morning." He turned to Cassandra. "I guess I'll have to go back to crashing in the truck. Look, I was going to put up your storm screens in the morning, but now I won't get to them until late next week. I gottta go. We got another outage. Some drunk rammed into a substation. I'll get to your screens early next week."

"Thank you, and you know you're free to come here anytime."

Yolanda nudged her brother. " 'San just works for Reverend Doc, and until she makes lasagna you know ain't nothing going on."

Finus's eyebrow shot up.

Brown filled in the blank. "At our home church Cassandra's lasagna is requested almost as much as her singing."

Yolanda playfully nudged her sister. "You haven't made us lasagna in a while. Don't you *luv* us anymore, big sis?"

Cassandra laughed. "Keep safe, Brown. Goodnight, Doc." She waved the men out of her house.

Finus and Fred sat in the sunroom of the bishop's official residence and enjoyed the early light as they skimmed through the Sunday *Tribune*.

Fred looked up from the sports section. "What time did you get in last night?"

He scowled. "Around one. But I'm not tired."

"I shouldn't ask, but where'd you go after the dinner? Broadnaux and some of the fellas came over to catch the replay of the Bulls game."

Finus looked out of the window at the rising sun. "Yeah, I planned to check that out with you but I went by Cassandra's and—"

"Cassandra, Cassandra. What do you think about Miss Cassandra? You spend a lot of time with her, and all I hear from you lately is Cassandra, Cassandra."

Finus poured another cup of coffee and filled Fred in on his visit.

"It's no wonder she accepted Whitney's invitation. You know what they say about all work. But I also hear about another." Fred acknowledged that some of the gossip had reached his ears. "But it was you who looked like you were missing something or someone last night." He paused. "What say you give the offertory prayer this morning at eleven?"

Finus recognized one of his father's old techniques. Lay it on thick, then abruptly change the subject to avoid back talk. He picked up the business section so Fred wouldn't see his grin. "I won't be there. I'm escorting Cassandra to Mean's church. She has been visiting there and wants to go back for another look."

"Cassandra, Cassandra," Fred sang. "Well, I'll say this: I respect her for not joining the Assembly just to chase after you. I've got enough of those on my rolls, thanks to you."

An influx of young professional women had joined the church once Finus began attending services on a regular basis after his mother passed.

"I wish she would join us. She'd be a tremendous asset." He set the paper down and pointed his index finger at his godfather. "And you can stop your little ditty. Cassandra and I are just friends. Bulls win?" He'd mastered the technique, too.

Fred glanced down his nose. Finus smiled. It wouldn't do to show annoyance with Fred, not on a Sunday morning when he had other plans.

"Ever hear tell of friendship caught afire?" Fred pondered aloud.

That would have been the last comment, but Inez came in and sat down.

"The traffic at our table last night was almost unbearable. Even Gladys complained. So many ladies walked past or stopped at the table last night as soon as word spread you were alone. I didn't enjoy my dry chicken at all." She poured herself a cup of coffee. "And what happened to Cassandra? I heard Ellen Whitney's got quite a bee up her bonnet because she and James Jr. never showed up."

His leg shook under the table while he filled Inez in.

Inez's face lit up. "And after all that talk from Ellen at choir rehearsal. You know, Gladys and I thought for certain you had accepted one of Iva Payton's many offers and were off courting her."

Finus scowled. "All I did was walk Iva to her car." He snatched up another section of paper.

"I'm just letting you know so you can be prepared." Inez stood up. "Fred, isn't it time we go?"

"Yes, ma'am." Fred stood for the only person he'd take an order from. "Son, know that the house is always open to you anytime you don't feel like driving back to the city."

"We'd rather you stay here than…" Inez finished her husband's thought.

"Cassandra, Cassandra," Fred sang as he strolled away from the breakfast table.

Slightly past eleven Finus and Cassandra arrived at Northside Baptist Church. She walked in behind him as he followed the usher. She should have gone first. He was just the type to follow an usher straight to the mourners' bench. Midway up the center aisle, she spied some space. She reached forward and tugged at his coat tail. They settled into a pew in the middle of the sanctuary.

After the opening prayer, Rev. Paul Means rose to greet his congregation. He made some cursory remarks, then focused on one particular guest. "Rev. Gates, that can only be you in your signature bow tie. Northside, please welcome the Reverend Doctor Gates from the Baptist Methodist Assembly. Reverend, our pulpit is open and you are welcome in this place."

Finus stood but declined the courtesy of a pulpit seat. The service progressed with a distracting amount of aisle walking. Mainly young women, who'd sometimes pause and smile at him before they passed. Could they go anywhere in Chicago without this happening? Cassandra studied her clasped fingers.

Northside was famous for its contemporary gospel choir, and this morning they didn't disappoint. Cassandra's salon-fresh curls bounced softly on her shoulders as she enjoyed the spirited singing. During a round of praise clapping, Finus leaned in close. "Your hair looks really nice this morning."

When the visitors were formally acknowledged he poked her in the ribs twice. But she refused to stand up with the rest of the morning visitors. "I've been here before."

The ushers packed their row with a few more late comers. His firm thigh pressed against hers and a thrill tickled her spine. She shifted in the pew. She looked around the simple sanctuary as the various announcements were read. Northside reminded her of her home church: simple wooden pews and a classic communion table, with the standard inscription, 'Do this in remembrance of me.' She jumped and turned towards his nudge. He passed her a note written on the back of the church bulletin.

Dinner at Sullivan's?

They'd had dinner there several times after church. It was hard to enjoy a meal there with him. Too many tigers, fellow ministers, and other acquaintances sought to have *just a word* with him. Then he'd get cranky when his plate turned cold.

No, I cooked, she wrote and passed the paper back.

Lasagna?

Chicken, now stop!

He emitted a low chuckle at her reprimand and whispered, "Yes, ma'am."

She tried to focus on the sermon, but his nearness and the smell of his cologne kept turning her thoughts to places they had no business going, especially in church. Sitting next to him in church was too close for comfort. She squirmed.

During the invitation he nudged her again. In the remaining blank space on his bulletin he wrote. *Are you joining today?*

Cassandra turned towards him and made contact again with his thigh. She shook her head.

He smiled, retrieved the program, and scribbled, *Good!*

After service many Northside members, mainly female, came over to meet or be remembered by Finus Gates. Some of the ladies acknowledged Cassandra, but many looked right past her. One young lady stepped on her foot trying to get his attention. Cassandra sat down and watched the show. This spotlight of his was tiring. When the sanctuary was nearly empty he took her arm and escorted her to the front to meet Rev. Means.

"Man, don't you know who has been sitting in your sanctuary? This is Dr. Brownley from Westmore High. She's been visiting you, and we came this morning because she may be interested in joining you. Unless I can talk her out of it." Reverends Gates and Means shared a laugh.

"My pleasure, Dr. Brownley. I certainly know of you, but I don't believe we've met. And I don't recall seeing you in our services."

She nodded. She'd been there a few times in the last month, but always left right after service. They had a bit of small talk until they were interrupted by one of Northside's members. Cassandra took a small step backward.

"Excuse me, Rev. Means, Rev. Gates, Dr. Brownley. Dr. Brownley, would you mind having a word with me?"

Richard Stephenson, the father of the first student she'd expelled, towered above her. The last time she saw him, the man had cursed her out eleven different ways and called her a hundred kinds of black bitch. She took another step back and brushed against Finus. "I think that would be okay."

Finus's face twisted as concern flashed in his eyes. She gave a small nod and walked over to the mourners' bench.

"I just wanted to apologize and thank you for not having me arrested that night," Mr. Stephenson began.

"Apology accepted. How's your son?" Rich Stephenson, Jr. was an above-average basketball player with a permanent record filled with violent behavior, some of it sexual. She'd had no choice but to expel him. His last offense was violent, sexual and there had been some hint of bondage from the girls involved. She'd strongly suggested counseling to the family. She'd been close to turning the matter over to the police.

"I wish my wife and I had taken your advice. We sent Rich to Texas to live with his aunt and now he's in jail, well, juvenile detention. I'm surprised they didn't tell you." His head hung low. "He repeated the actions you expelled him for. We should have known better than to send him to Texas. My wife's down there now trying to see what she can do." Richard Stephenson looked up. "You didn't know?"

"No, Mr. Stephenson, I didn't know. Information of that sort would go through the district's legal counsel. I am so sorry to hear about this. I'll pray for your family, and I hope now that Rich will get the help he needs." She turned in the direction of the familiar hand on her shoulder.

"Miss Cassandra, are you ready?"

They said their goodbyes to Rev. Means and she agreed to stand if he wished to acknowledge her the next time she visited.

Back at Cassandra's house, while they ate the simple meal she'd prepared, Finus peppered her with questions until he got the full story on Rich Stephenson.

"Yet it sounds like something more. What else is going on?"

She realized how perceptive he was. *Is he asking more about what's going on at school? Or what's going on with me?* "I just hope that I am not in charge of discipline for too much longer."

"I thought you would have an easy time with discipline at Westmore."

"There you go again. You have a good way of making me refocus. I should be counting my blessings. Westmore is not like the city schools. Most of the problems we have are rudy-poot things that happen in high schools, except for the sex."

He let out a long low whistle. "What?"

"It's awful. These children continue to find creative places in the school to make out. No, I'm sugar-coating it. Have sex. I'm so tired of having to shift though and listen to the sordid details as part of the discipline process that I could scream."

"How bad can it be? Is this something the former vice principal dealt with?"

She looked away. "It's pretty bad. We're not talking about straight sex. We're talking about all manner of sexual acts. It's sickening. I feel so sorry for these children. Oooh, I can't even stand to think about it, and I can't tell you the half of it."

"Why, because I'm a reverend?"

She sighed and looked at him. "I couldn't even begin to describe it. No, I take that back. I have two levels of language for most of the acts that I have to document in my discipline reports. The street language the students have to describe what they were caught doing, and the clinical language I look up to use when I write the reports or talk to parents. And I don't want to talk about it anymore. But God bless your listening ear."

"Just a part of the service, ma'am, but there is something I've wanted to ask you."

She held her breath.

"Why are you spending your Saturday nights working? You should be going out with friends. On dates."

His tone was so friendly she decided not to take offense. "You sound like Phyllis, and I should ask you the same thing."

"I have my reasons." A silent space crept around them.

She spoke into the void. "I know the only time you have to work on the Gates school is late on Saturday nights. I don't mind."

His face contorted. "You know, you can always tell me no if you have other plans. And you didn't answer my question." His mischievous grin spread across his face. "Attractive, educated, no children, employed. Why can't you get a date?"

She shifted in her chair. "I had a date last night."

He glowered.

"I get asked out a lot by tenth-graders, old goats, and married men."

"I see." He leaned forward in his chair.

"The men I meet that are our age are immature and have trouble and drama. The brothers know they're in high demand and expect a woman to woo them. And I'm not dating anyone's grandfather, thank you."

"I hear you."

"And I'd never touch another woman's husband because, when I *do* marry, I don't want anyone touching mine."

"A-men, sister. But there are some good thirty-something brothers out there that I suspect would meet your criteria. Every time I take you anywhere I get pressed to turn over your number. I had to put Reynolds out of my house to keep him from taking your number from my caller ID."

116

She shuddered. "That's how he got my number?" Isaac Reynolds had called her several times since the revival.

"I'm afraid so, but I'll take care of that." He sat back with an agitated look on his face.

"Doc." Cassandra called him by his pet name because she sensed his mood shift. "Thank you, but I think I already took care of it. Come on, let's go sit in the den."

He walked ahead of her into the den and flopped down in her chair. "I hope you know I'm being serious. If a righteous brother were to ask, I'd show him your way."

"You know, I'm not trying to get into any of that right now. My focus is on making my new *jobs* work. I just can't deal with anything else right now." She picked up a throw pillow and hugged it to her chest.

"You see, that's exactly how I feel. I have a lot on my plate, too. That's why I'm so grateful for your friendship. It's nice to have a pretty woman on my arm and not be worried about what plot or schemes she has. Did I tell you how grateful I am for your friendship?" He had the preacher's habit of repeating himself.

Her chest warmed from his compliment. "Yes, you do so often, and I'm grateful for your friendship as well. And my mother is glad that I'm getting out of the house."

"Glad to help. You don't know what it means to be with someone without expectations. Women these days have expectations I am not willing to fulfill."

"Is it the money? Because you make it quite evident that you have some, but not every woman is after that."

"I'm not talking about money or buying things; I can do that quite easily. I'm talking about *putting out*. Those women out there are true tigers, and if a man's not trying to have sex with them, they get outraged. I cannot tell you how many women in the last few years have tried to tease, cajole, and even trick me into bed with them. Not going to bed with them seems to be a blow to their egos. Each one is convinced that her love is strong enough to make me yield my faith. The pressure is terrible. And it's sad to see our women so bought into this sex-crazed culture that they feel the only way to build a relationship with a man is in the bedroom."

"I know what you mean. I get the same thing in reverse. I still can't believe what Whit tried to pull."

"I'm glad he did. I mean, show his true colors early before..." He paused. "Let's talk about something else."

"Okay, there is something I've been wanting to say to you. I think you work too hard. When do you take time to relax?"

"Have you been talking to Fred?"

"No, why?"

"Nothing. Just this morning he was telling me the same thing. So much is expected of me, but I'm getting used to it. If I'm not working, what am I going to do? I don't sit still well."

"I've noticed." She squeezed the pillow. "Doc, have you always been surrounded by people, like you were today?"

He sat at the edge of the chair and leaned forward. "And that's what you've missed. A lot of company doesn't prevent loneliness. Now that Mom and Dad are gone I don't have anyone who truly knows me. You know what it's like when you and Yolanda get together and talk about growing up? There's no one for me to share those kinds of stories with. I listened at your graduation party when they were telling stories and discussing old times. I don't have that. And I am envious of how your family just comes over and the way you all work together. I don't have that."

"Are you talking about the family that comes over and disturbs my peace?"

"No, they come over and you share your lives."

"They come over here to eat and get into my business," she insisted.

He reached over and placed his hand on the arm of the sofa. His head tilted to one side. "It's a blessing to have family to share with. I wonder if I would be as generous in your shoes. I am often referred to as selfish and spoiled."

There was such sincerity in his eyes, her face softened. She nestled into the sofa cushions and hugged her pillow close. "Only those who don't know you would ever accuse you of selfishness. I think you're kind, generous. But…" she tossed the sofa pillow at him, "you can be a spoiled brat at times."

He caught the pillow, placed it behind his head, and closed his eyes. "Mind if I relax? Take a little nap?"

And so he did until late Sunday evening. Cassandra stood on her porch listening to the sexy little hum of the Boxster's engine as Finus sped away. Even after the chill of the autumn evening sent her indoors she continued to think about that sexy little car and its driver.

Chapter 9

Just as Cassandra finished writing final comments on the week's disciplinary report, Brenda Thomas, one of the math teachers, poked her head into her office. She waved her in.

"Why weren't you at the NAACP dinner dance?" The teacher plopped down in front of her desk. "Dr. B, you better watch your man cause your sorority sister Iva Peyton was all over him Saturday night. They say he left with her."

Cassandra put down her pen. "Brenda, if you are talking about Rev. Gates, we're just friends."

Brenda leaned forward. "Maybe it's nothing, but I hear she wants him bad." She leaned back and made herself comfortable. "How did you and Rev. Gates enjoy the services at Northside yesterday?"

"Brenda, how do you…" Cassandra rolled her eyes toward the ceiling.

"You and Rev. Gates are the hot topic in the Assembly. It's all the talk, the amount of time he spends at your house and how you go everywhere with him. He even took you to dinner at the bishop's house. They say you two have been together since this summer." Brenda paused. "Most of the old ladies are looking for him to settle down, and all of the young ones are praying it's not with you." Brenda stood up and walked toward the door. "You know, Rev. Gates is the only child of our favorite bishop. We're just looking out for him. That's one of the tenets of the Assembly."

"It seems to me that you all are all up in the man's business. Not that he has any business with me other than the consulting work I'm doing for the Gates school. And don't you have a class to teach?"

"They're in the media center. But before I go, Principal Brownley, are you still going out to dinner with us on Friday night?"

"Yes, and I didn't mean it like that."

"Okay, boss lady. I'm going to get to work, but don't say I didn't warn you." As much as she enjoyed Brenda's weekly Monday interruption, today the visit had rubbed her the wrong way.

When Cassandra turned into her subdivision at seven o'clock, she looked at her neighborhood with different eyes. She'd chosen Somerset because of the number of African-American families she saw while house hunting. She'd had no idea at the time that she was buying into a BMA community. Now she knew at least two BMA families lived on her street and another half a dozen within two blocks. While she understood the historical significance of the church's tenet that encouraged the Assembly members to live in close proximity, she had a sneaking suspicion she was being spied on.

❧

Cassandra was still fanning her hands to encourage her nails to dry when the doorbell rang. He was earlier than expected. According to Yolanda he was going to be late. She'd just hung up from speaking with Yogi, who'd called her during the social hour at the Pan Greek convocation. Her sister had called to make sure she knew how many women were in Finus's face. The convocation was an annual meeting ritual for all of the members of the African-American fraternal organizations. According to Yolanda *everybody* was there, and she practically had to stand in a line to have a word with him. She reported also that Finus was effervescent and flirted with all the ladies in classic Kappa fashion.

Cassandra ran downstairs and stopped with her hand on the doorknob. She felt as if she were playing the Mystery Date board game. But unlike the board game she had when she was twelve, there was a black man on the other side of her door. But since that man was Finus Gates, she couldn't be sure which of his personalities would greet her.

She peered through the peephole to check him out before she opened the door. Yolanda said he looked rather natty this evening, in a red jacket with his fraternity crest and a crimson and cream-striped bow tie. *Yogi was right.* She turned the knob. He looked good, and his broad smile signaled a good mood.

"Hello." He walked straight into her den and sat in her favorite chair. "You missed a nice event. You should have come with me to the convocation. Yours truly gave the prayer." He leaned back and made himself comfortable.

"I heard." She smiled and took a seat on the sofa opposite him.

He shot up. "I spoke to Yolanda tonight."

She lifted an eyebrow. "I know."

"We had a nice chat." He rubbed his hands together. "She was trying to look out for you. She warned me that you've been hurt."

She let out an exasperated breath.

"Cassandra, I just need to make sure we understand each other."

She stood up and walked over to her patio door. "I'm so embarrassed. What did she say to you?"

"Nothing out of line. She was just attempting to check me. But how anyone could harm a sweet lady like you is beyond me."

She turned around and walked back to the sofa, praying the flush was gone from her cheeks. "No, the mystery is why anyone would leave you."

"So you've heard." He sounded a little annoyed.

"Only snippets from Brenda Thomas, who makes a weekly visit to my office to check on me. Some people just can't understand our friendship."

"Tell me about it. I'm not unaware of the gossip. And I assure you, I do all I can to dispel it. Everyone knows I'm not dating, and that's not likely to change."

She stood up again. "I...I need some ice cream. Care to join me before we start working?"

"Not if it's chocolate." Finus sank further into the easy chair and put his feet up on the ottoman. "I'm not in the mood to work. Why don't you fill me in on what Yolanda hinted at. Tell me your story."

Cassandra walked towards the kitchen. "Only if you tell me yours."

"Mine is short. She cheated."

She stopped and turned. "Same here." She shook off her memories and went to the refrigerator. She scooped up three mounds of ice cream and poured a glass of ice water for Finus.

"You know you're not getting away with that. I need more detail," he said as she sat down on the sofa.

"What woman in her right mind would cheat on you?" she shot back.

"There's so much you don't know about me. I'll give you the abridged version. Pheadra's a textile artist. We lived together in Hyde Park while I was working on my doctorate. Mother hated her. So, to keep down confusion, I stopped taking Phea to church. I came home early one Sunday afternoon and caught her. End of story." He took a long draw from his glass. "What's your tale of woe?"

"Mine is even shorter than yours. There were clues, but I missed them. But at a certain moment when your fiancé calls you Mary…"

"When your name is Cassandra," he interrupted.

"Yes, well, that's a hint you can't ignore. That was in July, and our wedding was scheduled for August. I called everything off. In September I started my doctorate and a year later I accepted a position in the administrative offices of District 314 and moved out here. End of story."

"No, not the end of the story, just a sad chapter."

"I hope the same for you." She pushed her melting ice cream around in the bowl. "Do you think you'll ever fall in love again?"

He shifted in the chair. "Sure. It will be fast, like a flash of lightning. I'll meet her and boom, that will be it."

"I don't think that's love, maybe another word that begins with an L."

"Okay, then, what are your thoughts on the subject, Miss Brownley?"

"I think it starts slowly. You meet someone and they grow in your regard. Then, over time, you realize that this is the one person you want to be with. Slow and steady, patient and kind." She waved her spoon in the air.

He slapped his thighs and laughed. "Cassandra, you're going to be an old maid."

"And you'll be right there with me, my friend, lamenting about your lost lightning lust."

They continued talking for several more hours about why it was so hard to find the right person. Finus talked about his parents and his perception of their relationship.

"It always seemed so stable, kind of boring. Dad basically went along with whatever Mom wanted at home. He always said he was grateful to have a woman with sense enough to make good decisions. He argued enough with his deacon boards. He wanted peace at home, so he let Mom run everything."

Cassandra looked wistfully towards her sliding glass door. "It sounds like a true partnership. My parents were just the opposite. High adventure, passionate romance and one day, after three kids and a stack of bills, my father left. Mom wasn't much fun after that. I have to have something stable, like what your parents shared. I've lived through the quick passion and high excitement. It's not so good for children."

"So you want children."

"Oh, yes, a houseful, at least five." *Well, that will ensure he never has an interest in me.*

He sat up and leaned forward. "Finally, a woman after my own heart. Five's a good number, a whole team. I don't want my children to grow up lonely like I did."

"I've told you siblings are overrated."

He settled back into the comfort of the chair. "And I'll remind you family is a blessing."

"Yes, Reverend," she responded, and quiet settled around them. It was comfortable just to sit with him.

"What say we make a pact?" he said after a few minutes.

"What kind of pact?"

"If you will continue to go places with me and help ward off the tigers—and I needed you tonight—" he wagged a finger at her, "I will, if you let me, keep the 'hounds' away from you. We can also work on that shyness of yours."

"Sounds fair, but if I have to work on my shyness, you have to work on your schedule."

His lip twisted. "And what does that look like?"

"Well." She contemplated for a minute. "It's a trade. I step out of my shell and you take something off your schedule." Cassandra sat still while he pondered his options. She had been trying to work up the courage to ask him to spend some time with her socially, but after his 'do we understand each other' speech, she couldn't. She had probably just done Iva Peyton or some other damn woman a huge favor.

"All right, my friend, we have a deal. And there's an event next week you should attend with me. Why don't you bring Yolanda with you?"

To ensure there's no misunderstanding.

Driving in downtown Chicago was always a challenge, and Cassandra was running a little late. "I should have given myself more time," she told herself as she circled the long city block for the third time. Frustrated by the parking situation, she pulled into the drive of Finus's building on Stetson Drive.

A uniformed doorman stood by her door as soon as she brought her car to a stop.

"Excuse me, ma'am, are you Dr. Brownley?"

She nodded.

"Dr. Gates is expecting you. I can take care of your car. He asked that you go right in and make yourself at home."

Cassandra thanked the doorman and followed his directions to the elevator bank. She looked up at the mirrored ceiling of the elevator and smiled at herself.

I do look nice tonight. She smoothed the skirt of the tea-length black taffeta bell-shaped skirt. Yolanda had really come through tonight, loaning her the skirt, a slinky silver silk sweater, and a pair of teardrop diamond-like earrings.

She stepped off the elevator when the doors quietly opened on the thirty-fourth floor. She looked around, unsure which way to turn. In the months that she had known Finus this was the first time she had been invited to his home. Cassandra looked down the hall and saw only four doors in the beautifully decorated corridor. The hallway was strikingly modern with a taupe and black color scheme, very classy.

"Hope this is right," Cassandra said aloud as she pushed at a door at the end of the hall that was slightly ajar. She stepped into the most beautifully appointed living room that she'd ever been in. This was his apartment. The living room was decorated in black and white with just a touch of British tan. The room was stylish, yet masculine, with lots of leather and polished wood. She looked around and admired all of the expensive furnishings and art. *Perfectly lovely, but nothing personal. Reminds me of the Reverend Doctor.*

"Hey, girl, thought I heard you. Like my place?" Finus came partially into the living room. "Come on back to my room."

What? I know he's not standing in front of me smelling all warm and sexy from the shower with the tails of his tuxedo shirt hanging out and asking me to come back to his room. Well, it's about time. Bed, bath, beyond anywhere you want, baby.

"Cassandra, is that all right with you."

"Oh sure, yeah," she replied, not knowing what she was agreeing to.

"Good. You'll enjoy La Trattotria. They have excellent old world Italian food. Come on, I need to finish dressing and return a call before we go. You'll be more comfortable in here."

She floated on his scent down a short hall into a corner room with a fantastic view of Chicago's lakefront.

"Here's the remote. You can switch off the music if you like and watch TV. Be back as soon as I've completed my duties." Finus handed over a small wooden box.

You are too silly, she chastised herself as she looked around the room. *This* is Doc's room. Warm, friendly, well appointed, strong but not overbearing. She wondered if she was describing the man or the room. She took a deep breath, trying to calm down even though the air was humid with his scent.

She sought distraction by inspecting the bookshelves. She spied a silver-framed graduation photograph of Finus with his parents. A picture of Bishop Gates hung in the Cathedral conference room and Gladys Herbert had pointed out a lithograph of Wilma Gates on the plaque acknowledging her contribution of the stained glass windows in the Cathedral, but this was the first family portrait that she'd seen.

Wallace and Wilma Gates stood on either side of their only child, beaming with pride. Finus, in his academic regalia, grinned broadly and displayed his diploma. She held the photo closer. She couldn't decide which of his parents he favored more. She turned her attention to his books. The contemporary gospel music CD on the player caught her ear. The soundtrack had a mellow groove. *Nice. Religious but not intrusive.*

Finus, fully dressed in a classic black tux, casually strolled into his den and took a seat in one of the two leather club chairs that looked out onto Lake Michigan. "It's been a busy day. Let me sit down and catch my breath for a minute before we go. Why didn't Yolanda come?"

"Last-minute date. How did your meeting at College Station go?"

"Very well, thank you." He smiled broadly. "I was pleased with the receptiveness of the deacon board." His afternoon had included a meeting with the leadership at the College Station church. Bishop Sutton was getting ready to appoint a new pastor. He shared his excitement about the possibility that it might be him.

"So, when will you know?"

"Fred meets with the board early next week, and they'll have a new pastor by next Sunday."

"I'm excited for you."

"Well, hold on. It's between me and David."

"But it's Fred's decision."

"Ultimately, but Fred's a democratic dictator. He'll most likely go with the wishes of the board." Finus looked at his watch. "We need to be going or we're going to miss the overture."

"Okay. By the way, whose CD are you listening to?"

"You like it?"

"Yes, it's nice."

"Good. That's Amaria, an artist Will's representing. He has her signed with an independent label. I put up the money to get her album completed and then into distribution. I haven't had the chance to work with Will on any of his projects, so I'm glad to do this because he does so much for me. But I'm still trying to decide if her music is faith-based enough for me to publicly associate myself directly with her project."

He continued talking about the possibility of working with Will on a musical venture as they rode in a limo to Symphony Center. In addition to being Finus's closest friend, cousin, and fellow 'damm' girl enthusiast, Will served as his principal legal advisor. While there were other attorneys that handled his affairs, Will ultimately supervised everything.

Finus chattered on as they settled into a prime opera box and waited for the concert to begin. "My mother was among the first patrons of the Symphonietta. She increased her support in her later years because she thought it important to support real African-American artistry, and not just singing and rump shakin'."

When the lights dimmed Cassandra got a full view of the house. Symphony Center had undergone a total renovation since the last time she'd been there. She looked at the choral box and remembered the many times she'd sung there as a part of the university chorus.

The Symphonietta was lovely, a classical music company with an African-American conductor leading a multicultural orchestra. *I've got to bring Jalen and Yasmine.* It would be good for them to see this side of the African-American experience. She turned her full attention to the performance to get her mind off the man sitting next to her. She took a deep breath. *Now if I could turn off my nose.*

After the overture the conductor asked to have the lights brought up. He made several general remarks about the program and gave a tribute to the patrons.

"While tonight's performance is dedicated to all of our wonderful sponsors, I want to dedicate this next piece to the memory of our first sponsor, Wilma Gates. As a younger man I would spend summers at Wilma's lake house complaining about the dearth of opportunities in the classical field for musicians of color. Every year she would tell me to do something about it. And when I finally did it, she kept her word and gave me a generous donation. She's one of the reasons we're here today. Wilma's son, the Reverend Doctor Finus Gates, has continued to support us, and he's in the audience tonight."

There was a round of applause as Finus stood and their box was spotlighted.

"Thank you, Finus, for your continuing support. This next piece is a special tribute to Wilma."

Finus gave a slight bow and sat down.

"This was one of mother's favorites," he said as the orchestra began the opening strains of 'Ava Maria.'

Cassandra lost herself in the performance, unconsciously joining in softly.

"That's beautiful," he whispered and placed his hand on the arm of her chair.

Cassandra stopped singing.

"Oh yes, they are very talented."

"No, I was talking about you. Please continue singing."

"Oh, I'm sorry, I didn't realize." Cassandra nervously moved her hands to her lap and began to fuss with her skirt. Her stomach turned flips. After he remarked on her singing he didn't say another word. He shifted restlessly in his seat and stretched and shook his leg.

After the concert she didn't know what to expect as they waited for a private elevator to take them downstairs to the patrons' reception. As they stepped into the elevator he turned to her.

"Walk slightly behind me when we enter the reception hall."

What? What an odd request, and there's that haughty tone I hate. "Whatever," she replied as the elevator doors opened to the fourth floor. "You look very handsome tonight," she added to make up for her smart remark.

"I'm walking like a penguin and you know it," he snapped.

She fell in line behind him as he led the way to the reception.

"Will you please stand on my left side tonight?" he asked as they stood in the reception line.

"Are you all right?"

"I'm fine, fine."

Phoney.

She stood at his left, noting his slight tremors. She marveled at how well he was remembered by so many people. His manner was a little snappish but still stately. He introduced her by her formal credentials to everyone they met, even to several ladies who made it clear their only interest was in establishing an acquaintance with him. After a short time he looked down at the endless receiving line and frowned.

"I'm going to sit the rest of this out." He motioned for her to follow him to a small sitting area.

An elegant woman in a tight black dress followed them to a table. "Dr. Gates, I would really love to discuss your thoughts on the influence of the church in modern music."

He gave the lady his card, then brushed her off.

"Rev. Gates, if you're interested, I'd be happy to play for your church." This attempt for his attention came from a seriously Afrocentric sister with a crown of long, blonde goddess braids.

He also gave this lady a card and instructed her to call the office on Monday.

"Finus Gates, I have been dying to meet you." The third person introduced herself as Vivian Marsh, the newest addition to the Symphonietta woodwind section. "Since joining, I've heard so many wonderful stories about our patron saint."

"My mother?"

"No, you." Ms. Marsh replied as she sat in the empty seat to his right.

"Oh, now, I'm no saint, Ms. Marsh."

He's blushing. Cassandra sat quietly at his left. Vivian Marsh was a musician who looked like a model. She was tall and had a pretty face and the confidence to wear her hair in a short pixie cut. *I'm no judge of women, but I think she might fit the description of a 'damn girl.'*

"I can see how that might not be the best choice of words, Reverend," Ms. Marsh stumbled. "But what other words can describe your generosity? Here's my number. I would love to continue our conversation any time." Vivian Marsh passed Finus her card.

"Well… yes… thank you." His hand shook slightly as he slipped her card into his jacket pocket. "Let me introduce Dr…"

Vivian Marsh cut him off by waving at someone behind his back and added, "It was very nice to meet you, Finus Gates." Without a word to Cassandra, she jumped up and walked away.

Got to admire her game. Light a spark and move on. Finus didn't seem to get it. He turned in his chair to speak to some other patrons. She remained quiet during the remainder of the reception. She just nodded and hello'd when necessary. She watched him closely and wondered if something was medically wrong with him. He was uncharacteristically clumsy tonight. After the third time something slipped from his grasp, he stood up. "I'm ready to go. We won't be able to keep that dinner reservation."

Something was definitely wrong. He'd been so busy and snippy in the past hour she'd dared not ask. She wondered if something was wrong with her for putting up with him.

As they rode back to his building, she knew she needed to align her heart. Tonight the tigers were clearly on the prowl, and these women were much bolder than the church crowd. He didn't turn down any of the 'business' cards that were given to him, and he indicated to a couple of the ladies that he would follow up with them.

"Finus, tell me which of those ladies you are going to call." She hoped her voice sounded friendly and casual.

"None of them. Why?"

"What do you mean? At least three of them were your type."

"Now what do you know about my type?" He sounded a little less cranky. His left leg quivered. "I'll not call any of those women for the reasons you are suggesting."

"Well, that Ms. Marsh was giving me the eye like I was blocking her."

"Now that was a real tiger. What reason did she have to be unkind to you? Obviously she did some recon and knows we're friends, but she still chose to disrespect you. Did she think I wouldn't notice?"

"No, she thought she was so cute you wouldn't care." Cassandra shifted in her seat. "Two of the ladies seemed nice."

He closed his eyes. "You want to drop it?"

"Can I ask? Do you have some kind of medical problem?"

He templed his fingers and then placed them on his nose. "Well, my dear, there's something the matter with all of us. My problem, as Pheadra would say, is that I'm more trouble than I'm worth."

They rode in silence through the wintry Chicago night. She couldn't figure out what to say. There was something he wouldn't tell her. For the time being she chose to let it be.

At last the car pulled into the circular drive of his building.

"It's been a long day, it's late, and I can't let you drive home by yourself. My driver will take you home. If I had known earlier Yolanda wasn't coming I would have sent a car to pick you up," he announced.

"I'm perfectly capable of driving myself home."

"No, and next time I'll send a car to pick you up when I can't. I won't have you out this late by yourself." He spoke in slow, measured tones. "I will see to it that you have your car back before morning."

Cassandra opened her mouth.

"Don't argue. I haven't the strength."

Before she could formulate a question the car door opened and Finus reached out for the assistance of the doorman who'd parked her car earlier. He turned and supported himself with the door.

"You won't win with Mario. He has your keys and dares not cross me. Goodnight, Cassandra."

"I'll make sure they take good care of your car, ma'am. Goodnight," Mario said as he closed the limo door.

Stunned, she watched Finus shuffling towards the elevator banks inside his building as the car pulled away.

"Ugh," she exhaled when the car moved forward. Not having to drive gave her the chance to think critically. Her student services training pointed to a few clinical reasons for his trembling and ill moods. She bristled at his dodge about something being wrong with everyone. He'd been so wonderful at his apartment. What could have triggered his symptoms during the concert? Her head pounded. She sat back in the comfort of the leather of the limousine and fell asleep.

"She looked lovely tonight." The fresh minty scent of her hair, that silky, sexy blouse and softness of her hand when she touched his. And her eyes were definitely enhanced with eye make-up, which she did not normally wear. *Was all that for my benefit?*

His manhood pressed against his zipper as he leaned against the cold glass of his window pane and looked out at the lights of the city, hoping to clear his mind.

He sighed, deeply. "Any woman dealing with me would have to be a saint." He strode over to his briefcase and took it to his bed. He'd work just a while longer. At half past two, he turned off the light, knowing his alarm would ring at five for his morning prayer. In the quiet of his bedroom he heard his mother's persistent admonition that he always get enough sleep.

"I know. I know."

Early Sunday morning Cassandra stood looking out of her front door, half listening to Finus as he talked over the phone. *How'd he do that?* Her car sat in her drive. He'd called to make sure she'd found the keys in a pouch on her porch. She listened for him to apologize or explain his behavior last night.

"Are you going to Northside this morning?" he asked.

"Uggh." The phone hit the floor.

"What was that?"

"Nothing, just dropped the phone. Gotta go, have a nice day." She switched off the phone and fought the temptation to fling it across the room. *Can he be so unaware of his impact on me? He didn't even consider that he might owe me an apology for the way he spoke to me last night. He might be the prince of the BMA, but sometimes he acts like a hellion.*

Chapter 10

On the first Saturday in December, Cassandra sat in an ornate banquet hall looking up at the dais and Finus Gates. These ballrooms with gold filigree wallpaper and red regency patterned carpet were beginning to run together in her mind. She'd lost count of how many she'd been in over the past months.

She glanced at the program to remind herself of the occasion and their location this evening. When she looked up again, Finus flashed her a Cheshire cat-like grin. In spite of their *understanding*, she hoped their friendship could turn into something else.

She returned his smile and focused on her plate of banquet chicken. The program began and yet another mistress of ceremony attempted to introduce the enigmatic Reverend Doctor Finus Gideon Gates. She'd heard him presented in the usual way so many times her mind wandered. *Why so many of these things?* He wasn't the kind of preacher that set a house to dancing. His popularity seemed due more to his generosity than his oratory skills. It was common knowledge he never accepted an honorarium for speaking and that his personal donation to a worthy cause would exceed any love offering that might be collected on his behalf.

The hairs on the back of her neck rose with awareness. All of the attention in the room was focused on her.

"Cassandra, please stand," Finus said from the dais. "My friend, Dr. Brownley, was kind enough to accompany me this evening and I just wanted to recognize her."

Cassandra stood briefly and smiled politely. She mentally kicked herself for not paying attention. *Well, tonight was better than last week.* Last week when the mistress of ceremony introduced her as his girlfriend, she didn't stand when requested because she wasn't paying attention then, either. Finus recovered that moment with a little joke about his friend who happened to be a girl. She'd vowed last week to be more attentive. But her head was lost in the clouds, thinking of him.

She shifted in her chair and tried to focus on his after-dinner speech about the value of education. But she'd heard this sermon a dozen times already. She hoped he didn't want to stick around after dinner.

They had an established pattern. After the event they would hurry back to her house and hammer out several hours of Gates school project work over a pot of coffee. She pushed her chair slightly backward. *Yolanda would die laughing if she knew how much I look forward to spending my Saturday night working with him.*

The tone and cadence of the speech shifted. Finus's voice rose to the standard preacher's close. Sometime within the past month her ear had become more attuned to him and his emotions. While his words were still highbrow and haughty, the underlying sentiments were warm and caring. He loved his church and its people. And she loved him, sometimes.

She rose with the banquet attendees in the usual ovation and applauded enthusiastically. Butterflies fluttered in her stomach.

As usual she stood politely by Finus's side at the end of the event and endured a few comments from Assembly women about their friendship while he made the necessary corrections about their relationship. He handled the Nosy Rosies in a gentle but condescending way.

"Cassandra, the car is here. Goodnight, ladies. I trust I'll see you in church in the morning."

He reached around and touched the small of her back to escort her from the ballroom. His brief touch warmed her more than the wool coat he retrieved from the coat check. It was nice to be in the company of a gentleman. She turned toward him and smiled. "Thank you."

She walked with him through the outer doors of the banquet hall and stepped into his Mercedes. She didn't really need to put her coat on, his cars were always warm. He drove expensive cars and tipped well. Valets made sure his cars were always warm. His help with her coat was her tip for the evening.

Cassandra glanced over in the darkness at his profile as he sped through the clear, cold December night. Yolanda's voice ran through her mind. *All you want to do with him is work?* His cell phone rang and silenced Yogi's scoff.

"The bishop's ring," he said as he reached down into the console between them. He pulled over to answer the call.

Even riding in the large car did not diminish the intimacy of being alone with him. His cologne, combined with his personal energy, charged the atmosphere.

This is getting tough.

"Cassandra, would you mind," he lowered the phone. "Andrea Dixon, one of the faithful members of the Cathedral's singles group, is in urgent need of pastoral counseling. Fred wants me to take this call. I need to go, but it's a cardinal rule to never go to a woman's house alone. If you can't or don't want to, Fred will come."

"Not at all." She sank a little lower in the seat while he completed his call. Guilt pricked at her soul as she prayed a self-serving little prayer that whatever the situation, it would be resolved quickly.

Finus reprogrammed his GPS, changed direction, and sped towards a neighboring suburb.

On his first knock the door to a second-floor apartment flew open. Andrea Dixon, clad in a black satin robe, appeared and propped herself up against the door jam. Behind her what looked to be a thousand candles and burning incense filled the room with a smoky haze. A conflicting cloud of fruit and herbs swept over them.

Finus exhaled in frustration. His arm reached backward and caught Cassandra. He wobbled slightly and then crossed the threshold, drawing her into the candlelit room. He coughed. Then he stepped back outside. Cassandra and Andrea stood with their mouths agape in the candlelit foyer.

"Andrea, please go through your rooms and extinguish all of these flames. Miss Cassandra and I will start in here." Finus issued a firm order from behind her.

For five minutes Cassandra and Finus walked around the small room extinguishing flames. Then he stood by her as she sat on the sofa to wait for Andrea. His foot tapped like a metronome, sixteen beats per measure, sixteen beats per measure. Anger and joy sparred in Cassandra's soul. *How dare this woman attempt to set him up like this? Thank God I'm here.*

She could have sung two hymns in the time it took Andrea to return. When she did, he stopped keeping time with his foot. "Shall we pray?" He extended one arm toward Andrea and one backward for Cassandra.

She stood and frowned at the smile that came across Andrea's face when Finus's hand touched hers. Cassandra took a deep breath, then turned her lips down and bowed her head when Finus squeezed her hand. *How can he so calmly pray for this woman to find peace?*

"Andrea, spend some time meditating on these scriptures. Shall I ask any of the ladies from the women's society to come and sit with you?"

Andrea shook her head no and accepted the scripture card. Finus placed his hand at Cassandra's back and ushered her toward the door. Once outside he grabbed her hand and hurried down the steps.

"You're moving too fast," she protested as she nearly stumbled during their descent.

He slowed. "I'm sorry. I can't get away from here fast enough. It's so disheartening to know that Andrea would attempt to set me up like that. I am grateful to you for being here with me."

He apologized again when they got in the car and sped away from the apartment complex. As he drove to her house he talked and sped. He couldn't say thank you enough. She sat half listening and considered the difference between them. When she was disturbed, she slowed down and became very quiet. Apparently when he was disturbed, he moved fast and talked even faster.

Back at her house he exchanged the speeding for pacing.

And he was still talking.

Finus kept recounting information she already knew. He was leaving on Monday to spend the holidays in L.A. He really wished he could go to her home church in the morning to hear her sing, but he was assigned to preach at the College Station church. College Station was still without a pastor.

She sank into the comfort of her favorite chair and watched him pace and preach.

"Cassandra, did you hear me?"

She blinked. She'd missed the end of his blathering.

He'd stopped in front of her chair. He held something aloft in his hand.

"I know you don't like stuff, but I wanted to give you something during this season to thank you for your kindness toward me."

"You didn't need to do that, but I have something for you, too." She jumped up and brushed past him. In the living room she searched out a small gold box under her tree. As she kneeled to pick out the right box, she lingered. He stood right behind her. The heady scents of pine and his presence caused her knees to wobble. She accepted his hand to help her up.

"Merry Christmas, Finus."

"Thank you. This looks too nice to open." He twisted the elegantly wrapped gold box in his left hand, then handed her the three red envelopes he held in his right. "These are for you to put under your tree. Now don't open them until Christmas."

"Okay, then same goes for you." She had wanted to see the expression on his face when he opened his gift, but this was better because she didn't know how he would respond to it.

"That is not a problem; you know I am a well-disciplined man." He glanced at his watch. "And now I guess I need to go. You'll need rest in order to be in good voice in the morning."

"You're right." Her heart flipped in her chest. She was thrilled to hold a gift from him in her hands. A slight frown crept over her face. He'd be gone until after the New Year. "Well, goodnight and happy holidays," Cassandra said as she opened the door to an arctic blast.

"It's Merry Christ-mass, Miss Cassandra."

"Wait a minute, Finus." What she'd been thinking since they arrived at her house tumbled out. "Are you sure it's okay for you to spend time with me alone? Doesn't that violate a tenet?"

He chuckled. "Thanks for looking out for me. No, that rule applies to business. I'm allowed a personal life, and I'd like you to consider that while I'm away."

Cassandra spent Christmas at her mother's house, as usual. In the midst of her extended family and old friends, she missed him.

Yolanda had the yuletide anthem for lonely hearts, "What Do the Lonely Do at Christmas", on repeat.

"Special dedication to all the lonely ladies in the Brownley household, and that's all of us," Yogi sang as she danced and laughed around the scattered piles of Christmas presents.

God is good and he continues to bless us, Cassandra thought as she viewed the excessive piles of gifts. Growing up they were lucky if they received three presents each, and two of those were usually something practical like socks and underwear. Christmas had been good again to Jalen and Yasmine, and, from what she gathered, her brother's house also looked like a toy store this morning. It felt good to know that the family prospered, but something was missing.

Several hours later she sat on the floor helping Yasmine set up a Barbie dream house. Their mother's small bungalow pulsed with the sounds of her extended family.

"Whose purse is this?" Aunt Gloria lifted the Coach bag up with her cane. "This thing's getting on my nerves with all this beeping and chirping inside. What going on in there?"

"That's mine. I forgot to turn off my cell phone. I'll do it now." Cassandra knee crawled over to her aunt and reached down into her bag to find her phone. Before she could pull the phone up from the bottom of her bag it rang again. "Hello."

"Merry Christmas! I finally got you. You all must be having some kind of good time."

"Merry Christmas, Doc!" She stood and rushed out of the living room.

"Girl, I've been calling you all day. I wanted to thank you for your gift. I opened it first thing after I prayed. Where did you find them?"

She'd given him a pair of antique cuff links emblazoned with an original BMA crest. "Perfect gift, something I did not have."

"I'm glad you liked them, but the source…that will have to remain a secret." She wasn't about to tell him she'd found them on eBay. "Did you really wait until this morning to open your gift?"

"Yes, ma'am, it's all about discipline. What about you?"

"I had your cards opened before you got to the air-port."

He laughed.

"So did you like your gifts? I know how you feel about stuff."

"Oh, yes, and I thank you for the next twelve months." His gifts were memberships in the fruit, flower, and cake of the month clubs. He'd also sent fruit, flowers, and cake for the holiday season to her family. "I hope you have plans to help eat through a year's supply of cake."

"Glad you asked. I knew you'd share."

Christmas in L.A. obviously was going well for him. He seemed to be in a grand mood, but, then again, he was with Will.

"I wanted to tell you it looks like my investment in the music business is going to pay off."

"What?" She knew he would soon be calling Will's name. *But what business of mine is it?* "Sounds fun." She really didn't have much to say because she tried not to overstep the boundaries of their friendship in two particular areas: her feelings and his money.

"We're going to the Tabernacle in a few hours to hear Amaria sing again. The artist I told you about." His voice was animated. "And then she's coming to Aunt Jo's for Christmas dinner so we can talk."

Her? She'd missed something in the conversation. "That sounds like a good plan. Hey, Doc, I'm curious about something. Why do all of the BMA churches carry such grand titles, or is that a secret?" She didn't want to discuss his financial affairs or think about him sharing his Christmas dinner with a female musician.

"It's no secret that Assembly members are constantly trying to outdo each other. The bishop of the western states builds a tabernacle; the bishop of the Midwest builds a cathedral. By the way, I'm preaching Sunday at the Tabernacle."

"That sounds like a great honor."

"Either that or, as Fred said, 'Bishop Jones is trying to get some free labor.' Either way I don't mind."

"I'm sure you'll be brilliant."

"Of course I will. I'll bring you back a videotape of the service."

Yolanda barged into the bedroom they had shared as girls, closely followed by their mother. "There you are. What are you doing all holed up in here?"

"Excuse me." Cassandra placed her hand over the receiver. "I'm on the phone."

"Oh, we thought you might be in here crying your eyes out. And you're talking to whom?" Yolanda asked the question as if she knew the answer.

"Finus is calling from L.A. to wish us a Merry Christmas." Cassandra carried on the required three-party conversation, transmitting messages between her sister and Finus.

"Finus says Merry Christmas."

"Yolanda wanted to be sure and remind *you* that Kwanzaa starts tomorrow." Phyllis and Yolanda sat at the foot of the other twin bed. Clearly they weren't about to leave.

"Well, Doc, it's apparent that I've been away from my family for too long. I've got to go. Enjoy the rest of your holidays."

"You, too, but…Cassandra, there was something else I wanted to say to you. I'll call again before New Year's. Merry Christmas, my dear."

The smile that filled her face turned to a scowl when she looked at the pair stationed at the foot of Yolanda's bed. "What?"

"You were on that phone an awful long time. What was Doc talking about? Was the good reverend previewing his Christmas sermon?"

"He called to thank me for his gift."

"Did you thank him for all of that fruit and cake he sent?" asked Phyllis.

"Of course I did."

Phyllis stood up and leaned on the door jam. "You know, he can be so nice and then sometimes he has the nastiest attitude. I don't know about him. But I do know that if he wanted something with you he would have said something by now. You need to stop spending so much time with him. You're wasting what little time you have left."

"What's that supposed to mean, Phyllis?"

"Put together you two would be one perfect woman. Yolanda's artistic, spontaneous, and the life of any party. Cassandra, you're accomplished and studious, the family's success story, but you have no idea what to do with a man." Phyllis walked away.

Cassandra's cheeks burned and she lay back and buried her face in her pillow. Phyllis was wrong; she knew what to do with a man. She just didn't do it with every man she met. Running water gushed from across the hall.

Phyllis yelled from the kitchen. "You might show a little cleavage."

"Mama, he's a minister," Yolanda shouted back.

"No, he's a man. Now both of you come in here and wash these dishes."

Chapter 11

Cassandra sat in her den on February fifteenth reviewing the week's discipline reports. Far too many girls had misinterpreted Valentine's Day and had been caught having sex on school grounds. Her thoughts drifted to her own loveless life.

For the past month she'd been full of hope. Finus's invitations had shifted from church to social events. She'd attended a MLK Day breakfast, luncheon, and dinner with him. He'd taken her to his faculty dinner at Moody Bible Institute, a Chicago Bulls game, and one of her sorority's events. He'd acted like a boyfriend. Actually, better than any man she'd ever dated. He'd treated her with great care and always saw to her comfort first. When they dined out he made sure her food was prepared to her liking, and at the movies he never forgot to buy her Raisinets and put extra butter on her popcorn. She barely felt the effects of a cold Chicago January until, at the end of the month, he went back to L.A. She jumped at the ring of her cell phone.

"Where were you? I called last night. Hot Valentine's Day date?" Finus quipped.

She sighed deeply. "I wish. I was here, having a private pity party."

"What's wrong?"

She melted at the genuine concern in his tone. "Sometimes single girls get weepy on romantic holidays."

"Sounds like a song lyric. Mind if I share it with Amaria? And, my dear, I do not believe *you* didn't receive any valentines."

Her heart sank. In one breath he could make her heart sing and in the next crush her with his mocking superiority. She stood up and stretched. "Actually I received a marriage proposal."

"Really?"

"From a tenth-grader. And I got flowers. A carnation from Jalen." She winced at the ingratitude in her tone.

"Poor Jalen. I empathize with the young brother. I had roses delivered for Aunt Jo and Cherie and they both sounded about like you. I guess flowers from a nephew don't rate." He chuckled. "The only person who showed me any appreciation yesterday was Mari."

Her eyes narrowed.

"The launch party for the single went very well. We took Mari to dinner last night to celebrate." Finus went on and on about the stars he'd seen at a posh L.A. restaurant, Amaria's single, and the good time he was having in the California sunshine with Will.

She'd hoped to receive a Valentine from him, and listening to him talk about his dinner with a woman she suspected to be just his type was just too damn much. She rubbed the back of her neck. "I really should be grateful Jalen thought to bring me that flower instead of worrying about what I don't have. You know, it's been snowing here." She kept up her nervous ramble.

"Brown was kind enough to shovel my drive and walks this morning." She took a deep breath. "Thank you, Reverend, for helping me focus on the people that love me. And now I'm feeling a little ashamed of myself."

"That was not my intention." He paused. "I called last night to ask you to go somewhere Saturday night."

She glanced out the window onto the pristine blanket of snow covering her back yard. Cold outside, sad inside, she wrapped an arm around her waist. "Another speaking engagement? No, thank you. I think I'll make a pan of lasagna and invite my family over. They all do so much for me."

"Even Phyllis?"

"Yes, even Phyllis." Her face burned with shame over having told him so much about her relationship with her mother.

"Cassandra, I called last night to ask you to go to the Will Downing concert at the Park West on Saturday night."

"Will Downing?" *Oh, my God! How romantic.*

"I don't know what you ladies see in that bald head."

"Are you serious? I'm his biggest fan. I don't know anything about a concert. Are you sure?"

"Yes, ma'am. It's a private show, fans only. Will got us a reserved table."

"Then my family can have lasagna some other time," she practically sang.

"We'll take David and Lydia with us to celebrate his elevation. Lydia's in love with that ole bald-headed singer, too."

Her smile flattened.

"Good, good. Then it's a date, but Saturday is going to be a busy day."

Did he say date? Her thoughts wandered as he prattled on about Saturday's agenda. Pride swelled in her chest at the grace he showed in defeat. He hadn't let his disappointment in not getting the pulpit at College Station affect his friendship with David.

"Cassandra?"

"Yes?"

"Goodnight, my dear." His voice was a sweet song in her ear.

"Goodnight." She grinned and placed the phone on its charger. "Don't get excited and over think this," she said aloud. Her brow creased. "Saturday's a celebration for David and Lydia, but…" She ran upstairs singing, "I'm going to see Will Downing. I'm going to see Will Downing."

The setting was too intimate. The booth at the Park West too small. Finus sat too close. She squeezed her thighs together. She smiled across the table at David and Lydia, who both looked a little worn. She glanced at the man beside her. He was in a rare mood, almost hyper. Tonight he'd abandoned the Reverend Doctor's bow tie and stuffed shirt. His black leather-clad thigh pressed against hers. *A man of the cloth has no business wearing all revealing leather. I'm going to hell for my thoughts.*

Will Downing took the stage and opened the show with a sultry version of "A Million Ways to Please a Woman." She melted into the shelter of Finus's shoulder as the warmth of Will's songs washed over the crowd. His fingers moved slowly up and down the sleeve of her ruby silk blouse.

Lord have mercy. She shuddered.

"Watch, he's going to bring Gerald Albright out here in a minute." His cognac breath brushed against her ear. She turned in his direction and flushed as his eyes traced the direction of the cascade of gold chains that lay against the V-shaped neckline of her blouse.

He brushed a lock of hair away from her ear as Will Downing announced Gerald Albright was in the house. "Told you."

She scooted an inch closer to the far end of the small booth to fight off the temptation to run her hand up the length of his thigh. She rested her arms on the booth's rail, closed her eyes, and listened to the smooth jazz emanating from Gerald Albright's alto saxophone.

How did he do it all? They'd started the day co-facilitating a workshop for the Gates school committee on the criteria for hiring an administrator, then rushed to the Southside where he keynoted the scholarship luncheon at the College Station Church. They barely had time to fellowship with David and Lydia afterwards because Finus had a late afternoon meeting at the Cathedral to authorize the formation of a support organization for young professionals. Instead of attending the meeting she went home, took a nap, and waited for Yogi to come over and dress her for tonight. The tension she held in her thighs released with the smooth sounds of the sax.

Will Downing returned to the stage and began the we-won't-be-together segment of the show. His velvety tones soaked her bones. Tonight's rendition of his hit, "Sorry I", numbed her.

Next Will sang "I Can't Make You Love Me." She sighed, despite Yolanda's clothes and coaching, the words of the song rang true. She couldn't make him love her.

"Hey, are you okay?" Finus's hot breath caressed her ear. She turned into his shoulder and he drew her into his arms. She lifted her head to look into his eyes. Dead dark pools devoid of emotion. Her eyes burned hot with tears.

"I didn't intend for the concert to make you sad. Excuse me." he whispered and ended their brief embrace.

Cassandra turned back to the booth rail and tried to tuck her feelings away. She glanced over at David and Lydia, who were lost in the romantic music. She closed her eyes to the jealous tears.

The table shook. Finus squirmed, twisted, and rocked out of time with the music. She didn't move or respond when David asked if they were okay. They sat in silence at opposite ends of the small booth and, as the performance reached its finale, the house lights came up on a contented couple and a disjointed pair.

"Lydia, why don't you and Cassandra visit the ladies' room?" David stood up and playfully tapped at Finus's legs to swing around to let her pass. She turned to look at Finus. His countenance was cold and impersonal.

She made her way through the crowd with Lydia to the ladies' room. When they returned, David stood alone at their table.

"Gates is waiting in the car."

"What's wrong, David?" Cassandra asked.

"He's tired. Let's not tax him further, okay?"

The Gates code for "don't ask any questions." David helped the ladies with their coats and they stepped out into a blustery Chicago night.

The valet held the back door open for her while David escorted his wife to the front passenger seat. Once David settled behind the wheel she overheard his whisper to Lydia. "Baby, it's going to be a long drive, so I won't mind if you fall asleep."

She settled into the backseat of a cold car with Finus huddled as close to the opposite door and as far away from her as he could get. Before David put the car in motion, he barked, "David, I'll call my service to take Cassandra home."

"No," David volleyed back from the front seat.

"You can't do all of this driving and still be fresh in the morning."

"Um-hum."

"Take Lakeshore Drive."

"I know where I'm going. And please stop talking. You're disturbing my wife."

Finus bristled and made a few more snide remarks, which David ignored. Finus's whole body shook as they rolled down Lakeshore Drive. He twitched and squirmed in the seat.

"Why were you crying during the concert?" he demanded when they started south down the Stevenson Highway. "Were you remembering what's-his-name? He didn't love you."

A giant lump formed in her throat.

"Cassandra, real love is faithful through any circumstance."

She closed her eyes tightly. Now he mocked her. "People say they love the Lord every day, but they are not faithful to his word," she shot back.

"I was not discussing God's love."

"Love is indefinable and abstract," she whispered more to the window than to him.

"You can tell love by love's actions."

And what do you think your actions say about you? She didn't want to argue. She wanted to know what was wrong. Did he think she didn't notice his sudden mood shifts and jitters? Or that she didn't care?

"Did ole boy run the 'just because I'm not faithful doesn't mean I don't love you' line on you? Did you believe it?" Gone were the soft, sexy undertones in his voice from earlier. His words grated on her ears like the scraping of sleet from an icy car window. She turned away from her window to face him, sure her face burned as ruby red as her blouse.

Finus stretched a trembling hand toward her. "Love and fidelity go hand in hand."

"Do you two always have such deep conversations?" David intervened from the front seat.

Cassandra leaned forward, grateful for the distraction. "David, I am so sorry. I've gotten totally spoiled.

Usually we have these types of conversations when there's a hired driver. I forgot we were with friends."

He withdrew his hand.

She turned and hugged her window.

They rode onward in silence. David turned up the volume on the car stereo. The Will Downing CD they'd listened to earlier in the evening still played.

She shivered in the cold leather seat. Halfway to suburbia and the backseat hadn't warmed up. Maybe the chill was emanating from Finus. He continued to quiver and hug the passenger door.

She sang softly the opening lines of Will Downing's hit, 'I Try'.

"Lord, woman, you can surely sing," David hooted from the front seat midway through the second refrain.

"David, take me to the bishop's house first. Cassandra, please stop singing," Finus ordered from his side of the car.

She shook with anger and buried her face in her hands.

Late into the night, as she polished her toenails, Cassandra reminded herself of Finus's condescending attitude and the way he showed off his wealth. There was no reason for him to speak to David as he had tonight. Ordering David to take him to the bishop's house was just rude. And the nerve of him to think he could tell her to stop singing just because they were in his car.

She wallowed in confusion. Beneath that bow tie the man had a nice body. She'd checked him out. Well-toned legs, tight chest, strong hands, plus his brilliant mind. He absorbed information like a sponge. Finus studied hard to make the school a successful project, and his leadership with the board was masterful. He was a steadfast, strong and uncompromising leader, and he did it all with a certain finesse.

She lay across her bed, toes pointed toward the ceiling. After such a long day she was tired, yet restless. Something was definitely wrong with him. Or her. She flexed her toes. "Why am I putting up with this?"

Later, when she slid between the sheets, she answered her question. In spite of it all, he had a beautiful spirit. She tossed and turned, thinking about how gently he handled fragile spirits like Andrea Dixon, the children at the cathedral, and her own niece and nephew. He was generous with his time and money, swift to aid anyone in need. But then, there were times like tonight when he was just ugly.

Cassandra looked over at her alarm clock. It flashed five a.m. She turned over and tried to sleep. Ever-faithful Finus was scheduled to arrive at ten-fifteen to escort her to church. If he was still in his foul mood she'd only make it worse by being late. *Fool that I am, I'll be ready.*

Cassandra snapped shut the hymnal and looked at her watch. It was only eleven forty-five. She was hopping mad and ready to go home. Instead of coming himself, Finus sent a car to pick her up this morning. If she hadn't been dressed and in need of prayer, she would have stayed at home.

She looked up at Finus as the congregation continued to sing. He looked a bit of a mess. His bow tie was not perfectly straight. His shirt cuff hung below the edge of his sleeve. He appeared to have a five o'clock shadow, and he was wearing glasses. Compassion mixed with her confusion. He appeared so vulnerable.

Through twitching lips he gave a short smile. She hoped that crooked smile was meant for her. She wasn't sure because Iva Peyton sat directly behind her. Finus only stood briefly through the hymn. He looked exhausted, and he couldn't keep still. He twitched, fidgeted, and shifted in a seemingly choreographed pattern. The church bulletin he held waved like a sail under a good wind. This time when she caught his eye he didn't smile.

Following the choir's B selection, Bishop Sutton rose to deliver the morning message. Per custom, all clergy stood while the text scripture was read. Finus expended a great effort to stand. Partway through the passage, he tipped over. Several congregants gasped. She stood. The assistant pastor caught him and dragged him through the door at the back of the pulpit. The church mother seated to her left reached up, took her elbow, and urged her back into her seat.

"He'll be all right," Mother Pierce whispered.

Bishop Sutton changed direction and led the congregation in a chorus of the prayer chant, 'Lord have mercy.'

Inez rose and left the sanctuary.

Bishop Sutton rarely preached, and she'd been look-ing forward to hearing him. But she couldn't focus. The internal dialog that kept her from sleeping last night played on. She shifted and fidgeted through the rest of the sermon.

The service ended with no sign of Finus or Inez. Cassandra shook a few hands and received several hugs of reassurance from the ladies in the patch. Everyone kept telling her he'd be okay. Even Iva Peyton gave her a brief word of assurance.

"Excuse me, Dr. Brownley." Deacon Jones tapped her shoulder. "Will you come with me, please?"

Without waiting for her reply, the deacon started to-wards a side door.

She followed the deacon through the long inner hallway Finus called the ushers' passage. *Am I being es-corted out of the Cathedral?* She looked up at the beau-tiful stained glass windows, the tangible part of Wilma Gates's legacy. Her eyes were drawn to the window rep-resenting the third tenet of the church, respect for the clergy. The Assembly members were certainly faithful to that one. These were a peculiar people. They could gossip all day about a non-existent relationship, but no one would tell her what was wrong with Finus.

"Dr. Brownley, I don't think you should keep him waiting."

Chapter 12

Cassandra stood at the antique oak door to the bishop's study with Deacon Jones. He knocked, they waited. The door opened and she stepped into the inner sanctum alone. Her eyes flew across the room to Finus, who reclined on a small sofa, surrounded by clergy. As she moved toward him she overheard Inez, who was hovering anxiously over him.

"You really need to tell her."

The boundaries he placed around their friendship didn't permit her to pick up on Inez's comments. "Are you all right?"

Finus sat upright and slowly spoke. "I'm fine, but…" He motioned for her to come closer. As she neared, the others stepped away. "I won't be able to take you to dinner or work on the project this afternoon. If you don't mind, I've asked Inez to drive you home."

Cassandra looked around the room at the others. She didn't understand what was going on, but because of the measured tones he used and the concerned frowns on the others' faces she decided not to question him. "That's fine. Just call me, when you can."

"I will do that." His tone flattened. He turned his head.

Like a tenth-grader dismissed from the principal's office, she walked across the room to Inez, who stood by the desk, jingling her car keys.

Cassandra spent the first part of the week trying to sort out her feelings. Things should be clear, she decided on Monday night. *The man told me to shut up on Saturday night and dismissed me on Sunday. Something is wrong with him, and he doesn't trust me enough to share it when it's clear everyone in the Assembly knows.*

"I bet if I called Yolanda she could find out in a New York minute." *I can't do that, they gossip about him enough.* She went to bed early and struggled throughout the night.

During an endless scheduling meeting Tuesday afternoon, she decided all she could do for Finus was pray. She penciled the midweek prayer service at Northside in on her weekly agenda.

Brenda Thomas caught up with Cassandra while she was walking to the auditorium for the Wednesday afternoon faculty meeting. "Is Reverend Gates still in the hospital?"

She stumbled. "Excuse me?"

Brenda rolled her eyes. "We all know that he was admitted Sunday after service. I was just wondering how he's doing."

I should have called.

"I hope you don't mind my asking. I know he tries to keep certain things secret."

She wasn't sure how to answer Brenda. She certainly wasn't his secret keeper. Not knowing he was in the hospital was further evidence he offered her only a limited friendship. She'd made the mistake a few months ago of mentioning to Brenda that she and Finus spent most Saturday nights catching up on their reading. The mess of gossip that came out of that remark was unbelievable. She drew a deep breath and chose her words carefully.

"I haven't spoken to Reverend Gates today." *That's true and unrevealing.*

Instead of attending prayer service, she called Finus, left a message, and waited. She fell asleep in the den and dreamed she stood in a field of flowers. Each time she picked a bloom, the wind blew away the petals. As the petals drifted away, they sang, "You love him-you love him not."

On Thursday morning, her cell phone rang just as she turned into the faculty parking lot. Her breath caught in her throat. Late night and early morning phone calls usually brought bad news. She lifted the phone and exhaled. The caller ID read F.G. GATES.

"How are you?" she blurted out before he could say hello.

"I'm fine. I'm calling because your picture is in the *Black Pages.*"

Unbelievable. I wish I had the chutzpah to bless him out.

"Cassandra, did you hear me?"

"No, what was that?"

"I'll read it aloud," he said in a chipper voice. " 'Who was the mysterious beauty seen with the very eligible Reverend Finus Gates at Saturday night's Will Downing concert?' "

"Me? A mysterious beauty? It is a picture of me, right?"

"Yes, ma'am."

"Another picture in the *Black Pages.* Phyllis will be thrilled."

"You're not mad?"

"I'm mad at you," she muttered.

"I'm sorry about this, Ca-San. I'd almost forgotten about the gossip in the *Black Pages.* It's been a while since they had an interest in me."

"Millionaire playboy preacher no longer a hot topic?"

"You offend me. And I'm fine; you don't need to worry about me." He spoke casually, as if nothing had happened on Sunday. "We're a little behind on the

169

school project, and I need to cancel today's meeting. I hope you won't mind working tomorrow night."

"I can't tomorrow night. I have to supervise the varsity game."

"Then I'll see you Saturday night, unless…" He paused. "Cassandra, I…"

"I'm available." *I shouldn't be*. She deliberately cut him off. "See you Saturday." Cassandra clicked the END button and sat in her car for a few minutes. *What am I doing?*

In preparation for a rare fifth Sunday in February, the senior choir and gospel chorus of the Cathedral held a joint rehearsal on Thursday evening. The musicians and section leaders were so frustrated after an hour of trying to blend the voices and keep control of the sidebar conversations that they called an early break.

Brenda Thomas rushed for the opportunity to talk. "Dr. Brownley didn't know Rev. Gates had been hospitalized." The gossips chewed voraciously on that juicy tidbit.

"You didn't tell her why, did you?" Gladys Herbert hated to get involved, but she had made a promise.

"No, that's not my place," Brenda replied.

"Good. It's none of her business. She's not a member," Ellen Whitney chimed in.

From there the conversation took a new direction: the picture in the *Black Pages*. Ellen spoke critically about Finus for attending a secular concert "…and the way she was dressed. Very inappropriate."

"There's nothing wrong with Rev. Gates taking his lady to a concert," Mother Pierce interrupted. "We discussed this yesterday at the regional missionary circle meeting. Rev. and Mrs. Broadnaux were with them. I'm glad to see them get out; I always thought they were spending too much time reading."

There was a general laugh from the gossips.

Gladys Herbert tried to change the tone of the discussion. "They are both scholars."

"Reading. Humph, that's certainly better than the stuff I hear from my daughters and granddaughters about their Saturday night dates," one of the senior ladies commented.

"If they're doing that much reading, maybe he's still available," a much younger member of the gospel chorus said hopefully.

"I heard Iva Peyton is starting a Cathedral book club."

Ellen Whitney added a final two cents for the conversation. "That's one desperate child."

"Gossip break is over," the choir director's voice boomed from the back of the sanctuary. "Musicians, take your seats and let's focus on the business at hand."

The doorbell rang at precisely nine p.m. on Saturday. She paused for a moment to check him out through the peephole. Since he hadn't rung the bell six times in two minutes, she surmised he'd be in a pleasant mood. She watched him through the tiny lens for a second. He looked sound, no twitching and, tonight, no suit. Was the pious Reverend Doctor wearing blue jeans? She hurriedly opened the door, hoping he smelled as good as he looked.

They settled into their favorite places in the den and began reviewing documents. Temptation to demand answers to her questions about his health crowded her brain. But she decided to wait. If he trusted her, he would tell her. If he didn't, that would tell her something, too. After an hour he broke the quiet.

"Cassandra, I need to tell you something."

She stuck her index finger in the air. "Oh, sure, just wait one minute."

Tap. Tap. Tap. His fingers drummed the coffee table.

She looked up. "Could you please stop that?"

"No, this is what I need to talk about." He continued drumming.

She set her papers on her lap. "Okay, but please stop tapping."

"I'll try." He placed his hands under his thighs, opened his mouth to speak, then stopped.

"Yes, Doc?"

"We spend a lot of time together, and there's something you need to know about me."

A chill settled over her shoulders. *Steady, girl.*

He raised an eyebrow. "Cassandra?"

She let out a nervous giggle.

"Madame, this is serious." The Reverend Doctor spoke the words.

She leaned forward.

He stood and drew his frame up to his full height. "Cassandra, I have epilepsy."

His announcement sat heavily in the air for a minute.

"Some things make sense now." Her words came out calmly, though her heart raced.

"Like?"

"You never sail alone."

Relief flashed across his face and he sat back down. "Right."

"The car service and…the fidgeting?"

"All correct. Just some of the ways I manage. But try as I might, some of the side effects from my medications are not so easy to control."

"But it doesn't seem to be a chronic ail—" She stopped short. She couldn't bring herself to pronounce an ailment on this strong, vital man.

"Thank you, Cassandra. I don't think of it as an ailment, either. It's just the cross I have to bear. It's been called the sacred disease. I wanted to tell you for two reasons." He moved over to the sofa and sat next to her. "I've wanted to tell you this for some time. I realize now that it would be unfair to catch you unaware if I were to have a seizure. I need to ask if you would like to know what to do in that event. I hope you care enough to want to know what to do in case…" His voice trailed off.

"Yes, of course. What a heavy burden for you."

He covered her hand with his. "No, no greater than anyone else's troubles. I've had this since childhood; it is pretty much a part of me. And," he took a deep breath, "there is something more."

Her shoulders tensed.

"I've told you the worst of it."

She exhaled.

"I also have a bad case of anxiety. That's really the manifestation you see most. I get so frustrated and anxious that I might lose control, I overreact sometimes at the slightest indication from my body. If I have been abrupt at times, I apologize. I don't like to lose control, especially in public."

She sat back and nodded. His words 'in public' pounded in her ears. She scratched her head. *What am I going to do?*

They spent the next hour talking about his condition and how she should respond in the event of…

"They all know, don't they?"

"Yes, everyone in the Assembly knows about the epilepsy. I'm surprised and humbled the gossips had not informed you by now. To think I've garnered enough respect to not have my illness grist for the gossip mill is a blessing. But only a very few know about the anxiety, so I'll trust you not to discuss that."

"Of course not."

He stood up and shook his leg out as she'd seen him do many times. Then he sat again in her favorite chair. "I've been lucky not to have had any major episodes at church since my college days. Until last week when, well, you know what happened." A wicked grin crossed his cheeks. "I was in the hospital and you didn't call, come by, or send flowers."

She rolled her eyes.

He laughed and launched into a story about the last *gran mal* seizure he'd at church and the tongue-lashing his mother gave him after he recovered. "Lack of sleep is not good for me. That was one wild summer, one of the last Will and I spent together before last year. After that I slowed down and Daddy finally accepted my petition to enter the ministry. After I proved I'd gotten on the right road."

"Kind of like a Damascus experience?"

"Not quite, but I see you're studying."

She winked. "I've learned a few things hanging out with you."

"Good, good, glad to be a positive influence." Finus reached for his paperwork. He stood up and moved towards the front door. "I have strict orders from Ms. Inez. I have to be home by eleven."

She followed, inhaling his cologne. "Home?"

"I'm staying with Fred and Inez for a while. I haven't had a curfew since I was eighteen, but I have better sense than to mess with Inez. I'll be with them until they feel I've fully recovered." He paused with his hand on the doorknob. "Thank you, Cassandra. It's never easy to discuss this, but, as always, it's easy to talk to you. Thank you for your friendship, it means so much to me."

"That's what friends are for. May I ask one more question before you go?"

"Sure. What mysteries remain unveiled?"

"Is this the reason Phaedra told you that you were more trouble than you're worth?"

Finus grimaced and stepped through the door. "Yeah."

Over his shoulder she could see his driver waiting beside his Town Car. It was close to eleven o'clock and the streets were quiet, but she felt like yelling, "Phaedra's wrong." He lingered at the threshold. She reached out and wrapped her arms around him. He leaned into her embrace, then released her with a kiss on the forehead.

She spent the rest of the weekend content; he trusted her. She melted when she remembered the warmth of his embrace, but bristled at his kiss. A cousin's kiss wasn't what she wanted. His unfulfilling kiss reminded her too much of the last days of her relationship with Greg. He'd come home late, give her a familial peck on her cheek, and turn his back to her in bed. She broke off the engagement when she found out Gregory frequented every gentleman's club in northern Illinois and did God only knows what in the back rooms. He'd said there were things he desired that he wouldn't ask the future mother of his children to do.

Finus's kiss reminded her that she'd been down this road before.

Chapter 13

"Cassandra, what's your fax number? You need to see this." The command in Finus's tone was not pleasant this morning. She had barely sat down at her desk following a Friday morning pep rally when the office clerk informed her of this urgent call. She ticked off the number and then rushed to stand over the fax machine. She gasped as she picked the pages up from the machine; it was another item from the *Black Pages*.

"Is everything all right, Dr. Brownley?" one of the student office assistants asked as she rushed past to the privacy of her office.

"Sure," she muttered. Heat from the faxed paper burned her fingertips. She blinked twice at the pages that featured two pictures of her and Finus. The first frame showed them attending a charity dinner. She was dressed in a black business suit with her hair in its usual bun. The second frame captured Finus whispering in her ear at the Will Downing concert. The caption underneath the photos read, 'The freak comes out at night'. She took a cleansing breath before she picked up the phone. "I've got it."

"Read the copy," he demanded.

" 'Mystery Solved—the woman seen with our boy—' "

"No, not out loud. I don't want to hear it."

Her eyes rolled up to the ceiling.

Mystery solved—The woman seen with our boy, Rev. Finus Gates, at the Will Downing Concert is none other than Dr. Cassandra Brownley, Vice-Principal at Westmore High School. Dr. Brownley has been seen frequently accompanying Brother Gates to various social functions, but BP has never seen her looking like this. P.S. Thanks, tipster P.I., for the ID.

"Cassandra, I've already been on the phone to the publisher and my attorneys and have demanded a retraction and an apology. This is unacceptable, and I wanted to alert you before anyone called," he yelled.

She held the phone away from her ear to protect her eardrums. "Like my mother, after the way she paraded that picture of me last week?"

"Especially your mother."

"She's going to be so embarrassed."

"I promise to fix this." He drew in a deep breath. "What about you? How do you feel?"

She held the phone against her chest for a moment and closed her eyes. Now his tone shifted to concern. "Well, I don't like being called outside of my name, but how much harm can be done by the *Black Pages*?"

"That remains to be seen. I need to call Fred and send him this picture. I'll call you tonight and let you know where I stand."

"Oh, God, I didn't consider what this might mean for you. I'm sure this will blow over."

She hung up the phone and stared at the intimacy the photo conveyed. "A picture tells a thousand lies."

She sat at her desk and stared at her nails. Her index fingers were both chipped. It was time to make some decisions about her relationship with Finus. She ran the nail of her pinky finger under her thumbnail.

During the week she suffered more than a few rude comments from some of the teachers as the photos circulated around the school. Brenda told her the word among the students was that maybe if she let her hair down more often she would get some and wouldn't be so hard on them. She shook it all off until the call from the superintendent of personnel.

For the next two weeks she used every excuse she could think of to avoid seeing Finus. She attended a school board meeting via conference call and even went to a Saturday night house party with Yolanda. All of his calls went immediately to voicemail, and she answered all of his questions via email.

Phyllis called her silly. Yolanda questioned her maturity.

"Oh." She yawned and stretched out on her sofa. It was only eight on Saturday night, but she was tired. It took a call from Janice to pin her down to accept this late Saturday night working session. She sank further into the comfort of her favorite chair. Wrapping her arms around her waist, she remembered the way it felt when he put his arms around her to position her in receiving lines. Oh, how her heart craved the intimacy of a ride in his Boxster. "Oh, God, the way he whispered in my ear at the Will Downing concert. Stop it! You need to stop torturing yourself." She stood up and paced around the room. "It's getting harder for me to breathe around him." She looked down at her freshly painted toenails. "I miss him, but we need to stay away before we get hurt."

She yawned and looked at the clock. Finus was late. "I'm tired of waiting on a man who has no interest in me. I ought to go out, if only to the store."

The doorbell rang.

After he arrived she couldn't keep still. She paced around her den while he sat lounging in her favorite chair. They were supposed to review budgets and grant funding proposals, but he said he didn't have the energy.

Finus placed his hands behind his back and yawned. "What's wrong?"

"I'm nervous about Monday."

He relaxed further into the cushions. "You should have come out with us this evening. Iva did a really nice job of arranging the networking dinner. I even made some contacts with the business community."

She rolled her eyes. He was late because he'd attended a networking dinner set up by Iva Peyton, the first activity of the new professionals networking group she'd started. Iva's name was coming up too much in conversations. According to the gossip she heard from Brenda and Yolanda, Iva had been seen everywhere he was in the past two weeks.

"I have a meeting with the superintendent of personnel first thing Monday morning."

"Oh, that." He waved her off. "Don't worry, my dear. They can't fire you over a gossip column. Are you sure you don't want me to do anything?"

She shook her head. "No."

"I'm praying for a positive outcome, but you just never know who sits where." He sat up and took off his glasses and rubbed his eyes. "Do you realize you haven't gone anywhere with me since the concert?"

As she sat on the sofa opposite her guest, her breath caught in her chest. He looked so tired. She took a deep breath. "I've decided to keep a low profile." She glanced over at the wall clock and stood up.

"Isn't it time for you to go? That's all I need." She raised her hands to highlight her words: "*Black Pages* headline: 'Finus Gates seen leaving Cassandra Brownley's house after midnight.'"

"Okay, okay, I'm leaving. I know how you feel about men in your house at the midnight hour." He started to gather his things. He moved slowly towards the door. "I almost forgot. I have an update for you. We've decided to accept Amaria's offer and host a benefit concert for the Gates school project."

She followed, inhaling in his wake.

"Care to attend church tomorrow? Then Sullivan's for dinner?"

I'm trying to stay out of the public eye. "No, thank you. I'm going to church with Phyllis."

He looked down at his shoes. "I will continue in prayer about the situation, but don't worry, Ca-San. I'll call you Monday as soon as I land in L.A."

She heard the genuine concern in his tone and sighed. After she closed the door behind him she stood breathing in the remnants of his cologne. It was just after midnight, but just spending a few hours with him had ignited her. Suddenly she had enough energy to write the budget alone.

Over the next two weeks the details for the benefit concert quickly finalized. The time crunch left no opportunity to see Finus when he returned from L.A. and she spoke to him only once to tell him her good news. Her job wasn't in jeopardy from the *Black Pages* article. The excitement for the fundraiser for the Gates school intensified when Amaria's single hit number one on the inspirational charts.

For the concert the youth choir from Amaria's home church in Tuscaloosa, Alabama, was invited to come and sing backup. Cassandra declined a formal invitation from the Gates School committee to sing, but she did volunteer to serve on the hospitality committee with Gladys. To save on cost, the choir members were housed with different Assembly members. She signed up to host five teenage girls.

It was a busy Saturday. She spent half the day chauffeuring the girls around. First rehearsal, then the mall. Each girl wanted to buy something of the latest fashion from Chicago. They barely made it back to the Cathedral in time for the concert.

Since she was at the church early, Cassandra went into the kitchen to see how she might help out.

"No, dear, we really don't need your help. You should go in and enjoy the concert." One of the nicer members of the kitchen committee gently tried to urge her out of their space. Finus had tried to warn her. The kitchen at the Cathedral was the sole province of the eight senior ladies. Cassandra stood in the door of the kitchen and watched as the church mothers bustled around. They had their systems together.

Mother Pierce took a break from her duties and walked toward the door. "There's really not much to be done. Rev. Gates had all of the food catered, and we have already set up the buffet lines and laid out the linen."

Ellen Whitney waved at her from the restaurant-sized stainless sinks. "We really don't need *your* help. We've run this kitchen for years. Bishop Gates didn't call us the Great Eight for nothing. You go sit in the patch. But after the concert you can help us take care of the trash and spills once the people start eating, if you will."

By the time Cassandra went back to the sanctuary the building was filled. In less than a week, Amaria's single had crossed over and was in heavy rotation on the local R&B stations. The house was packed. She spoke to a few people that recognized her and waved at the members from the Black Student Union at Westmore as she looked around for a seat. She spied Finus on the front row next to Inez, the bishop, and Iva

Peyton. No place for her. She sucked in her upper lip and took a seat in the back.

David Broadnaux, the master of ceremonies, got the program off to a laughing start with his easy wit.

She focused her attention as David introduced several prominent Assembly members who traveled with the choir.

"Bishop Emeritus Joshua Morton is my personal mentor."

The senior cleric stood up and was applauded.

"It gets so cold here in the winter I've got to ask you, sir. Is it a blessing or punishment that you sent me to cold Chicago?" She laughed. Poor David and Lydia had complained all winter about the ice and snow.

The program began with a spirit-filled contemporary gospel selection from Amaria's CD. While the sanctuary swayed and rejoiced she pondered the conversation she'd had with Amaria that afternoon. She looked down at her grey dress and sensible shoes, another reminder that she was not like the 'damn girl' who looked like Chaka Khan burning up the choir box. Amaria and the choir brought the house down when they sang her hit song. In appreciation the offering baskets overflowed.

During the final acknowledgements, David asked all of the fund raising committee and school board members to stand and be recognized. Cassandra remained seated.

"We would be remiss and I would lose a friend if we did not thank Dr. Cassandra Brownley, our educational consultant, for her work on this project. Because of her leadership we have been able to secure some grant funds from both the state board of education and the federal government."

The house erupted with a round of applause. David turned in the direction of her usual seat in the patch. He didn't see her, so he continued. Luckily no one seated around her said anything. Finus stood up, looked around, and scowled. She sank down in her seat and thankfully escaped his notice.

"I understand Dr. Brownley is down in the kitchen helping out, which means, choir, you are in for a treat because the good doctor can do some mean things with a chicken." She hung her head as another round of applause and laughter rippled through the building. During the encore she left the sanctuary.

In the fellowship hall she donned an apron and went to work. She picked up empty plates, cleaned spills, and replaced fallen forks. She served on the kitchen committee at her home church and had served more than one large conference dinner. As the dinner hour dwindled she went to the head table to clear the remains. The only person still seated was Bishop Morton.

"Can I offer you anything else, sir?" she asked after she cleared away the elderly man's plate.

"No, but you can sit down and talk to an old man for a moment."

"I can do that."

"I bet you're a school teacher, aren't you," he began.

She smiled. *Okay, here we go.* "Yes, how did you know?"

He grinned. "I can tell every time. You look like a teacher. I see you are a single girl, too. Look over there." He motioned across the fellowship hall to where Finus stood in the midst of many female visitors. "Why aren't you over there with the rest of the gals vying for Gates's attention?"

Cassandra shrugged her shoulders.

"They look silly. Just don't know what's wrong with the young girls these days, always running up in men's faces. A lady ought to wait for a man to approach. Now what do you think about that?"

"Oh, I agree."

"Well, good, you got some sense, too. Stay right here and watch for a minute."

Cassandra pulled up a chair.

"I hear Finus has a girlfriend now. I suspect she'll be along soon to put an end to that nonsense."

She let his comment pass.

"I'm glad I made this last trip to the big city. The Gateses always treated me so well when I came, and they always did have the prettiest girls in Chicago." He winked at her. "I also had to come check on my boys. You a member here or College Station?"

He didn't wait for her answer, but rambled on.

"You are a sweet girl to sit here with an old man. Boosts my ego and helps with my digestion to talk to a pretty girl. Don't worry, I'm single, too. I lost my wife of fifty-three years just two short years ago."

She gave him a soft smile.

He continued talking. When he paused she stood up.

"I've enjoyed talking with you, and if you'll excuse me…"

"No, now wait a minute. That Finus is headed this way. Let's see what he has to say."

"Uncle Joshua, did you enjoy your dinner?" It was BMA tradition for the children of clergy to call the bishops uncle.

"Yes, sir, and I'm enjoying my after-dinner conversation as well."

"Good, I'm glad to see you talking to Dr. Brownley. I was looking for her to introduce you."

"Doctor who?" The older man gave her a hard stare.

Finus shook his head. "You didn't introduce yourself?"

"We just started talking. We hadn't really gotten around to names," Bishop Morton said.

"Then grant me the honor of formally introducing you to Dr. Cassandra Brownley."

"What? I thought you were a school teacher?"

"I am. Well, I was until a few years ago." She verbally stumbled when she saw the disapproving glower on Finus's face.

"Cassandra is a high school principal and the educational consultant on the Gates school project."

"You're the one we've heard so much about. You're the girlfriend. Why didn't you say so?"

"Uncle Joshua, I told you earlier," Finus began his usual refrain. "Cassandra and I are just good friends."

"Okay, then you made your point and you can move on." Bishop Morton waved a withered finger at Finus. "Young lady, sit down and talk with me a while longer."

Finus didn't move.

"It's all right. I'm not going to steal your girl." Joshua Morton placed a wrinkled hand on her knee. "Didn't say I didn't want her, said I won't take her. But if I were twenty years younger, I might just give you a run for your money."

"Yes, sir, I believe you would." Finus winked at her and walked away.

Bishop Morton lifted his hand and placed it back in his lap. "No wonder you weren't concerned about that gaggle of geese seeking Gates out. He comes seeking you. Daughter, you're doing the right thing. Don't you chase after him. You make sure he respects you. The Bible says he who finds a wife…"

"Rev. Gates and I are really just good friends."

"And if I heard that before half the weddings I performed I wouldn't have had so much divorce in my churches. Now you can go." He waved her off.

She looked around the fellowship hall and saw Finus sitting in a corner talking with Inez, so she returned to her kitchen duties.

As much as she offered, Finus would not accept her check for the fundraiser. He even told her if she slipped a check in the offering plate, he would have the counting team return it. So to contribute something, at the end of the evening she gave each member of the Great Eight a gift certificate for a pedicure from the Green Spa, a new salon where she was getting her hair done. She knew Finus would approve since the Green Spa was owned by an Assembly member.

Mother Pierce grinned from ear to ear. "Finus didn't have to do this. No one ever gives us anything. And he's supporting that young girl's business, too."

"That Wilma taught him well," Gladys said in praise of her departed friend.

Too shy to say the gift was from her, she let all the credit accrue to Finus and set about bundling the soiled linen.

"Excuse me."

She looked up to find Amaria standing in front of her.

"My Uncle Joshua was just asking me if I'd met Finus's girlfriend."

Cassandra looked around. There was no one else within earshot. She kept her head down and focused on the bundle of linen. Earlier Amaria had made a point of telling her all about all the time she'd spent with Finus in L.A. She glanced up at the beautiful, talented woman with the nasty attitude.

Amaria rolled her neck and looked down her nose. "You need to stop embarrassing yourself and just do your job." Amaria shook her Chaka-inspired tresses. "I've got to go. The radio station is waiting for me to call in and do some shout-outs. What's the name of your high school?"

"Westmore, why?"

"I'll be careful not to mention it." She turned and walked away.

Cassandra's head hung as low as a sagging clothes line. It was past time she left. At ten p.m. she went outside to wait for her girls.

"Cassandra, I've been trying to get a minute of your time all night."

She didn't need to turn around to know who was speaking to her.

"Let me drive you home, it's getting late. You can pick up your car after service tomorrow."

She turned in his direction. Finus stood with his hands in his pockets rocking back and forth in his shoes. He looked pleased. She closed her eyes to maintain her resolve. "No, thank you, and I'm not coming here tomorrow."

"If you aren't coming tomorrow and I can't drive you home, can I come over?"

She looked around the emptying parking lot. "No. The only reason I'm still here is to wait for my houseguests. Where are those girls?"

"Cassandra, I'd really like to talk to you tonight. There's so much that I want to go over with you."

"No," came out a little sternly. "You know I have these girls staying with me, and that's all I need. More gossip when these girls find your feet under my table." *Especially since I've been denying that I'm your girlfriend all day.* "I just want to go home, get the girls settled, and close my bedroom door because I'm sure they'll be up half the night giggling."

"If you are tired, let me drive you. I'll have someone bring your car."

There was the arrogant *don't-say-no-to-me* attitude in his voice.

She shifted from one foot to another. "No, Finus, please just leave it." *Just leave me alone.* She stopped moving when her feet fell into her singer's stance.

"Cassandra, you know we really need to have a long talk."

"Not tonight. I just can't." *Can't listen to you extol the value of our friendship, not after what Amaria said to me. And I'm too tired to hear about how angry you are about what the gossiping hens at this church are saying about me and you.*

"Hi, Rev. Gates. Hi, Cassandra," her houseguests chorused as they came giggling out of the building.

His shoulders slumped slightly and he jingled some change in his pocket. "Ladies, have a good night. Goodnight, Cassandra, and thank you."

She watched his back as he re-entered the Cathedral, where she was sure that damn Amaria waited.

Late into the night Cassandra sat on her bed polishing her nails. "Yes, girls," she said to her toenails. "We're definitely in love with him. And after what Amaria said to me, we're soon to have a broken heart."

"So," she announced as she applied a second coat, "let's keep our distance."

Chapter 14

Cassandra stood behind Finus while he unlocked her front door. She reached up and brushed a crumb from his grey herringbone wool English morning jacket. He'd melted her resolve on Good Friday with a simple pale pink pillbox hat and a hand-written note. *Share Easter with Me. Finus.*

She looked back at the Bentley he'd hired for the day. "What about the driver? He's been out all day with us." She inhaled. The masculine scent she'd missed filled her senses. She lifted her left foot. Her pink pump pinched her pinky toe. After two church services and dinner at Sullivan's, it was time to take these shoes off.

Finus winked as he stepped aside for her to enter. "Lucky for him I'm in a generous mood. I'm sure it will be a great day for him."

For a Sunday he's been unusually funny and approachable. She passed through the door. "Several of the church mothers commented on your generous spirit today."

"Because of you."

Grateful her back was to him, she shuffled her feet. Her face itched under her Easter hat. "Make yourself at home. I've got to take these shoes off now. And these hairpins are killing me. I'll be back."

She took the stairs two at a time and stopped dead at her bedroom door. Her bed was littered with shoe boxes and dresses in need of re-hanging. Nothing seemed to fit right this morning. Not even her new dress, which she ended up wearing anyway. She glanced over at the clock; it was almost five. She pushed a few more dresses to the floor and sat down on her bed to call her mother.

She took a deep breath while the phone rang. "Happy Easter."

"Hey, I thought you would be coming by. You missed the family. Everyone's just about gone." Her mother sounded a little put out.

"I'm not going to make it. I've been out all day and I'm tired. Did you all have a good service?"

"Yes, the same resurrection service the pastor preaches every year. What about you? Did you enjoy the services out there?"

"Services is right." Cassandra leaned back and described the Easter rituals of the BMA. She glanced at the clock again; five-twenty. "Oh, no, I almost forgot Finus is downstairs."

"I can't believe you agreed to spend Easter with that man. There are some nice young men at our church. Sister Fischer's son was there today. He asked about you."

"He's an ex-con, Phyllis."

She could hear her mother bristle. "Well, if you want him you ought to say something. We know you aren't giving any up, and it doesn't seem like he wants any. Sounds to me like a match made in heaven." Her voice dripped with sarcasm.

A long sigh of exasperation escaped her lips. "Phyllis, I didn't call you for all of that. Happy Easter. I'll talk to you later. Bye." She clicked off the phone. She wasn't sure if she was annoyed with her mother or herself. She dropped the receiver into the mass of clothes on her bed and went downstairs.

She stopped short at the threshold of her den and looked at Finus asleep in her easy chair. He'd taken a liking to her favorite chair, and now when she let him come over he'd plop down and refuse to move. In his sleep no worry furrowed his brow, no trembles or quivers affected his limbs. The softness of peace illuminated his face. The ends of the pale grey striped bow tie hung loosely around his neck. The top button on his rounded collar shirt was undone, and his eye glasses sat slightly askew. The stern Reverend Doctor would never abide this look. It had to be Doc fast asleep in her den.

"I've missed you," she whispered. Peace and relief passed over her like a gentle summer breeze. "I'll tell you later," she whispered as she covered him with a pink paisley silk sofa throw. She sat on the sofa and quietly flipped through the Sunday *Tribune*.

Finus reached up and adjusted his glasses. He opened his eyes and blinked to adjust to the soft glow of the early evening and the vision that sat opposite him. She looked so pretty with her hair down. *I should tell her.* He hesitated. *Maybe I should wait.* He wasn't quite sure why, but it was clear she'd been avoiding him since the fundraiser.

"Good evening, Doc."

He smiled at the song in her voice. "What time is it, Ca-San. I didn't intend to fall asleep."

"It's just after seven, but it's okay. You've had a long day."

"And I have a longer tomorrow. Cassandra, I've got to go." He sat up completely and spoke slowly. "I'm catching the red eye to L.A. tonight."

Her smile faded. "I didn't know."

"I'll be gone for almost a month."

She frowned.

"I have meetings with the architecture and engineering firm for the school. You did receive the agenda for Thursday's meeting?"

She nodded.

"Then I'm off to San Diego for the preparation meetings for our national conference." He paused and pulled in his lower lip.

Don't push.

"I need to get out of here. I'm due at the airport in a couple of hours."

He called for his car and they moved outside and stood on the porch to wait. He rambled on about the difficulty he'd had in arranging his schedule to be away for a month. She frowned when he brought up the success of Amaria's album. "There's early talk about a Dove award or even a Grammy."

Her face twisted.

"I'm all set for my trip except for one thing." He took a step back. "Will you take my calls while I'm away?"

She looked down at her feet. "Of course I will."

He closed the distance between them as the Bentley came into view. He placed his hands on her arms just below her shoulders. Instead of looking into her eyes he stared at the part in her scalp. He planted a lingering kiss on her forehead. "Thank you for Easter."

She frowned.

On the following Thursday, the Gates school committee and several members of the deacon board assembled in the Cathedral's conference room and studied the architectural drawing for the Gates school.

"Hello, sorry I'm late," Cassandra said to those assembled and took her usual seat next to Gladys at the conference table. Finus's secretary Janet Jones nodded her disapproval and tapped the call out button on the conference phone. The dial tone served to call the meeting to order. Everyone settled as Janet placed them into the conference call with Finus and the project architect. Almost in unison the attendees said their hellos.

"Is Cassandra there?" he asked when the hello traffic died down.

"Yes, I'm here." All eyes in the room fixed on her as she responded.

"Okay, good. I didn't hear your voice. Let's get started. I'll give a brief introduction of those here with me in L.A., then turn it over to the project manager to walk us though the plans."

The undertones in his personal greeting assured her he was well, so she pushed her chair back a little. Architectural diagrams were outside her area of expertise. As the project manager walked them through the design, he kept a focus on the exterior of the building and commented on how well the design complemented the grandeur of the Cathedral. The murmur around the table agreed it would be a beautiful building.

Cassandra remained silent as they were given a virtual tour of the building's interior. It had the requested number of classrooms and laboratory spaces, but...

Is it my place to say anything? They all seem so happy with the presentation. She looked to her left and read a satisfied expression on Gladys's face. Finus sounded pleased.

"We haven't heard from our consultant, Dr. Brownley. Cassandra, what do you think?"

There was silence. All the energy in the room focused on her.

"Cassandra," he called out to her from across the physical distance. "I'm interested in your opinion."

"Well, it seems to me to be more form than function." The words slipped out of her mouth. "I don't see a lot of flexibility in the interior plan for floating classrooms or assemblies. I was hoping to see more movable walls and open spaces, consistent with some of the district's experimental designs. Remember the buildings I took you to see?" His interest made her forget they weren't sitting in her den.

"This was designed," interjected the project manager, "to flow with the aesthetics of the Cathedral. We sought to provide as much classroom space as possible; we assumed the Cathedral would be used for group meetings."

"I understand that, but I don't think the bishop will be happy long term with students constantly assembling in his building." *In for a penny, in for a pound.* "And it's more than that. My concerns go beyond the outward appearance of the building. Where is the capacity for potential expansion? I hope some consideration is being given to that. And," she stopped midthought when her brain caught up to her runaway mouth.

"Go ahead, Cassandra," Finus said.

"And could the building entrance be on the opposite side of what's shown? The students attracted from the community shouldn't feel like they were driving through the church to attend school." She turned to face the bishop. "With all due respect, we must establish this school as an independent entity, and one physical way to do this would be to set the entrance on Butler Road."

"All good comments, Dr. Brownley." The project manager continued, "We are church designers, not public school builders. We followed the vision for a traditional school setting as outlined by Dr. Gates and the board."

I put my foot in it, now.

"One of the reasons we hired an educational consultant," Finus interrupted, "was to help us work through this kind of issue. Good job, Cassandra, I understand what you mean. Any other comments?"

"I'm in support of what Dr. Brownley is saying," Bishop Sutton boomed. "The schools should not have to rely on the Cathedral being open. It would increase our staff cost. Yes, ma'am, I think your counsel on this is wise." Bishop Sutton winked at her. "A woman of vision."

The conference continued with the firm taking notes from the entire committee on ways to place more emphasis on function and flexibility in the interior spaces. As the meeting dwindled, Finus thanked everyone for their input. "Sir, may I ask for a personal privilege."

Bishop Sutton chuckled and motioned toward the handset. "Yes, son. Cassandra, please pick up the handset."

She twisted her lips and reached across the conference table to lift the handset on the side of the pod phone.

"Fabulous work, my dear."

The warmth of a blush crept across her face. She took two steps back from the table and extended the cord as long as it would go.

"I just wanted to tell you personally. Are you going to be home this evening? I'll call later."

"Yes. Thank you, Rev. Gates."

"Why so formal? Is everyone in the room looking at you?"

"Yes, every eye and ear." She turned her back to the table. "I'll talk to you later." With a fully flushed face she returned the handset and Finus closed the meeting with a long-distance prayer.

Instead of rushing home to wait by the phone she went back to school to supervise the evening activities. When she walked into her house at eight-thirty with an armful of groceries and her dry cleaning, the phone was ringing. An eight-hundred number scrolled across her caller ID screen, but she picked it up anyway.

"Hi, it's me."

He'd always called from his own phones. Maybe he was onto her.

"Hi, Finus." Her voice echoed. He had her on speaker phone.

"Say hello to Aunt Jo. We're on our way to choir rehearsal."

"Hello, please take me off of speaker phone. I've been on speaker phone enough today." She waited until she heard the click. "And you shouldn't be talking to me and trying to drive in L.A.," she scolded him in her school teacher's voice.

"No one drives in L.A., beautiful. I hired a driver for the week." He laughed. "How are you?"

She chose not to acknowledge his endearment. "Don't you think it's kind of rude to carry on a conversation with me while your aunt is in the car with you?"

"Aunt Jo, Cassandra wants to know if you mind listening to my one-sided conversation."

She could tell he was holding the phone away from his mouth. He must be having a great time with wild Will, joking around, calling her beautiful.

"Aunt Jo says it's okay, and she can't wait to meet you. I really wanted to speak with you tonight before it got too late for you. I can't talk long as we're almost at the Tabernacle. Amaria is rehearsing to sing with her choir on Sunday."

So Amaria's the reason for his happy mood.

"I wanted to let you know how pleased I was with you earlier today. We were bound in some traditional ideas, but girl, you broke that paradigm. The firm already has plans to make the changes you and the board suggested."

She frowned. "I'm glad. I was afraid I was overstepping my boundaries."

"You don't have any boundaries, my dear." His tone softened. "You were priceless today, and you didn't answer my question. How are you?"

"I'm fine. You know me, every day the same, school, work."

"And no me to ask you to run all over town?" He paused. "I hope this means you'll be well rested and agree to accompany me again when I return. I miss your company."

She grinned. "We'll see."

"Not exactly the answer I was hoping for, but patience is a virtue I'm praying for." A second of silence passed between the phone lines. "Hey, I'm taking Aunt Jo shopping on Rodeo Drive in the morning for her birthday. I'd like to buy you a gift. We're going to Tiffany's. What would you like?"

"You don't need to buy me anything. Just relax and enjoy your trip."

He hooted. "What woman doesn't want a present from Tiffany's?" The phone clicked and his next words sounded like they came from an echo chamber. "Aunt Jo, what's wrong with her?"

"Boy, take me off that speaker," his aunt said.

"Ca-San, we're pulling up to the church now and I'm off to San Diego tomorrow afternoon. I'll call you back. Take care of yourself. Goodbye."

"Goodbye, Finus." She placed the phone back on the hook. "Why'd he call me beautiful?" she asked the refrigerator as she put away the milk. "Did he say he missed me?" she asked her coffee cup as she washed the dishes. "Can I survive for three weeks until I see him again?"

Chapter 15

When he returned from California in early June Finus didn't say a word. He just assumed she'd go anywhere he asked. And she did. They went to informal dinners with Fred and Inez, the movies, and all of Chicago's weekend outdoor festivals. He invited himself to her brother's birthday party. Cassandra told her mother it was a clear signal that he had a romantic interest in her. Yogi shared with her the talk from the end of year sorority meeting. It was all about his long visit to California and Amaria. Cassandra prayed she wasn't wasting her time.

Finus was uncharacteristically chatty as they drove down the city streets toward the expressway after Brown's party. "Let's go out on Saturday night."

"Where do you have to be?" She knew his schedule was still filled with the sermons, and church events he'd stopped asking her to attend.

"Nowhere. I was…" He glanced her way. "I am formally asking you out. On a date."

Cassandra turned her face towards the window so he couldn't see how far her smile stretched. "Yes, I'd like that very much." *Finally*.

He exhaled. "Good! What's your pleasure?"

She hugged the soft leather of the seats with her legs as the mile markers whizzed by. They were on the highway now and she wasn't sure if she should reply. Finus didn't care to talk while he drove on the interstate.

"I don't know. You make the plans. Just tell me what to wear." She hoped that sounded as blithe as she felt.

"Wear your prettiest dress." He gave her another sideways glance and stepped on the gas.

It was a blue sky day and she was flying high. She'd successfully completed her first year at Westmore. The Gates school project was on track. And Finus had just asked her out. If he had the top down she'd raise her arms in a roller coaster salute. Whoo!

"Now that that's settled I want to ask you about teacher credentialing."

Her stomach muscles constricted as he took the off ramp and downshifted the Boxster.

Cassandra spent the balance of the week anticipating their first official date. Yolanda coached her on what to wear, and she openly shared her excitement with Brenda Thomas at a post-graduation faculty luncheon. The only thing that gave her pause was the question of who would pick her up Saturday night. He could shift so quickly from the easygoing Doc to the stodgy Reverend Doctor.

At precisely six p.m. on Saturday the doorbell rang, once. She took a deep breath before opening it. Yolanda and Phyllis had cautioned her against appearing too eager. One ring in two minutes. That was Doc.

"Wow, you look beautiful." He stepped into her foyer and took in the full view.

She swirled around in the flowing turquoise dress so he could see the back detail. "Thank you. You look as handsome, as usual." He was resplendent in a dark grey suit with a lavender shirt and coordinating tie.

She reached out to accept the bouquet of exotic flowers he held. "These are *beautiful*." They stood transfixed in the moment. Then his cell phone chirped and broke the spell.

"I'll get a vase for these while you answer that."

Perfect, she thought as she walked toward her kitchen, glad for the distraction. *Okay, girl fix your face, take a deep breath, and simmer down. This is it.* When she returned to the living room perfection had fled.

"I am very sorry, but…"

"You have to go?"

He shrugged his shoulders and turned towards the door. "I was really looking forward to our time together this evening." He rocked from side to side in his shoes. Disappointment clouded his features.

She twisted her lips. "I was, too, dear heart, but if you're needed elsewhere…" Whatever news had called him away clearly disturbed him.

"Cassandra, may I kiss you?"

She looked into his eyes, soft brown pools of sensitivity, Doc's eyes.

"Doc, I…" She inhaled deeply. "It's certainly nice to be asked, and I've never been asked so nicely. But

I don't think so." *If you kiss me, I might not be able to let you go.* She slowly shook her head no. "No, I can't wait another minute." She wrapped her arms around his neck and pressed her lips against his.

"Now go where you're needed. I understand."

She watched him pull out of her driveway and contemplated the price of being with him. *Am I unselfish enough?* She kicked off her shoes and wandered into the kitchen to find some dinner.

Finus kicked himself all the way to Edwards Hospital for having to break their date. His mouth opened in a grin as he remembered her kiss. It was as soft and sweet as he'd dreamed it would be. He slowed down as he entered the hospital zone, then whispered a prayer of thanksgiving for the depths of her trust and respect. She didn't even ask where he was going or why.

Cassandra spent her evening idly watching network TV, reliving kissing Finus. It wasn't a long kiss, but it was everything she longed for. It took all of her strength to pull away from his embrace and send him on his way. The teaser for the ten o'clock news tweaked her interest and she decided to check it out and then turn in.

A few minutes later, the phone rang.

"It's me. Have you eaten? We can go out and get a late bite."

"If you're hungry you should get something. I've already eaten."

"Me, too. I ate with Iva."

"What? You were with Iva Peyton?"

"Yes, she needed my help."

"You left me for Iva Peyton?"

"I went to fulfill my calling. Iva is a dedicated member of the Assembly and she, she needed… Look, I'm coming over."

"Don't do this to me."

The click of the phone let her know she was being switched to speaker phone. "Do what? This isn't about you." His annoyance crackled across the distance.

Bitter thoughts filled her brain. "I can't believe I'm so stupid. Floating around all week on cloud nine, telling everyone my business."

"It was a legitimate call for pastoral care. Iva was in a car accident, and by the grace of God it wasn't fatal."

Tears warmed her face, and she sobbed in self-condemnation.

"This is something you must know might happen from time to time, although I did not expect a call tonight."

As she spurted and gurgled on about being selfish, she heard the familiar roar of his Porsche. She peeked out of her bedroom window as he pulled into her driveway. She raced downstairs and opened the door.

He hurried into her open arms. "I'll make this up to you."

For a long while they sat cuddled up in her easy chair. He kissed the top of her head and her temples before claiming her mouth again.

"Cassandra, as we go forward, I do not intend for you to be last on my list."

"I know."

"I wish I didn't have to go with Fred in the morning to inspect the Chapel," he murmured in her ear.

"At least you'll be at the lake." She kissed him softly and stood. "After you finish with Fred tomorrow promise me you'll relax."

After she walked him to the door he planted another lingering kiss on her lips.

Late Sunday afternoon Finus sat in his mother's garden preparing to call Cassandra. He fussed for ten minutes about her not going to the Cathedral this morning and about the condition of the building at the lake before he told her about Iva Peyton.

"Iva's with you at the lake?" Her responses slowed.

The phone lines were silent. He hated when Cassandra went mute. "The Bakers are all here having what Lucy is calling their last blast. It's like old times. Lucinda brought her along. With her injuries, Iva needs some help."

She didn't respond. He stood up and shook his leg out.

She was so quiet he thought she'd slipped away. "Cassandra, are you listening to me?"

"What's this Bobby Caldwell? 'What You Won't Do for Love,'" Fred exclaimed as he pulled an album from the stack. "That's one Finus needs to hear." Finus had actually asked Fred and Inez to leave the lake a week earlier than planned so Cassandra could have the house. "Just friends, my eye. She's got his nose wide open." Because it was Finus's birthday, Fred decided to take it easy on him and skip that song.

Fred stood up and sauntered into the house in search of record player needles. "What your son needs now is a wife," he said to the departed Wilma as he found the needles in her cabinet in the great room. "In my opinion, old girl, Cassandra would make him a very fine wife." Fred grinned as he went back to sifting through the records.

"Cassandra didn't seem his type at first. But the right woman has a way of making some changes, like you did with Wallace. Yes, ma'am, it would seem that she's changed the stripes of your little tiger. Ah, Ray Charles. What say I play a little Ray for you and me right now?"

"All right, all right how the young folk do it? Bishop Freddie S on the mic and tonight, tonight," he intoned in his preacher's voice to get the party started, "tonight we're going to do this thing like me and Wallace did back in our heyday. One artist all night with something to say. I got it lined up, and there's a special dedication for each of you in the stack. Now, boys, if you haven't danced with your wife all year, tonight's the night. But you had better catch her before I do." Fred winked at Cassandra, who sat on one of the Adirondack chairs that lined the patio.

Cassandra turned and smiled at Finus. So often he lamented there was no one he could reminisce about the good old days with. Good for Fred bringing out a Gates family tradition to make the night special.

"Giving honor to whom honor is due and because it's his house and he bought all the food. This first one for you, Doc. Happy birthday."

Everybody laughed, as Stevie Wonder's "Sir Duke" filled the patio. It was a fitting tune for the guest of honor. Finus stood and extended his hand to Cassandra. The party was off to a great start.

"He's Misstra Know It All" played next, a second dedication to the birthday boy. While they waited for dinner, Stevie Wonder and DJ Freddie S kept everyone dancing and laughing.

Cassandra looked up into the darkening skies. It was a perfect summer night.

After many dedications and much dancing, Finus stood up. "I've waited long enough. Where are my birthday presents? And when are we going to eat?"

The catering company was a little behind in the kitchen, but they kept promising the food would be worth the wait. Finus stood in the center of his patio and addressed his small party.

"When you present your gift you have to give the birthday boy a blessing. And I'm not serving dinner until I get my presents," the spoiled birthday boy announced. "Okay, now who's first? I've been good and patient all evening. Now, whatcha bring me!"

The entire party roared with laughter while Fred and Inez stood up, ready to salute their entrusted son.

Cassandra sat back on a chaise lounger. She tilted her face to the heavens to thank God she was among those sharing his birthday. He seemed so happy. She sent up another prayer that his mood reflected peace and happiness and not the beginning of an aura.

One by one they presented Finus with simple, thoughtful gifts. But it was the beauty of the blessings that his loved ones bestowed upon him that lifted her heart.

"And last but not least…Cassandra." She could tell by his voice that he was eager to receive her gift.

"All right, keep your collar on," Cassandra joked as she slowly rose from the lawn chair.

"Doc, I'm giving you the only thing you ever asked of me. Your blessing is contained within this gift. David, are you ready?"

Finus looked over at his friend. "What kind of conspiracy is taking place on my patio?" He smiled broadly and rubbed his hands together as David stood by the sound system.

For his gift she sang the "Mother's Prayer" in English and Italian. Her voice was strong and sweet and everything she felt for Finus came through as she sang. She froze when she opened her eyes and met his gaze.

"Thank you, Ca-San, that was beautiful." He rose from his chair and hugged her as everyone else applauded her gift. Blinking back tears she held onto his embrace while she accepted the compliments of the others.

"I finally have the pleasure of hearing your voice. I was beginning to think it a myth," Fred said.

"Stop teasing her, Fred," Inez quickly chided her husband.

"Next time you are among us, I'm calling upon you to bless us with song," Fred added.

"Don't say that, Fred, or I'll never get her to come to the Assembly with me again," Finus said as he slipped his arm around her waist. "Thank you again. It is a beautiful gift."

"I don't know half of what she said, but it sure was pretty," David chimed in. Finus laughed so hard his arm slipped down to her butt.

"Well, sir, I believe the food has been blessed and the chef has been standing in the door for the past ten minutes trying to get our attention. Can we eat now, Gates?" Cecil Ford said.

"Sure, let's go in." Finus grabbed her hand. "I'm starving," he said as they walked into the house. "Where did you find recorded music that so perfectly complements your voice?"

"That's actually your gift." Cassandra was glad to have something to talk about as they sat down for their meal. "The music is from the Westmore High orchestra. Through me you made the donation that allowed them to complete the purchase of their concert dress. In appreciation the band director agreed to add the song to the spring concert. Afterward he recorded it for me."

He laughed. "That's perfect."

After dinner the party moved back to the patio for more Stevie and cake.

"Cassandra, come into the garden with me. I want to show you something." Finus took her hand and led her down the garden path.

They walked behind the hedge and he motioned to the only seat in the garden. "This is where I sit every night when I talk to you. Do you remember what we talked about last night?"

She looked up into the heavens and tried to discern stars from satellites. "Yes, there's the North star." She pointed. Last night he had given her a biblical history lesson on the stars.

"No, ma'am, that's a satellite." He stood behind her and caressed the length of her bare outstretched arm. "Were you listening to me last night or were you half asleep?" he murmured in her ear.

For months now when her ears fell asleep her heart continued to listen.

"*Viajou na maionese,*" he whispered.

She closed her eyes at the Portuguese expression that literally meant for her to get her head out of the mayonnaise.

He reached up and repositioned her hand to point out the true position of the North Star. Apprehension crept across her chest.

"Are you here with me?" He brushed the side of her cheek with his the back of his hand. "Let's sit for a minute." He guided her to his chaise lounge chair.

"Is this where you sat last night?" She had to say something to relieve the urge to turn and kiss him since he chose to sit behind her.

They sat in silence as they so often did, listening to the music and the sounds of the conversation from the patio.

A soft, sweet kiss brushed the side of her face, followed by another. In the back of her mind she heard her mother's voice. *Girl, turn around and kiss the man.* She turned and melted into his arms. His delicious little kisses covered the side of her face from her hairline to her cheek.

"Gates, whatcha doing out here?"

She jumped. The booming base of David's voice stilled his hand. They looked left to see David enter the garden, preceded by Cecil Ford.

"Can we finish this later?" she said.

Chapter 16

"Well, good people, we've dined, danced, and been delighted by two great singers; Mr. Stevie Wonder and Ms. Cassandra Brownley. The very fine pastor at College Station needs to be in his proper place in the morning, and I'm sure the first lady of the College Station will want to look her best."

Clearly Bishop Sutton meant to break the party up. Cassandra glanced over at Finus in time to see his smile shift into a grimace.

"It's late and tomorrow is our work day, so let's start saying goodnight," Fred concluded.

"Finally," Finus said as stood up and motioned the four guests that were leaving his house toward the gate.

"Ladies, goodnight, and I don't want to hear a lot of giggling from across the hall. I'm an old man and I need my rest." Fred playfully kissed Inez goodnight before he sent her and Cassandra up to their room.

"I don't understand, why are we sharing a room?" Cassandra asked after she and Inez settled into the guest room.

"There's enough talk about Finus in the Assembly, so Cecil Ford was adamant that if you stayed in this house tonight both of you be properly chaperoned.

Just thank God he didn't have his way or you'd be Alice's houseguest tonight." She laughed.

"He is old-fashioned. Doesn't he realize we're alone all the time?"

"Of course you're adults, but it would be unseemly if word got out that you two were together under the same roof as the bishop. That wouldn't be good for Finus or Fred. I'm sure by now you know our church is very political and gossipy. There are positions within the church both Finus and Fred are being considered for, and this is the kind of thing that would give certain people a reason to speak against them." Inez sat at the foot of the twin bed and rubbed night cream on her elbows. "There are some people that don't respect Fred because he's on his second marriage and hasn't been in the ministry for long, and some who don't like Finus because they think he's been too privileged."

"He tries so hard not to be arrogant about the money."

Inez set the jar of cream on the nightstand. "It's not just the money. Some people think that he doesn't deserve his position and only has it due to his father. You know Finus doesn't advertise all of the good things he does. Many people still see him as the pampered prince and a playboy. It's very hard to change the opinion of people who've known you all your life."

Cassandra wrapped her hair around her head and secured it with an oblong scarf. "I think it's the one thing that disappoints him. But having a slumber party with me is not quite fair to you."

"Cassandra, let's talk about something else. That was a beautiful song that you sang. You gave away all of your secrets when you sang. I heard some things in your voice that you surely need to say to him."

Cassandra looked down at the floral bedspread. "I guess it's like that song Fred played. I'm too shy."

Inez stood and looked into the mirror above the room's small dresser. "I almost made the same mistake with Fred. I thought that there was no way a man like Fred would be interested in me. I was passed over on the first marriage go-round and I was prepared to be a single, never married sister. But a wise woman gave me some sound advice and I'll share it with you. Talk honestly with Finus. Whatever the outcome, you'll know."

"I liked the way Fred did the music tonight. Stevie Wonder does have a lot to say," Cassandra said, changing the subject.

"That was vintage Wallace Gates, and the advice I just gave you came from Wilma."

She smiled. "The music made the party special for Finus. He gets so melancholy about being alone in the world."

Inez picked up her tweezers and plucked at an errant chin hair. "I don't see him as alone anymore. At least, he doesn't have to be."

Inez and Cassandra talked and giggled for the next hour. They laughed about the gossiping hens in the church, and Cassandra told tales of her adventures accompanying Finus to various church and community events. "Women are so bold."

"Yes, when it comes to an attractive, rich, single man, and he's a preacher… Girl, you don't know what you hold in the palm of your hand, and you don't know how many women are trying hard to snatch it out."

"Like Iva Peyton?"

"Ohhh. If she joins one more committee to try to get next to Finus, I'm going to lay hands on her." Inez lifted up her hands to the ceiling in mock ritualistic fashion.

"It's so funny to see them try, particularly when they are rude to me in the process. And they don't know what I'm prepared to do to keep him. I'll cut 'em," Cassandra said a little too loudly after she finished laughing at Inez's antics. She covered her hand with her mouth. "Oops, did the westside girl in me just slip out?" she laughed.

"Ssshh, don't wake Fred," Inez warned. "He's a light sleeper and a bear when he's disturbed."

Cassandra's lips parted, then closed. She wanted to ask Inez what it was like to be the bishop's wife, but shyness prevailed.

She slipped under the covers of the twin bed. Cassandra drifted off, content tonight to sleep under the same roof as Finus Gates.

Finus sat fidgeting on the patio long after the house had gone quiet.

"Boy, what are you doing?"

He jumped. It wasn't the soft, quiet tone he expected.

Fred pulled up a chair next to him. "I thought you'd turned in for the night."

"I'm waiting for Cassandra. Any minute I expect she'll sneak out of that room and come looking for me."

Fred slapped him on the back. "Son, Cassandra's asleep. Inez said she was very tired. Guess that summer school is really wearing her out. Or is it staying up half the night talking on the phone with you?"

His brow furrowed. "Half the time I think she's asleep and just holding the phone. She doesn't like to talk a lot about her job, but I do think she's tired and ready for a vacation. I'm just sorry I can't share it with her like we did last year."

"And what were you two planning to *read* tonight?"

"Why did Ford follow us into the garden, and what took you so long to play 'Ribbon in the Sky'?"

"You know why. We need to make sure nothing negative could be said about what happened at this house tonight. You know how Alice gossips. So Cecil followed you. But I made sure you he gave you a minute. Just remember to thank David for shouting a heads-up."

"You heard that."

"Boy, they heard him in Chicago." Fred chuckled. "I love that loud 'Bama."

They laughed again.

"Okay, but I'll not thank you for sending everybody to bed. I thought we'd take a walk." Finus stood and looked out over his patio and grinned as he remembered how well the evening had gone. "I was waiting for the right moment."

"Humph." Fred patted Finus on his back. "Son, let me suggest that you stop waiting for the right song, right mood, right moment, and tell that woman what she's longing to hear. Life rarely gives you the perfect moment. Sometimes life only gives you a quick minute. And you've had plenty of minutes, and many more tonight."

Finus reached into his pocket and withdrew a small Tiffany box. "Did I show you what I brought her? I was just about to give it to her in the garden when…"

Fred opened the box and let out a low whistle as he removed a silver necklace with a trio of diamond pendants. The stones in the anchor, cross, and heart shimmered and twirled as he held them up to the light. "A sailor's prayer. That's nice, but it's not doing you any good waiting in your hand."

Finus reached out and took back the necklace that symbolized faith, hope, and love. "Yeah, you're right. I wanted her to have this tonight. May I go upstairs and place it by her bedside?"

"You can go into that room, but you better come right back out."

"Are you sure Inez won't mind?"

"Inez isn't in there. How you think I know Cassandra's asleep?"

Very early Sunday morning, Cassandra skipped downstairs. She thought she'd be the first one up, but before she reached the kitchen the aroma of fresh coffee greeted her. She poured a cup and set out along the garden path. She knew where to find him. She stepped around the privacy hedge and her heart skipped a beat. Finus sat very still on the chaise lounge they'd shared last night. Heat crept across her face as she remembered his kisses. He looked up. He didn't beckon for her. He didn't smile. He lifted up a flattened palm.

She turned and ran back into the house, unable to take a breath until she was safely back in the room she was supposed to share with Inez. Apparently, Inez was a sleepwalker because she wasn't in their room this morning. Behind the closed door, Cassandra tried to sort out her feelings. She just didn't understand. She fell to her knees and prayed for the grace to get through another day of loving Finus.

She sang and prayed as she dressed for church.

She jumped at the hard knock and the harsh tone that came from Finus on the other side of the bedroom's door. "Hurry up, Cassandra."

She zipped up her sundress. "God give me grace."

"See, I told you. Cassandra is always the reason when I am late." Finus fidgeted with this bow tie and complained to the Suttons while they waited on the front porch for Cassandra. He could not get his fingers to cooperate this morning. His tie was not straight, and it angered him.

Inez sat quietly on the porch swing. She gave him an I-*could-help-but-I'm-not-going-to* smirk.

"Reverend Gates, you were late before you ever met Cassandra. Don't put that on that girl. But I would submit to you, sir," Fred said with a new smile on his face, "that she is worth the wait."

He turned around and agreed with Fred. Cassandra looked lovely. This morning she wore a black and white polka dot sundress and a black and white lampshade hat with spectator pumps. She looked every bit the first lady. She walked straight towards him and reached up to re-knot his bow tie. While she did him this small favor, her stomach growled. "I'm sorry about this morning. You caught me off guard while I was praying," he whispered.

"Come on, we need to start walking or pull out a car. I can't be late for church," Fred announced.

"Okay, I've got to lock the door and get something from my room," Finus answered.

Fred rolled his eyes up to the heavens, offered an arm to each of the ladies, and set out for church.

It took Finus an entire block to catch up with them, but he didn't mind walking behind them. As pretty as Cassandra looked this morning, he preferred the way she'd looked last night. Instead of placing his gift for her on the nightstand as he was supposed to, he'd sat on Inez's bed and watched her sleep. He didn't understand the physics of it, but the way she had a scarf wrapped around her head had to be how she kept the bounce in her hair. He sat for too long watching the moonlight play on her face. He remembered how she smiled when he yawned. He left the room. If it ever got out he was in that room last night, the controversy could impact not only his but Fred's ministry.

He slowed his stride and grinned. *Why does she think her hips are too wide?* "Excuse me, miss."

Fred dropped Cassandra's arm and she fell in step with Finus.

"May I say that you are looking altogether lovely this morning? I thought you might need this." He offered her one of two things he'd gone back into the house for.

Cassandra smiled and reached for the banana he offered. "I was just wondering how I was going to make it thought the service on an empty stomach."

Finus returned her smile and tucked her arm in closer to his side and hummed a hymn, off-key, as they strolled towards to the Chapel.

When their walking party arrived at the church, Fred kissed Inez on the cheek and motioned for Finus to follow him around back to enter the building. He thought he might kiss Cassandra's cheek, but her hat was too wide. "See you later." He squeezed her arm before he released it and followed Fred to the back door.

Cassandra took a deep breath in his wake and looked around. They were early. Neither the regular parishioners nor the busload of members from the Cathedral scheduled to attend this service had arrived.

"Cassandra, you do look lovely this morning." Inez linked her arm with Cassandra's and they walked up the steps. "If you want to help Finus, please be extra nice to everyone you meet today. Even those that try very hard to unnerve you. Please don't cut 'em." She winked.

Just as they reached the top of the stairs, Alice Ford opened the door and joined them on the chapel steps.

"How did you girls enjoy your slumber party?"

"It was fun. I didn't know Cassandra was so funny." Inez stepped forward to give Alice a standard hug.

A syrupy sweet smile crossed Alice's lips. "Fred let you girls stay up all night gossiping and giggling?"

"No, I'm afraid I was not much fun. I fell asleep as soon as my head hit the pillow." Cassandra hoped to end Alice's fishing expedition.

Alice looked around and clicked her teeth. "I heard you were used to staying up late at night working with Finus."

"No, the only time we talk late into the night is on the telephone. Finus lives quite a distance from me, and he's not in the habit of staying out late at night."

Inez pinched her arm.

"Good morning." Several members had reached the top of the steps, eager to greet the bishop's wife. Through hugs and kisses, Inez introduced Cassandra to a dozen or so very pleasant people.

After they went in and sat on the front row, an elegantly dressed Iva Peyton approached. She extended a white gloved hand and sat down beside her.

Since Iva was now a board member at the Cathedral, she was entitled to a seat on the front row.

"How are you, Iva?" Cassandra asked. "You look well recovered from your accident."

"I'm well, but I'm going to need a plastic surgeon for my hands. Didn't Finus tell you? He was so wonderful to me that night, I just thank God for him."

Cassandra gave a half smile. Iva's boldness unnerved her. She was still trying to compose herself when Fred stood and gave the call to order. In addition to his usual commentary he admonished the congregation regarding the condition of the chapel. He issued a stern warning about the chapel's finances and some needed repairs to the building. "I've already turned down Rev. Gates's request to fully fund the renovation."

Cassandra looked up into the small pulpit at Finus as Fred continued venting his displeasure regarding the condition of the building. Finus winked and gave her a sheepish grin. She pulled the unmarked envelope he'd given her out of her handbag.

"It has come to my attention that we have a singer of some note with us today, and since I've pre-warned her, I'll ask Dr. Cassandra Brownley to come forward and bless us in song."

Cassandra's head jerked. She wasn't a member of the Assembly, but she knew better than to say no. Maybe that's what Inez had been asking. She rose and walked over to the tiny choir alcove to consult with the church musician. Finus stepped over as she thumbed through the BMA hymnal looking for a selection.

"Will you sing 'In the Garden'? It's number 105. It was one of my mother's favorites, and for some reason I want to hear it this morning."

She shifted into her singer's stance. "If you like."

He took the hymnal from her hands and sat down at the piano to accompany her. What was she going to do with this man who blew hot kisses at her at night and then shocked her with a cold wind in the morning. And he'd never told her he played.

She shifted her footing and took a few deep breaths while the Sunday school report was read. She resisted the urge to turn back and look at Finus even though she felt his eyes burning a hole in her back.

She looked out amongst the congregants and noticed the Bakers had arrived. She prayed the lump in her throat would clear when she started to sing.

Finus's hand was a little choppy, and after the first chorus he moved over and let the chapel's regular pianist take over. At the end of the selection he stood behind her and whispered thanks in her ear. He took her elbow and escorted her the short distance back to her seat.

After the short service Cassandra sat alone at a picnic table in the back of the Chapel. All around her the Assembly members and guests were buzzing with joy and delight. The offering was sufficient to make the needed repairs to the building. Everyone but her enjoyed the pound cake and coffee in honor of Finus's birthday.

Cassandra pushed the moist cake around her plate with her finger.

In less than an hour a car would come to take him to O'Hare. It would be over a month before she would see him again. Maybe now would be a good time for them to go back to the house. If they left now there would be a little time left for them to spend together.

She walked over to the cake table where he was charming the church mothers.

"Excuse me, Reverend, it's getting late."

He glanced at his watch. "Yes, okay. Just give me a minute. Have you ladies met Cassandra?"

While she chatted with the church mothers and deflected their questions, Finus slipped away. She looked around the church grounds to find him talking with some teenagers she recognized from the Cathedral. When he looked up and caught her eye he motioned for her to come and join him. She excused herself and walked across the yard and asked him again if he was ready to leave. He patted her arm and again she found herself trapped in a conversation without him. Time was running out.

Inez, trailed by Alice Ford, came and stood beside her. "Cassandra, where'd that Finus get to? It's high time you started back for the house. His car will be here in no time."

Alice pointed towards the picnic table. "He's over there. Who's that hugging him."

"Iva Peyton," Inez spit out.

Cassandra spun around to see Finus accept a hug from Lucinda Baker.

Inez put her hand on her back and nudged her forward. "Be a dear, go remind him it's time for him to go. Now."

Bless her heart, that's a go-get-your-man move if there ever was one. Cassandra walked over in time to hear Finus laughing about how much he'd enjoyed his party. She wrung her hands together and said hello in her best trained voice.

"Finus, I really would like to start back. We don't have much time left before…"

Finus held out his hand for hers. "You don't have to press your way with me, my dear."

She turned and walked away from his patronizing tone.

Chapter 17

"Cassandra, please don't start being silly. Pick up the phone. I know you're home." Finus paused and pursed his lips. "Well, no. I don't. I'm not sitting outside your door like a stalker. Come on, don't do this." He ended the call for the tenth time in less than an hour. "I just don't understand," he yelled at his phone before placing it in his pocket.

"Nephew, what's gotten into you?" Aunt Jo looked up from her *Essence* magazine.

"I'm all right. I just want to get in touch with Cassandra. We had a bit of a conflict before I left, and I am anxious to speak with her before it gets too late."

"What did you say to that girl?"

Finus flopped down onto an easy chair. "How'd you know it was something I said?"

Aunt Jo put her magazine down and eyed him. "Because I know you."

"Whoa, hold your horses, man. You talk like you're caught up." Will strolled confidently into the sitting room in their posh L.A. home.

Finus rolled his eyes at his cousin. "It's not like her not to answer." He reached for his phone to dial again. "She should know I'm trying to call."

Will let out a low whistle. "Come on, Caught Up, let's go eat. Maybe by then you'll get in touch with your Cassandra."

He shot back. "Just let me call Fred to make sure he got her home safely."

Will shook his head and escorted his mother into the dining room.

After dinner Will kept him occupied with legal matters and talk of his escapades with Hollywood starlets. By now it was well after midnight in Chicago, but he dialed her anyway.

"It's about time. Why haven't you answered before now?" The question raced out of his mouth as soon as she picked up.

"Oh, it's you." Her voice trembled.

"Who else? Why haven't you answered? I've been calling since I landed."

Her voice was only a whisper. "I can't do this; I can't take any more right now." Her voice faded.

"Sweetheart, what's wrong?" he asked softly. He'd only heard her use this slow, deliberate tone once before, and that was when she was speaking with a parent from her school.

"Jalen's father was stabbed this afternoon over a ten-dollar bill. I've been at Cook County hospital for the last ten hours. He's not expected to survive the night." She stopped. "I only picked up the phone because I thought it was Yolanda with the news."

"I am sorry to hear this. What can I do?"

"There's nothing to do. I just want to go to sleep." She took an audible breath.

232

He started to pace the floor of the bedroom he used at his aunt's house.

"Oh, Finus, this is the worst mess. Jay made a mess of his life. There were several children and babies' mamas at the hospital all trying to make sure Jay's mother recognized them as a legitimate part of his life. There were quite a few scenes. Phyllis and Yogi had several arguments with each other and those women. It was so ugly. And Jalen had to witness all of this mess. He's only fourteen, and he's sitting there waiting for his father to die."

He slowed his stride.. "How can I help?"

"There's nothing more to be done."

He stopped. "There is always prayer."

"You pray if you must. I'm going to sleep."

A dead silence fell on the line. Her comment put him off. He'd always seen her as a woman of great faith. "I'll pray and call you tomorrow. Goodnight, Cassandra."

It wasn't yet noon and he was already aggravated. To blame jet lag wouldn't be honest. In the past hour, while her publicist presented the game plan for capturing at least a Dove Award, Amaria had all but exposed her breast to him. He'd also received a troubling text from Cassandra. Jay had died during the night, but that had only intensified the family's drama. He recited the Twenty-third Psalm as Amaria and the publicist prattled on about media plans. When his pulse rate slowed he left the meeting to call Cassandra.

"Hello, Finus. Can you hold on for a minute"

She sounded calm, but in the background he heard crying and shouting. He repeated the psalm again in his head.

"I'm sorry—"

"No, don't apologize. Are you all right?"

"I'm fine," she said.

"Tell me what's wrong."

She gave a long sigh. "They're arguing about where to send the body. Of course there's no insurance. Jay never really worked."

He resisted the urge to speak.

"His mother wants to use Minor, but they won't take the body without a policy or unless Yolanda signs a note. That's Phyllis and Yogi you hear in the background. We're telling her not to do it, but she says she can't live with herself if Jay doesn't have a proper burial. She can't afford to do it. She's already struggling."

"Who are you talking to?"

Finus picked out Phyllis's voice.

"Wait a minute, I'm going to step outside. If I drop the call, I'll call you back."

He waited until she could resume the conversation. Yolanda's guilt and pain were overwhelming. She had to put her financial well-being at risk in order to provide the comfort and closure of a funeral for her child's father, she reported.

"What about his church? Has the pastor been called?"

"Finus, these aren't church people."

There was an annoyed lilt in her voice.

"I see."

"We called our pastor and he said no. Suddenly he's decided, and I quote, 'not to lay another hoodlum out before his altar.'"

Finus coughed. "I'll call Fred. I know he'll extend the courtesy of one of our churches to your family."

"I couldn't ask—"

"*You* aren't asking for anything. Are you sure you want the body to go to Minor? We use Riley's. Are you all at home with your mother? I'm going to call David to come over. And I'll make arrangements to come home."

"No," she whispered.

"No to what?"

"You don't have to come. I can't ask you to do that."

"Cassandra, you can ask me to do anything. You know I care for you."

She sniffled. "If you call David that will be enough. Thank you."

His face twitched. *Why doesn't she want me to come home?* He'd have to deal with that later. There were more pressing issues at hand. He had at least a dozen calls to make. "Listen, go back and tell your mother and Yolanda not to worry about anything."

"I wasn't telling you all of this because I wanted you to fix anything. I just needed a friend to turn to."

Friend? "I know, and I also know you. You'll wind up signing that note and it's not necessary. Let me

235

help. Everything will be all right. Give my condolences to your family and I'll call you later."

After he hung up, he called Fred to request pastoral support for the family. Then he called Janet to send his personal expressions of sympathy.

Several hours later he received a voice message from Cassandra.

"Jay's mother is so relieved. She said that the Gideons had taken care of everything. She was just beaming with pride. She thinks it's because of something good Jay did. I knew you wouldn't want me to correct her, so I didn't. Thank you from all of us. I'll talk to you later. Bye."

Just to hear some calm restored to her voice filled his heart as he went into a meeting with the Gates School architects.

Hours later Cassandra's phone was still going straight to voice mail. He'd replayed her message a dozen times because it made him grin. He set the phone down on Will's desk. He'd try again later. His hand trembled slightly, as he was anxious to see how her day had gone. Ten minutes later he dialed her again. This time the phone was answered so fast it sounded as if she snatched the phone from its hook.

"What?"

"Why do you sound so angry?"

"I am angry," she hissed. "I'm angry at Jay for living such an uninformed life, I'm angry at Jalen for the horrible things he's said to Yolanda. He's blaming her for Jay's death."

"Tell me more." Finus mentally put his pastoral collar on. This was not the conversation he'd anticipated having with her tonight. Fred was right about missing moments.

"Somewhere between baby number four or five, Jay claimed to want to get his life together and marry Yogi. She wouldn't have him, so in Jalen's mind this is her fault. He has never been able to see Jay's faults. He just sees this hero that came over occasionally with presents. He doesn't know that the real hero is the one who's there every day buying groceries and paying bills."

The anguish in her voice weighed on his heart. He wanted to take his collar off. He'd had good pastoral counseling training, but it didn't prepare him to listen to the woman he loved pour this kind of hurt out of her heart.

"He's showing no respect for the woman who sacrifices and struggles to provide for him daily." The hurt in her voice pierced his soul.

"Is that all that's troubling you?" he asked, collar still on.

"No." Her voice went up an octave. "I'm angry with my father for leaving us. All these years and it still hurts." She sobbed.

Finus held the line while she cried. His arms ached to hold her. He wanted to assure her that he would never abandon her, but this wasn't the appropriate time. Collar off. *Wait a minute. What am I thinking?*

"Tell me more," he offered from behind the safety of his collar.

Cassandra continued to pour out her anger and hurt. It took an hour, but he listened patiently while she unburdened herself. As she wound down, her tone assured him she'd found relief. He was filled with sorrow to be so far away when she needed him. *Collar on, Reverend*, he reminded himself.

"And I'm angry with you."

He sat erect in the chair at the unexpected personal attack. Since she seemed well enough to launch a personal assault, he took the symbolic collar off.

"Me, why? It's a bad night for the brothas with the Brownleys," he chuckled.

"I got your message from last night. I'm not a silly woman," she hissed.

"Cassandra, I'll ask your forgiveness for that message and ask you to consider the power of forgiveness for Jay, Jalen, and your father." He drew a deep breath and put his collar back on. He counseled her on the transformative power of forgiveness.

It took the better part of an another hour, and when she stopped crying, they prayed. "Just say the word. I want to come home and be with you."

"No, dear heart, you *are* here with me now, and I thank you."

"Just know that I may be far away, but never distant. Be blessed, Cassandra. Try to get some rest and I'll talk to you tomorrow."

After the phone clicked and the line went dead he sat for a while. He looked out at the L.A. skyline and reveled in his success as a counselor and minister. "Yes, successful as a minister, but a failure as a man."

As promised, Finus called the next night, again from Will's plush office. "How are you this evening, sweetheart?"

"Oumm," she moaned. "Please don't call me that."

His head jerked back at her rebuff. "Why not if that's how I feel?" His tone held an unintended harshness. "What did you call me last night? Oh yes, dear heart. I liked the sound of that," he ended softly.

"Greg called me sweetheart."

"I see." He ran his finger between his shirt and the clerical collar he actually wore tonight. "Cassandra, have you forgiven him?" *Am I asking this question for her sake or mine?* "If you haven't, you can't trust, and until you can trust, you aren't whole." The truth in his words applied more to himself than her. *How long does it ___ the heart to trust again?* "We can't move forward without trust." *Trust is why it's taken me so long to speak up. I'm reluctant to trust another woman. Have I forgiven Phaedra? Am I ready to surrender all to Cassandra?*

She broke into his thoughts. "Are you waiting for an answer from me?"

"Yes and no." Her silence reminded him of the distance between them. What he wanted to say shouldn't be said over the phone. But there was something he needed to know. "Cassandra, are you concerned about my... my condition?"

Her answer came in the warm tones that months ago softened his heart.

"How could you even think that?"

"I hoped not. But I had to ask." His face lit up as his mind wandered back to his birthday party when they sat in the garden. He remembered the softness of her skin as he danced kisses along her cheek and jaw line. "That night in the garden..."

She giggled.

His heart turned a flip.

"Ugh, I can't take anymore. Doc, you are caught up, bad."

Finus turned and smirked at his cousin. "I'm going to say goodnight now. Will's ready to go to dinner. He's letting me tag along on his date with some supermodel. But when I see you, the first thing we're going to do is have a very long talk."

She yawned and released a little tension. "Yes, Finus. That's fine." Just the thought of kissing him put her in an agreeable mood. She nodded.

For a second night she lay in bed caught between two opinions. His kindness made her heart sing. Because she was exhausted, his endearments jarred her frayed nerves. And she couldn't help remembering how insignificant he'd made her feel in front of Iva and Lucinda on Sunday afternoon. But he'd been so wonderful tonight. *Could I be wrong about him?*

Chapter 18

The atmosphere was charged with excitement as Cassandra waited with several dozen Assembly members to catch an elevator downstairs to the BMA conference's opening ceremony. Ladies dressed in all white and men in their best suits greeted each other, in acknowledgement they were all headed to the same event.

She checked her watch; four thirty-five. She waved off another full elevator car. Several of the others waiting squeezed in. She'd already let several overloaded elevator cars pass. Energy coursed through her veins at the thought of seeing Finus again. It had been almost four weeks since his birthday party. She shifted her footing and looked up at the lighted elevator locator panel. The opening ceremony was scheduled to commence at five o'clock, and she prayed for a moment with him before the Assembly was called to order. She squeezed into the next crowded car.

She followed the crowd to the great hall and hoped to find a familiar face. The hall was filled with members from across the nation. The happy sounds of greetings and the renewal of old friendships filled the air.

The pager at her hip vibrated and a huge smile covered her face. Over the past week every time she spoke with Finus he stressed the importance of using her pager so they could communicate during the week.

Meet me at entry number five, ASAP.

She stood up and moved towards the aisle. "Excuse me." She smiled her apology for disturbing the row to get back to the aisle. She hurried toward door number five and checked the time; four-fifty. *I'm going to see him before this all starts.* She slowed her pace just a tad. If she ran toward door like she wanted, someone would surly recognize her.

"Thank goodness. Rev. Gates would have my head if I hadn't found you."

She had to think quickly to remember the young man that met her at the door. "Julian? How are you?"

"I'm fine, thanks. But we've got to hurry. The processional starts precisely at five."

Julian started across another hallway. They walked into a back corridor and there he stood patting his foot.

"Hey." Finus moved toward her and wrapped her up in a welcoming hug.

She beamed as she looked over his shoulder through an open door filled with BMA clergy.

He stepped back and gave her a quick once-over. "Come on." He grinned. "I'm glad you're here. Where have you been? Poor Julian has been trying to find you for an hour," he whispered as he pulled her towards a moving line.

Her joy dimmed. Rev. Gates sounded annoyed, though his eyes gleamed with happiness. He squeezed her hand. The line stopped. Inez looked back and nodded hello. She looked around and recognized the

Broadnauxes, Fords, and several of the other ministers and ladies from the Midwest.

"Make sure you keep your pager on vibrate. It's the only way to communicate in this crowd." The line moved forward. "Are you ready for this?"

"I shouldn't be here," she whispered. "This is for the clergy and their wives."

"This is the BMA leadership and whom they choose to escort. We do have some female ministers and officers, miss. And I want you by my side or I wouldn't have invited you," he said and winked.

The processional led them back into the great hall Cassandra first entered ten minutes ago without notice. Now she felt a thousand eyes upon her as they marched down the center aisle. She gripped his arm a little tighter and inhaled. She'd missed him.

The line came to a halt. Finus circled her waist with his arm and exchanged their places in the line. They stood as the row filled up, then he motioned for her to take a seat at the end of the row filled with the midwest delegation.

"See you later." He smiled and continued up to the dais.

"The Reverend Doctor Finus Gideon Gates," bellowed the baritone of the announcer.

She stood proudly to see Finus confidently stride across the stage and address the Assembly.

"I greet you in the matchless name of our Lord and Savior. From the Midwest seventeen congregations strong are in attendance. We are prepared to report

our progress spiritually, physically, and financially."
Finus moved forward and took a seat on the dais.

Her heart soared. *What are you so proud of? He's not your husband!*

Doesn't matter, her heart responded, *you love him*.

Throughout the opening she stood at the appropriate times, bowed her head, and clapped with the others. But her mind focused on Finus; she heard nothing of the conference opening. Butterflies turned a hundred happy flips in her stomach when he stood to be recognized with the forty or so other conference conveners. Her cheeks pushed her eyes closed. It was obvious to her he had found favor among the conveners, and when the presiding bishop mentioned his name specifically, she closed her eyes and praised God.

After the final opening prayer, she stood with the audience for the recessional. She enjoyed the pageant as it reversed its way out of the hall. The pomp and splendor reminded her of a college graduation. Each member of the dais party was clad in the colors of his office. The bishops were regal in their purple robes and miters. The clergy and officers wore black with varying multi-colored stoles, according to their office and standing. And Finus was resplendent in his red conference convener's cloak. In awe of the precision, she missed her cue. She turned toward the tap on her arm. Finus put his arm around her waist and positioned her in the stalled line. He took her elbow and whispered, "Hold on to your hat."

She took several long breaths to steady her pulse. Just to stand next to him in this sea of people made her knees weak.

The recessional led them to an Assembly-wide reception where Julian waited. "Julian is working as my page this week, so make sure you call on him if you need anything." He handed Julian his robe and wrapped her up in a bear hug that lifted her feet from the ground. "Umm, it's so good to see you. You look good." He set her down and gave her another sweeping look of approval. "Everything all right at home?"

"Yes, my family is fine." *I'll thank you personally later in my suite.* She wiggled a little to keep her balance. The next hour passed in a blur of shaking hands and hugging. Did everybody in the Assembly know the Gates family?

Many people were happy to meet her. "You're the one we've heard so much about. It's so nice to meet you."

Others wanted to inspect her. "How long have you been seeing Rev. Gates?" Those questions usually came with a complete visual inspection.

And still others just wanted to pry. "I understand you two are just *friends*?" Those comments were usually from women, who gave her the visual inspection and a touch of attitude.

Tired from the flight, she kept a tight smile on her face and pressed her thighs together. She looked around the hall for a washroom as another Assembly woman interrogated her.

"Cassandra, if you don't mind, we need to go and greet some of the mothers of the church. They're sitting over there, and many of them were good friends with my mother." Finus took her elbow and directed her toward the tables where the little old ladies sat.

She took a deep breath. Two full tables of women all over the age of sixty, dressed in angelic white and undoubtedly dying to inspect her in Wilma's absence. *Oh, Lord!*

"Doing okay?" Finus asked as they crossed the room towards the matrons.

He expertly hugged and kissed each of the ladies while introducing each of them.

He's good, Cassandra thought.

"You look a little overwhelmed, my dear. Why don't you sit down with us for a moment." Matron Dearing, an angel in white pulled, a chair from beneath the table for her. "Don't worry, Finus, we'll take good care of her. You go ahead and finish politicking. You can't expect Miss Cassandra to meet the entire Assembly in one night."

"Thank you. This is a bit more than I expected." She fanned herself as she sat down and accepted a glass of water from Matron Dearing.

"This is your first conference, dear?"

"Yes, I'm not a member."

"I know you're the educational consultant for the school project. But I wonder," Matron Dearing patted her shoulder, "what do you call Finus?"

Cassandra choked on the water. Matron Dearing had to be well past seventy, but she was sharp. The answer to this question would reveal a lot about the relationship between her and Finus. Few people were invited to call the esteemed Reverend Doctor Gates by his boyhood name.

"You know, it depends on where we are." She smiled.

Mother Dearing nodded.

Several of the gray heads attending to the conversation cocked to the side.

"Did he tell you I helped Wilma pick out that lake house? We spent many summers there with the family. I have a son a few years older than Doc, and my daughter Belinda is like a sister. You know, he was always a fidgeting, nervous child but he was always calmer by the lake."

She relaxed a bit as a picture of him sitting in the garden at his birthday party flashed across her mind. "You know, you're right. He is a lot calmer by the lake." After a few minutes of getting to know the matrons she decided Mother Dearing was her favorite.

"Ladies, if you will excuse me, it was very nice chatting with you but I need to find the ladies' room." She stood up.

"Dear, won't you wait for Rev. Gates to come back to collect you?" One of the more seasoned matrons placed a hand on her arm.

"No, ma'am. I need to excuse myself now."

Cassandra made her way through the reception area and found a line for the ladies' room. At last she made her way into a stall. As soon she finished she overheard a conversation.

"Anyone know who that was that Rev. Gates escorted in the processional?"

"Are you asking about Reverend Fine-Yes Gates?" another voice answered.

"Girl, that man is so fine," a third woman chimed in.

"And rich," reminded the first woman's voice. "All I want to know is who is she, where'd she come from, and is she another cousin?"

"Settle down, ladies." Another woman emerged from the stall next to Cassandra's. "I hear she's his girl-friend."

Cassandra stood fixed in the stall, amused, shocked, and feeling a little selfish for holding up a stall when there was a line. She took a deep breath and turned the latch on the stall. *What will these women say when I walk out of this stall?*

"I just want to know how she can stand next to him wearing those cheap white shoes." The powder room exploded in laughter.

Her hand froze on the latch.

"They look like a pair I brought my daughter from Payless last year."

She looked down at her feet. They were Payless pumps. She hated the way her feet looked in white shoes. She owned these only because Yolanda had dragged her to a sorority event last month that required members to wear all white. She took a deep breath and summoned her courage.

She washed her hands to the stunned silence in the washroom. She left the ladies' room, pushed on by muted whispers.

Cassandra reentered the reception hall to be greeted by a familiar arm around her waist.

"There you are. I'm glad you're still here. Thought the matrons ran you off."

"The matrons were lovely, but there are some real tigers in the ladies' room."

He gave her a curious tell-me-later look.

"We need to find Broadnaux and let Lydia explain to you about going to the ladies' room. And Fred and Inez would also like to greet you." Finus guided her through the reception with a firm grip on her elbow. For every three steps they took their progress toward the bishop was impeded.

The meeting and greeting continued.

"May I present Dr. Brownley," he said to some members whom he greeted with the stiff pomposity of the Reverend Doctor.

"This is Cassandra," he said to a few with the wicked grin of Doc.

The pleather Payless pumps pinched her toes, but the warm reassurance of Finus's hand on the small of her back eased the pain.

The responses to those she met varied widely. At times Finus seemed attentive to the reception that she was getting, and other times he didn't hear.

"I hear you're just a friend."

"You make a nice couple."

"You're just the educational consultant, right?"

Since this was his church and she was among people who knew and respected his parents and where he would do his life's work, she decided to grin and bear it. *The best thing to do is smile sweetly and put my tongue on mute.* Her cheeks tingled from her pasted-on Miss America expression. Her pulse quickened from his increasingly tight hold on her waist.

"Well, Dr. Brownley, what do you think about the standardized testing of all American students using one national test?"

She smile and nodded. *Who is this again?* She blinked and racked her brain for information. The man had just been introduced. A lay leader, attorney from Atlanta.

"Surely you have some thoughts."

"Cassandra is very much opposed to that idea," Finus answered for her.

"You're telling us she has a doctorate in education, but she can't speak for herself?" the man responded.

Her smile faded.

She shifted her footing and Finus dropped his arm. She stood a little more erect. She aimed her focus at the tall, dark, and handsome attorney with the build of a pro athlete. His skin was smooth ebony and he had an air about him. Like a powerful, graceful animal whose energy was caged in an expensive suit.

"I'm sorry Mr...?"

"Quentin Jarvis."

"Yes, Mr. Jarvis, it's a very complex issue wrapped up in race, class, and community constructs."

"Like most things in America," he drawled slowly as his eyes traveled across her face.

"I'll address that very issue in my workshop. Perhaps you'll attend to receive the benefit of my fully researched answer."

Finus's arm snaked back around her waist and gave her a squeeze.

"I'll look forward to it," Jarvis drawled.

"Good, good, great. Please excuse us, Jarvis. Still trying to reach the bishop." Finus took her elbow and moved them forward. "Welcome back. While I don't like his approach," he hissed in her ear, "I appreciate Que for at least getting a rise out of you. It has been a lot like introducing a zombie queen."

She shuddered and extended her hand for the next round of introductions.

Within minutes a choir heralded the call for dinner. They followed the crowd into another hall for the opening banquet. Her smile evaporated as the familiar uncertainly regarding her relationship with Finus filled her soul. It took a few minutes to wade through the crowd to find their table, and Finus kept introducing people. She tried to be a little more animated.

Mr. Social couldn't seem to remain in his seat as the dinner progressed. He was away from the table so much during the first course she'd ordered for him when the wait staff needed to know if he would prefer the chicken or fish. It wasn't until dessert was served that Finus finally sat still. He kept reminding her that as one of the conveners he was obligated to ensure things went well.

Instead of retiring to her suite with him, Finus sprung his other plans on her. "Okay, make your way to the car. If we get separated, keep going." There was a limousine waiting to take them and the Broadnauxes out for dinner.

Lydia and Cassandra had no problem working their way through the crowd and soon settled into the waiting car. Cassandra chuckled as Lydia rubbed her hands across the soft leather of the car's interior and checked out the mini-bar. "I've never ridden in a limo, not even on my wedding day."

"Then I hope you enjoy the ride." Cassandra turned towards Lydia. "Lid, would you and David mind riding backwards? Finus can't."

The two women rearranged themselves in the car and waited.

Ten minutes passed before the door opened and David piled in. David looked at his watch and shook his head. "I knew Gates wouldn't make it, and we need to roll. The place closes at nine thirty and it's quarter of. Hey, Cassandra, if you walk through that middle door and turn to your left you'll run right into Doc. And if you want to have a little fun, call him darling."

She tapped on the window for the driver to open the door. "That'll start some mess. David, you're incorrigible."

"You can't call me that, girl. I'm a minister of the gospel. But I dare you to call him out."

"I'm so hungry, I'll do anything to get him out of there. Be right back." She drew back her shoulders and marched into the conference center, right up to Finus. She pasted on her beauty pageant smile as she approached the group of young women hovering around him.

"My darling, we really must hurry. Ladies, please excuse us. Thank you." She uttered in one breath. Shock registered on their faces as she took his arm and pulled him out of the building.

Within minutes they were on the rough side of San Diego at a Southern barbeque restaurant. An hour later the four friends sat contentedly around a diner table savoring the last bites of their supper.

"Man, you know this is some good Q if it's got the Reverend Doctor F.G. Gates licking his fingers." The table laughed as David began the usual round of jokes he and Finus passed when they were together.

Finus pointed a stained finger across the table at Cassandra. "Oh, and look, Dr. Brownley is soaking up sauce with her bread."

"You both can keep your jokes. I'm from the west side of Chicago and this is some good food. Besides, I was starving."

"Cassandra, we have just come from a reception and a dinner. Didn't you eat?" He winked.

"Unbelievable. Every time I went to take a bite, Mr. Assembly here was either introducing me to someone or asking me twenty questions."

"You'll get used to it, and here's a little secret. We all eat a little something before the opening ceremony," Lydia said. "I'm sorry, I would have told you but I wasn't sure when you were getting in."

Cassandra looked down at her plate and toyed with her fork. Would she be with Finus long enough to get used to the Assembly?

The night air was about ten degrees cooler when they left the restaurant. Cassandra shuddered. Finus wrapped his suit jacket around her shoulders as they waited for the driver to open the car doors. They settled into the comfort of the car and began the trip back to the hotel. Since she had been up since five a.m. Chicago time, the car ride lulled her to sleep. She scooted a little closer to him.

"Well, how do you do, Rev. Gates?" David spoke a few minutes into the ride.

Finus yawned and stretched his arm out around her shoulder. "I got my belly full, I'm hanging out with my 'Bama brother and his bride, and I got my wingman by my side. I'm a blessed man."

"Brother Gates, only you would mistake your rib for a wing," David shot back. "I'll say you're blind, not blessed."

Cassandra lowered her head and chuckled. As the other passengers in the back seat laughed she took the opportunity to snuggle into his jacket. His warmth and scent held her captive.

Finus squeezed her arm. "Cassandra knows what I mean." He turned toward her and spoke in a hushed tone. "I've missed you."

Her half-closed eyes flew open to meet his gaze. She leaned forward and planted her lips on his. His lips parted. Cassandra took the lead and deepened the kiss by sliding her tongue in his mouth. He responded and her heart sang.

Lydia giggled.

He moved back. "I'm encouraged." He winked at her and she settled further into his embrace. Finus muttered something under his breath but she was too content to worry about the admonishment she was sure he'd give her for kissing him so wantonly in front of his friends.

David's voice woke her up. "Gates, you coming with us? It's rather late and we have a long day tomorrow."

The car stopped in front of Tower One of the convention hotel and the Brodnauxes said their goodnights.

"No, I'll walk back over. I want to talk to Cassandra for a minute."

David slapped Cassandra on her knee as he exited the car. "Don't keep him up too late," he teased.

It was nearly midnight and they sat in the lobby of Tower Two talking. Finus declined her invitation to take their conversation up to her suite. He made it clear that her room was in Tower Two for a reason, and at no time during the week would either of them be seen anywhere past the lobby of their respective towers.

Disappointed, she nevertheless understood. He was running for a national office, and there was the Gates name. She sat wrapped in the warmth of his jacket and listened to him talk.

"I hope you understand how much the success of this week means to me. Bear with me just a little while longer. I don't want to start anything that I don't have the time to nurture this week. Although I thank you for the encouragement. "

As Finus reviewed the week's agenda, she drifted.

"Cassandra, dear."

"Yes?"

"Julian is here to escort you to your room."

"What?" Her head snapped back. She rose to protest. "That won't be necessary."

"I am not going to have you walking the halls of this hotel alone at this time of night." Finus's jaw twitched. "Come, Cassandra." Finus took her elbow and walked her to the elevator. "I apologize for keeping you up so late." His tone softened. "It's just so good to see you again and to be with you."

Finus stepped back as the elevator chimed the arrival of a car. "Cassandra, my jacket, please." He whipped the jacket off of her shoulder as the doors opened. "Goodnight, my dear."

The elevator doors swooshed closed with a blast of cold air.

Chapter 19

Cassandra pulled the wide brim of a frilly peacock-blue hat down over her eyes and posed in the mirror.

She tossed the hat aside and picked up another. "No, he'd say it covers too much of my face."

While they were out last night, Julian had filled the living area of her suite with dozens of yellow roses, fifty hat boxes, and a note from Finus.

A hat is required for the Crowns Tea.

Paralyzed by too many choices, she couldn't decide which hat Finus might like the best. She changed her suit for the fourth time. The sitting room was a mess of purple tissue paper, feathers, hats, and bows. She glanced over at the desk clock; nine-forty. She threw up her hands. "I'm done."

She reviewed herself once more in the full-length mirror that hung on the bathroom door in her suite. "He'll like this."

Within minutes she stood in the receiving line for the tea. Only polite good mornings greeted her this morning as she stood among the ladies waiting to be admitted to the Crowns Tea. Under the hat she'd regained her anonymity. She uttered a grateful prayer. She and Lydia had become friends. Earlier this morning they'd played dress-up like two little girls in her room full of fancy hats while Lydia filled her in on this morning's event. Proceeds from the tea would go to the First Ladies Fund, a charity led by the bishops' wives.

"Ticket, please," the usher at the door requested.

"I don't think I have a ticket. But I can buy one." The usher pointed her towards a small table to the right.

She didn't mind making a contribution. She hadn't paid for anything yet associated with the conference. Even her hotel bill was already covered, courtesy of the Gates Foundation. She waited for just a minute behind a few other ladies who had ticket problems.

"I'm sorry, but tickets are all sold out," a salty voice blurted out as soon as she stood first in line.

Cassandra narrowed her eyes a bit. She recognized one of the women she'd dragged Finus away from last night.

"And since this is a subscription event for our charity, you understand why we can't break the rules and allow you to attend."

Snickers erupted behind her.

"Then I'm sure I have a ticket. I'll just need to find it." She turned and walked away from the table.

"Cassandra, get in here." Lydia stepped out of the banquet room as she passed. "Come on, girl. The only reason I recognized you in this sea of finery was because of the color of that hat. I knew you would wear that one. It frames your face beautifully."

She'd settled on a blush pink cloche topper. "Thanks, Lydia. You're wearing that hat, girl." Lydia had chosen a bold and regal red lampshade hat, which she wore over a simple black suit.

"Inez is looking for you."

"I can't come in just yet. I need to go upstairs and find my ticket. I don't recall seeing one in all of my conference materials."

"Good morning, Mrs. Broadnaux." Two ladies from the College Station congregation approached.

Lydia greeted her husband's members and admired their chapeaus. "You all are wearing those hats."

"Will you take a picture with us?" the College Station ladies asked in unison.

"Yes, but if you don't mind in the banquet room. Mrs. Sutton wants to have a word with Dr. Brownley, and I need to take care of that now. Come on, Cassandra." Lydia turned back toward the banquet room.

"I don't have a ticket."

"*You* don't need a ticket. Finus is one of the largest contributors to the First Ladies Fund, and I'm sure if the member at the door had recognized you, she would have let you in right away."

But I'm sure she did.

Lydia motioned for Cassandra to follow her right back to the usher who would not admit her a few minutes earlier. Not accustomed to privilege like Finus, Lydia pleaded her case to the gatekeeper.

"I'm Lydia Broadnaux, First Lady at the College Station Church in Chicago. This is my friend Cassandra. Would you mind letting her through without a ticket?"

The gatekeeper smiled but didn't budge. "I have strict instructions."

Lydia flashed her best smile. "I'm sure you do, but Inez Sutton, the bishop's wife, sent me out her specifically to find Dr. Brownley."

The usher gave Cassandra a sideways glance. "You know this is a fundraiser for our First Ladies Fund?"

Robbie Xander, a tea committee member from the Garden Cathedral joined them at the door and gave the usher a nod. Cassandra overheard Robbie saying, "*You* know who that is, don't you?"

The usher waved her hand to let them pass.

Lydia pulled her into the ballroom. "Don't worry. I'm very sure the proper contributions have been made," she said to them all.

They stepped into a colorful profusion of flamboyant chapeaus. Lydia led her to the back of the room where Inez stood laughing with Iva Peyton.

"Cassandra, I love that hat. It's you. Simple, elegant, but with just a touch of flair. Love the color." Inez gave her a side hug and an air kiss.

"Hello, Inez, Iva." Cassandra accepted an unexpected hug from Iva Peyton.

"Cassandra, I'm hoping you'll do me a favor and grace the tea with a song. I know I'm trading a promise the bishop extracted, but Iva thinks it might give Finus a boost politically."

"I almost feel obligated to since I'm in here without a ticket."

Lydia stepped in to explain what took her so long to locate Cassandra.

"Finus failed to tell you, you don't need any tickets. You're his special guest."

Inez turned toward a table filled with orchid corsages worn by the first ladies. "Now let's get you pinned."

The attendant at the flower table sneered at Cassandra. "I'm sorry, but all the first ladies haven't checked in yet and I don't believe we have an orchid to spare."

"That's quite all right, I understand." Cassandra pulled Inez gently by the arm.

The older woman bristled. "You know I'm about to make a fuss."

"Please don't."

A woman in an extra-large brimmed yellow hat with a huge sunflower tapped Inez on the shoulder. "Can I take your picture, Mrs. Sutton?"

Cassandra and Inez moved closer together and posed.

"I'm sorry Cassandra, I just wanted Mrs. Sutton."

Cassandra stepped aside.

"Oh, that will be a nice photo," another member said as she approached. "Do you mind?" The woman in a black beret handed Cassandra her camera.

An ever-increasing number of cameras were placed on the table beside her. The Assembly women of the Midwest were enjoying their yearly photo shoot with the bishop's wife.

"That's enough, thank you, ladies," Inez laughed. "You make me feel like Tyra Banks. Excuse me, please. Enjoy the tea."

As Inez walked away, Cassandra kept busy redistributing the dozen or so cameras.

Attending the tea was rougher than the opening reception. The first hour was reserved for fellowshipping, admiring the wide array of hats on display, and picture taking. Cassandra found herself amongst the Cathedral crowd.

"Nice hat, is it from Catherine's?" Mother Pierce asked.

"No corsage?" Ellen Whitney pointed out.

"Nice shoes." Cassandra recognized the young lady from the ladies' room last night. Her comment was nice or nasty, depending on your stand on cheap white shoes.

Cassandra excused herself and walked toward Lydia and the ladies from College Station.

"Are you ready for that picture you promised us, Mrs. Broadnaux?"

"Sure. Is this hat on straight? You girls know I'm not a hat diva." Lydia's small group laughed and began pulling cameras from their purses.

"Come on, Cassandra, get in the picture." Lydia waved her over.

A large woman in a ridiculously wide white hat stepped in her path. "No, if you don't mind we want a picture just with our new first lady."

She smiled politely. "Then why don't you get in the picture with Mrs. Broadnaux and let me take it."

This went on for several minutes until Lydia stepped out of the frame. "Now I would like a picture of me and my friend Cassandra." She stepped over and stood next to Cassandra and whispered, "Finus will be furious if he doesn't get a chance to see us modeling these crowns."

"Beverly, would you mind taking our picture with your camera and giving me a copy when we get home?"

"Surely, Mrs. B." Beverly in her wide-brimmed white hat reached into her equally large white bag to retrieve a camera.

"That's a nice picture. I'd like to be in that one, too." Inez had made her way around to the ladies from the College Station Church.

After taking a few photos Cassandra drifted away from Inez and Lydia to avoid continuing as the staff photographer.

"Here you are." Robbie Xander stood behind her. "Mrs. Sutton has asked you to join her, Dr. Brownley."

Cassandra followed Robbie to the front of the room where Inez, Iva, and the committee chairpersons prepared to give their recognitions and reports.

"Ladies, this is Cassandra." Inez breezed through the introductions. "This will move quickly. Do you need to step outside and warm up or anything before you sing? By the way, what are you going to sing for us?"

"Uh, I guess I'll have to sing the last song I rehearsed. I'll just step outside for a second and warm up. If I get locked out you'll be standing here, right?"

"I will," said Iva.

Inez reached over and gave her a reassuring pat on the hand. "Tap lightly, but only take a minute."

Cassandra stepped outside to warm up her voice and when she reentered the room she had just a minute to wait before Inez addressed the group.

"Ladies, on behalf of the First Ladies Fund, thank you for your generosity and for the lovely display of crowns. You are all queens, and to add to our expression of gratitude for your contributions to our scholarship and service fund we have a very special treat. Our friend Dr. Brownley, who is serving the Assembly as the educational consultant for the Gates school project, is also a classically trained soprano. She has sung all over the world and she has agreed to sing for us this morning."

Ahhs filled the room, along with a *ha-rump*.

"One more thing. The table arrangements are courtesy of the Reverend Doctor Finus Gates in memory of his mother, Wilma, one of the founders of our fund. If you check under your tea saucer and find a purple dot, you may take the table arrangement home to enjoy."

Inez turned to Cassandra as the room filled with the exclamations of the orchid winners.

"As soon as the room settles," Inez said, then walked back to her table.

Cassandra took a few deep breaths as the room quieted. She stepped up to the microphone and began. Her voice was strong and clear as she sang the "Mother's prayer." She closed her eyes as she recalled the light in Finus's eyes when she sang to him for his birthday. The memory of his soft kisses stirred her heart. She sang the refrain twice. After the final note, silence filled the room as her song resonated. She opened her eyes at the first blast of the applause.

She bowed her head and when she looked up, Finus was walking toward her, smiling and applauding.

What's he doing in here?

When he came near enough, he reached out and gave her a warm hug. "Didn't you give that song to me? Don't you ever sing it for anyone else, except me."

She stepped back from his embrace. She couldn't tell by his expression if he was serious or joking.

"Ladies, good morning." He addressed the tea and reached back for her hand. "Well, I wasn't looking forward to being the lone fox in this hen house, but now I'm just happy. Mother taught me to be early or else I would have missed this special treat. Let's thank Dr. Brownley again for blessing us with her special gift." He propelled her forward as the ladies gave another enthusiastic round of applause.

Then he finished his comments on behalf of the Bishops' Council.

"We missed you for breakfast this morning." He turned toward her after dismissing the tea with prayer. "We've got to be in the exhibit hall at 11:30 sharp. Are you ready to go?" He took her elbow and they started to leave the room. This time she was held up.

"What was the name of that song? It was beautiful," one of the ladies from College Station commented.

"You have a beautiful voice," a crown of multi-colored feathers complimented.

A woman in a houndstooth fedora tried to recruit her. "Why aren't you in the conference choir? We're rehearsing again this afternoon if you can join us?"

"Darling, we really need to be on our way." Finus winked at her, payback for last night. "Ladies, don't forget to stop by the exhibit hall. The candidates will all be available shortly."

Finus didn't utter a word as they hurried toward the exhibit hall. By now she'd grown accustomed to his sudden mood shifts, so she just walked along beside him. He stopped short of the exhibit hall.

"Would you like to step in there and fix your hair and makeup?" He paused and rocked back on his heels.

She slipped into the empty ladies' room. If putting on a fresh coat of lipstick and combing her hair would reduce his stress level this week, she would try to live up to his expectations and look as perfect as possible. She smoothed the bottom of her skirt. She and Yolanda had carefully shopped and packed for this trip. She hoped that Finus would find her wardrobe acceptable. *But I'll have to do something about those white shoes.*

"You look very nice." He smiled at her when she emerged from the powder room.

"Thank you. Doc, I noticed your tie isn't straight. Would you mind if I…"

"Please do." They stepped over to a column of windows and she tugged gently at the end of his tie.

"When did you learn to knot a bow tie?" he said while gazing over her shoulder out the window. "It looks like such a nice day. I hope we'll find the opportunity to enjoy some of San Diego before Friday."

She turned to her left and saw a few people pointing and nodding in their direction. Retying his tie was a rather intimate act; maybe she should have left it alone. But appearances were so important to him. Finus liked his ladies pretty and his bow tie perfectly straight.

His right arm quivered. "You know you can keep all of those hats if you like."

"No, that's too much. I should offer to pay for this one."

"You know better than that. But you did give Lydia my favorite hat from the collection."

"There, perfect. Aren't you in a hurry?" Cassandra shot back. They started toward the exhibit hall.

As expected Finus had set up a very impressive campaign display. His booth featured a white picket fence complete with a working gate. The interior was set up like a country doctor's office. His campaign theme was "Rx for a Healthy Church". In addition to shaking hands and providing information about the candidates for leadership positions, each booth handed out some kind of token.

"These are really clever," Cassandra exclaimed when she examined his give-away: an old fashioned Band-Aid tin imprinted with his prescription for a healthy church.

Prayer Praise Progress

Finus flipped over a plaque that said, "The doctor is in," and exchanged his suit jacket for a white lab coat. Everyone who worked the booth wore a lab coat to expand on the theme.

"Doc, you want me to get Cassandra a lab coat?" David, the campaign manager, had spent the entire morning making sure that everything was prepared.

"No, she has on such a pretty dress, let's look at it." Finus winked.

"Okay. Cassandra, you would be so proud of your boy here. He actually picked up a hammer this morning to help me put this thing up." David often teased Finus about his lack of practical experience. Cassandra laughed as David gave her a big basket of tins and quick instructions on how to help.

Within minutes she stood in front of the white picket fence passing out tins and reciting his qualifications for church examiner to interested members. The amount of traffic surprised her. Assembly members took the election of their officers seriously. And then there were others.

"I'd just like a tin please. I know all about Finus Gates." Nice or nasty, depending on the emphasis placed on the word *all*.

"How are you connected with Rev. Gates?" Nosy.

"I'll just wait to speak with Rev. Gates myself, if you don't mind." Nasty.

"What a great display. Reverend, stand closer to the fence for a picture." The staff photographer for the BMA was making his rounds. "Now let's get one of the two of you together." The photographer motioned for Cassandra to get into the frame.

"Oh, that's great, the country doctor and his wife." Finus started patting his foot.

"Now smile." The photographer took several shots.

On the heels of the photographer, the elections committee arrived. "Very nice display, Gates. Did you go over budget?" the sole woman on the elections committee inquired.

Finus's foot worked double time. "My campaign manager, Rev. David Broadnaux, has all of the financial reports ready for review."

Cassandra took a step to the side to continue passing out the tins.

Within moments the din in the hall quieted. Assembly members straightened up as their presiding bishop and lady paraded down the aisle. The grand old couple stopped in front of the booth and admired the clever design. Finus stepped out in front and introduced her to Jasper and Charlotte Willingham.

"Come, soror, I'd like to sit down." Charlotte took Cassandra's hand and led her towards the back of the booth. Mrs. Willingham was a round woman and it took her a few minutes to settle into a metal folding chair. When she got comfortable she leaned forward on her pink and green-striped walking stick. "You know if, no, when he wins, it will mean quite a bit of travel, soror." Charlotte emphasized her knowledge that she and Cassandra were members of the same social sisterhood.

Cassandra looked at the older woman who wore the sorority emblem on her rings, necklace, and jacket.

"He has a good support staff. I'm sure he'll manage."

"No, dear. I'm asking about you. How will you feel about it? I won't let Jasper travel alone. Not in the Assembly."

Her jaw dropped.

Charlotte sat back in her seat. "Don't look so stunned. You've been with Finus long enough to know."

Cassandra leaned back in her chair and stared at the grand old lady. "It's not something I've taken the time to think about."

"Fair enough, but it's something you need to consider since you can't leave your job to travel with him."

"But?"

Charlotte held up her hand. "Did anyone tell you all the sorors get together to fellowship on the last night of the conference? You need to join us, since Inez can't." Charlotte gave a dismissive wave of her hand. "I'll have one of the girls call you with the location once it's set."

The curtain parted and Jasper Willingham, followed by Finus, joined them.

"I've been looking forward to meeting you." The older man walked towards her with outstretched arms. His path was cut short by Charlotte's cane.

"Now Jasper, you know I don't allow you to hug the unmarried women."

Bishop Willingham and Finus howled with laughter. "Welcome to the family. You see even I am subject to certain rules."

Charlotte pushed back her chair and leaned on the table. "Jasper, it's time we go. We wouldn't want anyone accusing you of favoritism. We've spent long enough here."

The presiding bishop reached over to help his wife stand. "But I didn't get a chance to talk to Cassandra."

"Well, I did. She's nothing like Wilma. I like her." The older lady reached over and hugged a smiling Finus.

Another "tell me later" look passed between them as they followed the older couple back to the front of the booth, where several of Finus's contemporaries waited.

"Pretty ambitious move, Gates. Church examiner. You know they're saying you're too young and you've never pastored." A tall, very handsome man jabbed Finus in the ribs.

"So you aren't supporting me, frat?"

"Man, you know I got your back. But you know that this is going to shake it up," he said, extending his arms to give Finus a man hug. "Hey, Cassandra."

She stared hard. No, she hadn't met him. She would have remembered him. He was an extremely handsome and very precisely groomed man.

"I know you don't know me, girl, but ole boy talks about you so much we might as well be old friends."

Finus introduced his friend and fraternity brother from Richmond, Virginia. Her mind was too full to concentrate on remembering any more names. She did, however, remember Isaac Reynolds when he arrived. She took a step back when he reached out to hug her.

"Gates, you and Cassandra should have dinner with me and Josie tonight." Isaac turned to Cassandra. "Didn't he tell you I'm engaged? Wedding's next month."

She raised an eyebrow.

A third friend joined the group and she went back to passing out tins.

Isaac sidled up next to her. "Will you put one of those Band-Aids on me?"

She shot bullets at him with her eyes.

Isaac reached into the basket when she did and bushed his fingers across her hand. "I'd like to examine you."

She snatched the basket up higher and passed out more tins.

"I think you'd like my bedside manner," he whispered when he thought no one was paying attention.

Heat rose in her face. She looked back into the booth, where Finus stood talking with more of his friends.

"Cassandra, Cassandra." A minister she hadn't met waved for her to come into their conversation. Glad to have a reason, she pressed the basket into Isaac's hands and walked away.

"Cassandra. I thought that was your name. All we've been hearing about since September is Cassandra, Cassandra, and that's from Fred. You don't remember me, but you sat near me yesterday at the opening. I wanted to introduce myself and my wife but," he turned toward Finus, "there was some joker in a red robe that totally held your attention."

Shamefaced, she focused on the floor.

"Reverend Gates, I might convince my bishop to support you if you promise to come down to Peoria and bring Cassandra."

Finus turned his lips up. "Fred's your bishop. What else do you want from me? I introduced you to your wife. Are you inviting me to come preach?"

Finus chuckled and formally introduced his friend from Peoria.

"No, I'm asking you to bring Cassandra to sing," Peoria teased, holding onto her hand.

Her mind drifted back to the night of the fall revival when she met Isaac Reynolds, and how he would not release her hand. Peoria was only holding her hand to mess with Finus.

Richmond stepped over and took her hand from Peoria. "Miss Cassandra, ever been to Richmond? I think you'd like it there."

Finus reached over and took her hand from Richmond and let it fall to her side. "You inviting me to preach your revival again?"

"I'm inviting Cassandra to Virginia. You can stay at home." Richmond flashed a perfect-toothed smile.

"Excuse me." She was tired of being teased and inspected. She stepped behind the curtain and sat down at the work table with David.

The teasing she could take. For a moment she wished she was more like Yolanda. Maybe if she flirted with the drop-dead-gorgeous Richmond, it might encourage Finus to move up his timetable. She laid her head on the table. Had she actually agreed to wait another week before they discussed where their relationship might be headed?

"Stay the course, sister." Good and faithful, David patted her on the shoulder.

She stood. "Maybe I should just go back to work." *No, I don't think I can stand another one of Isaac Reynolds's nasty little remarks.* She sat back down.

Chapter 20

Within minutes Richmond and Peoria invaded the small space behind the booth, followed by Isaac Reynolds.

Peoria extended a crooked arm. "Cassandra, Cassandra, my wife wouldn't mind if I escorted you to the leadership luncheon."

Rev. Richmond also offered his arm. "No, my brother, Doc said I could."

She shook her head from side to side and studied both linen-suited arms. She looked up and her eyes landed on Isaac.

"I'd prefer to walk a step behind." He winked at her.

Her eyes rolled up to the ceiling.

Finus poked his head through the curtain. "Reynolds, let's walk together. I want a word with you."

She smiled, assumed a little of Yogi's personality, and took the two proffered arms.

It took a bit of maneuvering for the trio to pass through the crowded convention hall. She looked around to confirm her suspicions about the true attraction of the exhibit hall. In addition to the candidates' booths there were vendors selling everything from BMA apparel to ladies' hats and fur coats. Their progress was slow; the Assembly was shopping. Members also stopped them frequently to speak to their minister or the candidate. Several women they passed rolled their eyes at her. She overheard one woman say, "Who does she think she is walking through here like the Queen of Sheba?"

When they arrived at the luncheon her escorts deposited her at an assigned table. She took a second to look at her watch. The Assembly kept a tight conference schedule. At twelve-thirty she was already tired, and after this there was a Q&A session for the candidates, a workshop, and a youth activity. Finus was right. His position as conference convener was all-encompassing. There would be no time for a private moment this week.

She watched as social Gates moved from table to table campaigning and reacquainting. She refocused her attention as David and Lydia, the Fords, the assistant pastor from the Cathedral, and his wife sat down. She glanced up at the dais. Fred and Inez stood next to the Willinghams. Both women smiled in her direction. She turned over Charlotte's message in her mind. *What will it mean when Finus wins his election?*

He had not made it back to his seat when the server needed to know if he'd prefer chicken or beef. So she ordered for him again. At some point after the salads were served he made his way to their table. He didn't sound very cheerful when he greeted everyone and took his seat next to Cassandra.

"I ordered the chicken for you."

"Who asked you to do that?" he snapped.

"Excuse me?"

Finus snatched up the luncheon program and held it in front of his face. "I can order for myself. I don't need for you to do things like that for me."

Her head jerked back. "I was just…"

"It was cute yesterday. Today it's old."

"What's wrong? Are you feeling all right?" She paused for a moment and studied the crisp white linen tablecloth. Awareness of the room disappeared as she looked up into his angry face. They were practically nose to nose. She looked deeply into his cold, dark, and expressionless eyes. The vein above his left eye pulsed.

He looked down his nose at her. "I just do not need you to—"

"Don't worry, I won't overstep again. I think I'll excuse myself…"

"Don't you move from your appointed place," he hissed through clinched teeth.

She turned toward the heavy hand that squeezed her shoulder. David poked his head between them and whispered. "Stop hissing and start kissing."

Finus's foot kicked out. He stood and gripped David's hand.

Cassandra's hand shook as she reached for her water goblet. She took a sip and twisted her face into what she hoped was a neutral expression.

"Excuse me," Finus said to the table, then walked away.

When he returned his salad was warm and his chicken cold. But he had regained his composure. Cassandra was not so sure about hers. Under the table her feet shuffled and shifted for the duration of the lunch.

Finus remained glued to his seat as the luncheon dismissed. "Which seminar are you planning to attend this afternoon?"

"I'm not. Lydia and I are going across the breeze-way to the mall."

He twisted his lips. He could arrange his schedule to escort them, to buy whatever she wanted, but she'd sat with such a stiff posture during the luncheon he decided not to push.

On Tuesday evening Finus waited by the elevators of Tower Two. Quentin Jarvis stepped off the elevator and walked toward him.

"Well, well, Dr. Gates standing on the corner watching all the girls go by…or are you waiting for a certain someone?" The man towered over him.

He looked up. "Que, good to see you, good to see you. If you must know, I'm awaiting Dr. Brownley. We're chaperones for the youth dance tonight."

"I see. I was kind of hoping to have a word with you about Ms. Brownley."

At that moment the elevator doors opened and un-loaded Assembly members on their way to the evening activities.

"Good evening Rev. Gates, good evening Mr. Jar-vis," members spoke as they passed.

Que motioned toward the sitting area of the lobby. "Let's step over there."

"Sure, sure. What's on your mind, brother?" Finus stepped away from the busy elevators and tried to keep his eye on the opening and closing doors.

"Just want to let you know I'd like to invite Dr. Brownley to have breakfast with me before the end of the conference, and wanted to make sure my invitation wouldn't be misunderstood."

Finus stroked his chin. *Ding, ding.* He turned around to see an empty elevator car. "What did you want to discuss with her? Our plans for opening the school have advanced a hundred fold with her counsel."

Que's head moved from side to side and he cracked a half smile. "I'm having some issues with legislation coming up in Alabama about athletic eligibility and testing. I heard she's good, and I might be able to use her help."

The elevator chimed again. Finus heard the signal but Que's comments distracted him. He wasn't about to let Cassandra consult with him.

"Doc?"

He jumped at the soft voice behind his ear.

"Good evening, Mr. Quentin," said the same soft voice.

"Good evening, Cassandra. You look lovely, as usual." Que reached around Finus to take her hand.

More conference attendees stepped out of the elevators.

Finus's face twitched. He took a deep breath. "Que, you're right, she is good and we'd be glad to accept your invitation to breakfast. My dear, you look marvelous. Shall we?"

❧

Shortly after ten p.m. Finus walked toward Cassandra's solitary figure. She sat by the far side of the pool and stared at the water. A few brave young souls splashed in the water and filled the night air with youthful joy. He pulled a deck chair closer to her and they sat in companionable silence.

He'd done it again. During the dance he'd allowed her to lean in too close. He'd held her too close. She sang and they got lost in Earth Wind and Fire's 'Reasons'. When she sang the second verse, he pulled her even closer and moved his hips against her. Before the song's end David tapped him on his back. He laughed and waved David off. He held her closer and gyrated his hips, inhaling the soft essence of mint in her hair and the hint of flowers in her perfume.

He slipped his foot between hers. He should have released her. Instead he slipped his hands into the back pockets of her jeans, a move from his high school days.

A second tap came from a patrician New England matron. "Reverend, I shouldn't have to chaperone you."

The breath caught in his throat and a raspy, "Stop singing" emerged.

His singing Cinderella fled the room.

He reached over and covered her hand with his. When he squeezed, she looked up and gave him a half smile. They went back to their quiet repose, only looking up at the occasional loud splash or laugh from the pool.

"There you are." Bishop Sutton stood before them, still in his business suit and tie. It was a busy conference for Finus, but Fred's burdens were twofold this week. In addition to fulfilling his ordinary duties he was being considered for the Assembly's highest post. The presiding elder was selected from amongst his peers but that didn't mean there wasn't a lot of behind the scenes politicking. Fred looked weary.

"Doc, Cassandra."

Finus ran a soft caress over her hand as he stood. "Good evening, sir."

Fred pulled up a deck chair and stretched out his long legs. "Cassandra, please excuse us."

She stood. "Sure. Good night, Fred, Doc."

Finus held out his hand to stop her and stood. "Give me a minute, Fred. Let me walk Cassandra to the elevator."

"Son, I think Cassandra's perfectly able to move her two feet on her own."

Finus plopped back down. His face twitched. "I'll call you later."

Cassandra looked back at both of them and waved.

Finus watched as she walked away, and then stretched out his legs like Fred. "Ahh, that feels good."

Fred pulled his long legs in and leaned forward. "Doc, I've known you since you were twelve. Tell me now, father to son. What's going on with you and Cassandra?"

"Did someone call you about what happened at the dance?"

"Something happened tonight? I can't keep up. You can't continue like this, not with the election."

Finus looked over at his entrusted earthly father. He chewed on his lower lip and chose his next words wisely. "Okay, I was a little on edge this afternoon."

Fred placed a finger on his temple.

"It must be the strain of trying to be a good host along with everything else. But I've been careful not to be rude or unfair to anyone this week."

Fred smirked.

He'd chosen the wrong words.

"Only Cassandra." Fred clasped his hands in front of his chest and bowed his head. "Son, when are you going to admit that you're in love? You spend every free moment you have with Cassandra or seeking her company." Fred's head bobbed in agreement with his own statement. "You remind me of a wide-mouth bass thrashing on the hook. Just like that bass, you might ought to recognize that you're caught because you ain't hurting nobody but yourself."

Finus sat straight up in his chair.

"Why don't you stop making excuses and tell me what you're afraid of."

Finus blew out the breath he hadn't realized he was holding.

"Well, sir, you need to fish or cut bait." Fred rolled his eyes then continued. "Son, she complements you in every way. I've observed the two of you together, and by the way she looks at you, I suspect she might feel the same as you. But you both need to get on with it. Word is that Cassandra is first lady material, and there have been more than a few unmarried preachers and some married ones that have looked her way this week. You better take care."

Finus stood up and stretched. "I'm not worried about somebody talking up on Cassandra."

"Don't forget who your brethren are. You are a learned and eloquent speaker, but the Assembly has some silver-tongued devils that have talked the skirts off many a serious sister like Cassandra Brownley."

He sat back down and smiled. "Cassandra's too smart to fall for something like that."

"Smart, yes, but is she lonely? Because smart and lonely equals vulnerable. I have heard tell of many a strange thing happening convention week. And you have not helped yourself this week with your constant proclamations that you are just friends. Now don't get me wrong. I am pleased with the circumspect way in which you have conducted yourself, but stop and think about the opening that leaves. And not just for the brethren. There are still some young women on the prowl for you. I understand some of those gals are plotting to catch you at the right moment so they can give you a taste of something that it's clear you aren't getting from Cassandra." Fred paused. "Boy, I've got mothers of the church worrying me about when and where the wedding will be. Mother Jones has already purchased a new hat for the occasion." Fred laughed out loud. "I threw that in to lighten your load."

"Women know they can move from zero to a wedding fast."

They shared a belly laugh. A few of the youth that lingered around the pool looked in their direction.

"I'll continue in prayer for you both, but it's past time you resolve this, and not to satisfy anyone other than the two of you." Fred reached over and slapped his knee. "Now, with that said, how are you faring? Are you at least taking your medicine because I know you're not getting enough rest. Conference week can be draining without all of the political stuff going on." Fred stretched. "We've done all we can, on all fronts. Why don't you take some time for yourself? Take Cassandra sightseeing or something away from the conference. From what I've heard she's had quite a time here herself."

"Thank you sir, maybe I will. Fred…" he hesitated, "you know you're sounding more like Pop every day." Finus closed his eyes. "I miss his wisdom. Know what? He would have told me the same things tonight."

"I know. Remember, he left you under my care." Fred stood up and motioned for Finus to walk with him. "Doc, I know both of your parents would agree on Cassandra. Don't you know your mother's most fervent prayer was that you'd shake off those silly 'damn women' and get a girl just like her."

As they walked toward the hotel lobby they looked up into the star-filled sky, a quiet acknowledgment of their faith that Wallace and Wilma were now counted among the stars in heaven.

"She does have some of Mom's qualities."

"Yes, she does. Many of Wilma's fine and gracious qualities."

They stopped just short of the Tower Two elevator banks. "Now I'm going to say goodnight. I'm sure Inez is wondering what I'm up to."

When the doors opened they stepped through together. "Where, pray tell, do you think you're going?" Fred placed his large frame in the elevator door.

"To talk to Cassandra."

"No, sir, not at this time of night. And not with an election looming."

Finus stepped off the lift.

"I'll meditate some more on our discussion."

"See, that's your problem, you think too much." Fred waved him off as the elevator doors swooshed to a close.

The next morning Finus sat beside Cassandra in the private dining room reserved for BMA leadership. A steady stream of church leaders paraded in and out. Their breakfast conversation kept getting interrupted by the flow of influentials. He repeatedly stood to shake hands and kiss the ladies. Even though he was in full campaign mode he refused every request to join them.

He sat again and reached for his coffee with two hands, a clear indication of his lack of sleep. "I'm off convention call in an hour and it shouldn't be a busy day. I'd like to take you to the exhibit hall this morning. They have a few booths you might enjoy."

He set his cup down and made a bit of a splash on the white tablecloth. "Books, Bibles, BMA apparel, and there's a Greek booth. Aunt Charlotte wanted to make sure you have an AKA shirt for the fellowship on Thursday night."

"Does your aunt ever wear red?"

"No, I don't believe so," he answered.

They laughed together over Charlotte Willingham's dedication to her sorority colors. He stood up as another couple approached their table. "Good morning, Gates." Isaac Reynolds stood before them with a lady he introduced as his fiancée. Josie was a rather ordinary-looking woman. Cassandra couldn't tell if her chin was round or square since she kept her head down and nodded her responses to the conversation. She didn't appear nearly powerful enough for a man like Isaac.

Isaac pulled back a chair and motioned for Josie to take the other one at the table. "I think Josie and Cassandra should get to know each other. We'll join you."

"No, absolutely not. Nothing against you, Miss Josie. Maybe some other time." Finus extended his trembling arm to wave the couple off.

When he sat back down he placed his arm around her shoulder and gave a little squeeze. "There's something about her, I can't put my finger on it…"

"She seems awful timid."

"Like a lamb to the slaughter." He laughed aloud.

"What's funny about that?"

"I'm laughing about something my mother always said. In her book there were only two types of women. Lions and lambs."

"I see. And what type am I?"

He grinned, picked up her right hand with his left, and kissed her knuckles. "I'm hoping you're a wolf in sheep's clothing."

Cassandra bent her head and looked down into her coffee cup. Before she could compose herself his cell phone vibrated on the table. The steady shake only meant trouble. She'd hoped he would make it through the next few hours without interruption since he'd committed to spending time with her.

"Okay, I'm on my way." He hung up the call. "I'm sorry, but we had a daughter go missing last night."

Her mouth gaped open.

"No need for alarm. The security camera caught her sneaking off with a boy. She's back, and I need to go speak with the mother."

She touched his arm. "Be gentle."

"I should take you with me. You probably know how to handle something like this better than me." He stood and walked around to the other side of the table and planted a lingering kiss on her forehead. "Ah, I was really looking forward to spending the morning with you. Relax and enjoy your breakfast. I'll catch up with you as soon as I can."

She watched his back as he retreated from the dining room. He stopped in the doorway to speak with a group of men entering the dining room, led by Quentin Jarvis. She looked down at her half eaten plate of eggs. Breakfast was nice while it lasted. She smiled again at his wolf in sheep's clothing quip; she loved it when he was in a playful mood. She tried to shake off her apprehensions about the tremble in his hand.

"Good morning, Miss Cassandra." Quentin sat at the corner of the table next to hers. "Care to join us?" She looked over at the table of six men and shook her head.

He laughed. "Come on, you should meet the Assembly's judicial council."

For Finus she stood up and let him introduce her around the table. None of the names stuck in her brain, but one man was a sitting federal judge. The Assembly was a male-dominated hierarchical organization.

"We have good news," Quentin said.

The judge looked cross-eyed at Quentin.

"We've already filed our report with the Bishops' Council." He addressed the unspoken concern and motioned for her to return to her table.

Quentin walked over and joined her without asking. "I'm sure you know there were several objections filed to Finus's petition based on experience, and there was a challenge to Bishop Sutton because of his divorce. Our rulings are in both their favor. I've been looking at those brothers all day." He scooted his chair up to the table. "I need a change of venue." Quentin leaned forward. "I always get what I want. I knew I'd have breakfast with you before the end of the week." Jarvis relaxed with his cup. "I heard he talks to you like you're his ninety-year-old auntie. That's not the way I'd talk to a woman." He flashed a seductive smile.

She leaned back with her third cup of coffee. With his every word and catlike movement she squeezed her knees tighter together. Aware of the deep longing within herself, she gripped the cup tighter.

How long had it been?

Chapter 21

Hours later Cassandra paced around a six-by-six emergency room holding her cell. Her wait for Finus to return from testing was frequently interrupted by the buzzing of his BlackBerry.

Without looking she pressed the send button for the one hundredth time in an hour.

"Let me talk to him." The voice on the other side of the line demanded.

She sighed heavily into the phone. "He's not here, Amaria. They took him up for an MRI."

"My poor baby. I should be there with him."

"I'm here."

"I know you're there for the conference, but I'm talking about being there for him in the midnight hours as he calls it. When he takes that collar off."

Cassandra shuddered. The innuendo and nasty tone sapped the air from her chest. "I'll let him know you called."

"Speak up, I can barely hear you. Remember, you're hired help, so you had better tell him I called and that I'm on my way. I'm trying to get an earlier flight. I'll be there as soon as I can."

She lifted the hot device from her cheek.

"And Cassandra, I will call him back." Click.

Her stomach contracted. She wrapped her arms around her body. As she looked out the window, her pulse raced. She suspected that something was going on between them. *The way he's been kissing me? Yeah, on the hand and forehead like he would an aged aunt.* She rested her head against the cold window pane and watched the sun setting on what had been a hopeful week. "He wants her with him 'in the midnight hour'."

The distinct gong of the bishop's ring tone demanded her attention. She clicked the answer button. "Fred, I shouldn't be here."

"No, child, we're confident you're the one who will see to it that he's properly cared for. But of course you will call me first if…"

"I'm sorry, Fred." She adjusted her tone. "He's seems fine. They're just taking a MRI to be sure. He's even complaining the hospital is trying to milk his insurance card."

Fred gave a hearty belly laugh. "I'll let everyone here know he's okay, but you call me if you need anything. And let Doc know that the entire Assembly's praying for him."

Who's praying for me?

She sat the BlackBerry down and dug into the bottom of her purse. She found her own phone and pressed one.

"Hey girl, how's it going? Engaged, still going together, getting any?" Her sister's cheerful ribbing lifted her spirits.

"Yogi, I'm sitting in a hospital emergency room. Finus had a seizure this afternoon."

"Is he okay? 'Cause you don't sound right."

"He's fine but…" The conversation with Amaria tumbled out.

"Game, all game," her sister hooted. "She's messing with you. You're the one he took to the conference, and like you said, even his family recognizes that. You need to call that witch's bluff. Tell him what she said."

She stood and turned towards the interior of the hospital room, but kept close to the window. She didn't want to lose connection to her sister.

"Excuse me, Mrs. Gates." The hospital social worker rushed into the room. "We need you to call upstairs."

She took a quick step forward.

The social worker stretched out her hands to signal stop. "He's all right. He's just causing a commotion. We can't get him to stay still long enough to get the test run. He's worried that you haven't eaten. Can I get you to call up there and get him settled?"

"I'm not his wife."

The hospital social worker picked up the chart at the end of the bed. She twisted one of her blonde dreadlocks with her free hand. "I'm going by the information on this chart unless you tell me otherwise. And if you do that, I'll have to stop talking to you." She gave a sista-be-cool head bob and picked up the house phone.

Cassandra walked over and reached for the receiver the social worker held aloft.

"Girlfriend, that's one fussy man you got there."

"I know."

It was another two hours before they brought Finus back to the ER admitting room. His maleficent charms were still in full effect.

"No, I do not want any ice."

"I need to contact my personal physician."

"I have already given you my insurance information."

In between his yelling at every nurse, clerk or orderly that dared come in the room, he fired questions at her.

"What happened when I fell?"

"Why?"

"My dear," he sat up in the hospital bed, "it's quite an honor to serve as a conference convener."

Her eyes narrowed.

He lay back. "I couldn't function like I needed to this week if I took all of that medication."

Her eyes shot open and rolled up to the ceiling. "You're in the hospital."

"Yes, ma'am."

They sat for a while listening to the beep of the heart monitor and the periodic hiss of the automatic blood pressure cuff.

"Cassandra," he began after a long silence, "did many of the members see my fall?"

"Is that what's concerning you at this hour?"

A weak smile covered his weary features. "Well, I do have reputation to uphold."

"The Reverend Doctor Finus Gideon Gates did nothing to embarrass himself or his office today," she snapped.

"Who called?"

She snatched a small piece of paper from the tray table. News had traveled fast. In addition to Amaria, she'd spoken to Will, Aunt Jo, Inez, David, and Fred twice. And those were the calls she answered.

He shifted and squirmed in the bed. Hearing the messages of love and support from his family seemed only to agitate him. The BlackBerry buzzed. She looked down at the name on the display.

"Turn that thing off and come pray with me."

"It's Amaria."

He sat up and positioned himself so he could lower the raised rail of the bed, a precaution the head nurse had insisted on. "Turn it off and come here." He patted the space on the bed where he wanted her to sit.

She freed herself from his BlackBerry and went to him. His left arm was constricted by an IV and another device was attached to his right temple. He maneuvered himself so he could hold her hand. Together they recited the Lord's Prayer.

"Sing for me."

With a still bowed head she sang mournfully, "Sweet hour of prayer, sweet hour of prayer—"

"Music does soothe the savage beast."

She looked up to see the attending physician standing in the room's entryway, grinning.

"You have a beautiful voice." The doctor moved into the room.

Finus scrunched up his face. "When am I going to be released?"

"We're going to let you go very soon, as a favor to our nursing staff. I don't mean to interrupt your prayers, Reverend." He stopped at the foot of the bed. "I conferred with your doctors in Chicago and they agree, since you have someone to care for you. But he wants you and your *wife* to come in as soon as you get home."

Finus shot her a look.

Now he thinks I'm an easy liar.

Then the doctor said, "Ma'am, may we speak to you in the hall." He led her outside. "As you probably already know, watch him carefully for the next twenty-four hours. If there is any problem at all, contact the hospital. The number is on the discharge paper. When you get back to the hotel, have him take these pills." He handed her a brown medication envelope. "It's just a mild sedative to help him get some sleep. If you like, I can order another dose for you."

"No, thank you."

The social worker covered her part of the meeting. "I need you to sign here and here, your legal signature, please." She gave a knowing nod. "My mama always said that there's a lid for every pot. Make sure you call us if you need to."

"Cassandra, I can't thank you enough for everything you've done for me this evening." Wearily he plopped down on the sofa in his suite.

"Don't speak of it anymore." She closed the door of his suite, grateful they'd made it to his room without being seen or stopped.

"I'll just call Julian or maybe David to escort you to your room."

Heat rose in her cheeks. "No. It's late and I'm here. Go and get ready for bed. I'll bring you a glass of water. They want you to take these pills before you go to sleep."

Finus sighed. He wanted to protest, but the hard set of her jaw warned him against it. He rose and went into the bedroom to change. Half an hour later he reappeared in his blue Bill Blass monogrammed pajamas.

"I knew you'd be just the type to have monogrammed jammies."

"Very funny. By the way, you have no business seeing me in my nightclothes."

"Your nightclothes are nicer than most students wear to school."

She gave a wave of her hand that reminded him that she was a high school disciplinarian. He turned and got into the bed.

"Here, take these." She poured two light blue pills into his palm from a small dispensary envelope. She stood over him like a teacher over an unruly pupil.

Since her words sounded like a commandment, he complied while she pulled a chair from the sitting room and settled by his bed.

"I'm sure it's not the proper things to do by Assembly standards, but watching over you tonight is the right thing for me to do."

Her voice carried such command and conviction he chose not to argue. "I don't deserve your kindness."

She switched off the light and took up her vigil. "It's not kindness, you know, it's because I love you," she said softly in the dark.

The events of his day collided with the little blue pills and began to exact a toll. The words of the bishop and his late father drifted into his head. His brain would not turn off. He wrestled against the effects of the sleeping pills.

His heart went out to sweet Cassandra. Conference week was probably weighing on her in ways he had not imagined. Most of the Assembly members had graciously accepted her as his good friend, but, from their nightly conversations, he'd learned some of the women had been ruthlessly rude to her.

A wave of happiness washed over him, like the sense of euphoria that often preceded a seizure. Could it be joy? He was ready to talk. He wished he could talk to her all night. He looked over and tried to see her face. The dark form in the chair sat so still, she had to be asleep. He couldn't wake her. That would be selfish. But wouldn't it also be selfish to let her sleep in that uncomfortable chair? The form moved backward slowly and crashed to the floor.

"Owww," she cried.

"Come here to me," he whispered as she struggled to gain her footing. Without hesitation she crawled up into his outstretched arms. He planted a slow kiss on the top of her head.

"I shouldn't be here. Oh, God, I've got to get out of here. People will talk. Doc, I'm so sorry. What was I thinking? What will this do to your reputation?" she sobbed.

He stroked her hair, kissed her forehead, and held her as tightly as he could. "It's okay."

"But, but—" she sobbed.

"Sleep now, we'll work it out in the morning," he whispered softly in her ear. As he drifted away she was still sobbing.

Finus stirred and looked over at the alarm clock. Five-fifteen a.m. He reached over and switched off the alarm. He didn't want to disturb the angel sleeping soundly in the shelter of his arms. He inhaled the scent of her hair. "I love you, too," he murmured and relaxed. When he looked at the clock again it was close to seven. The Assembly would be active. He had a problem.

Chapter 22

Finus slipped out of bed and plodded to the sitting room of his suite. He searched in vain for his Black-Berry. Then he remembered. It was in Cassandra's purse. He picked up the hotel phone to place a distress call. "Fred, it's me."

"Morning, son, how are you? You gave the Assembly quite a stir."

"I'm fine, but I've got a problem."

"What's wrong? Isn't Cassandra taking good care of you?"

Finus frowned. "That's the problem. She stayed with me through the night and now I'm wondering how we can get her out of here."

"Are you worried about the wrong thing? After the way that girl looked after you, should anything be more important to you?"

"It's not that. She was a little upset—no, hysterical—last night. I never saw her like that. I don't know what she'll be like when she wakes up."

"Wonder what brought that on?"

Finus began to pace. "My guess, stress, plus she fell out of a chair. I think that startled her."

"Hysterical? Well, I hope you kissed her. That's the best way to calm an hysterical woman."

"Don't joke. I'm serious. It was bad."

"Okay. I'm on my way, we'll figure something out. I'll bring Inez. She'll know what to do."

"Don't bring her. I'm still in my bedclothes."

"You are one funny brother," Fred laughed. "Relax, Reverend, I'm on my way."

Slightly before ten a.m. Cassandra entered the final general plenary session of the thirty-eighth Baptist Methodist Assembly Convention. The delegates would be voting later this afternoon, and, for the sake of Finus's campaign, she wanted to be seen. A young lady wearing a conference page robe caught her at the door. "Dr. Brownley, Bishop Sutton would like to see you before the meeting begins."

She followed the page to the front of the room where the Bishops' Council stood waiting for the convener's signal to take their positions and preside over the session. Fred stepped away from his conversation as they approached. He surrounded her in a huge hug.

"Thank you, thank you."

She screeched and startled three elderly bishops.

He released her with a concerned frown.

"Escort Dr. Brownley to the Assembly's medical team." He barked out the order to the page. "And I'll expect a report back."

An hour later she sat next to Inez and listened to the endless stream of committee minutes and reports. The pain in her shoulder had subsided thanks to the Tylenol 3 the Assembly's nurse gave her. Regret for sharing her most closely guarded secret with Finus grew like an untended weed.

She shifted in her seat and recalled Inez's earlier calm efficiency. "For both your sakes," Inez had said when she hustled her out of Finus's room. On the journey between the two towers the bishop's wife answered all questions. When one observant church mother noticed the sweat suit Cassandra wore was embroidered with Finus' monogram, Inez reminded the older woman that in her day girls wore their beau's lettermen jackets.

Cassandra's pager vibrated in her bag. She shrugged off the looks she got and rooted around in her bag. It hadn't been a full twenty-four hours since his seizure. What if…? She clicked the right button to still the device and read the text message.

Let's go sailing!

Cassandra covered her mouth to stifle her laugh as she rose to leave the meeting.

The captain of the boat he'd hoped to hire could not make ready under short notice so they went for an early lunch at the marina. Finus seemed a little preoccupied, but she didn't press. He was well rested. Sound in body and personality, charming and funny. After lunch he insisted they visit the antique and gift shops in Old Town.

She refused to let him purchase the gifts she'd selected for her family. By early afternoon the pain returned to her shoulder. She used one arm to cradle the other, smiled to mask the pain, and asked him to carry her packages. It was their only real time together and she wasn't going to let a little pain ruin it. They strolled around the marina and found a bench overlooking the ocean. Crisp salt air mixed with the chirps of sea gulls. They sat side by side and enjoyed the view.

"Cassandra, I should have told you a hundred times before now how I feel about you. In all the time I've known you, you've always said and done the right things. We all just adore you. I've never heard you say a cross word or complain about the way we live. I can't express to you how grateful I am that you have so carefully guarded my privacy and never retaliated against anyone, no matter how rude they were to you. I am very sorry for the way some people have treated you this week." He picked her hand up and kissed her fingers. "Thank you for your loving kindness last night."

Finally!

"You know we're quite the power couple." He chuckled.

What's he talking about?

She turned slightly and cocked her head to one side as he finished.

It was like looking into his beautifully appointed living room, very nice but nothing personal. *He hasn't said one word about all of the private times we've laughed and talked. Not one word about sitting and watching the stars together or the way it feels when I am in his arms dancing or even those silly kisses on the forehead.* Clearly, it was the Reverend Doctor speaking. But what about Doc? How does he feel?

His BlackBerry chirped. He looked down at the device and smiled. "That's Mari, she's here. Let's go meet her."

He stood up then reached out for her hand. "My dear," he said softly, "I want you to take a more public role in my ministry."

The pain in her shoulder shot up to her head. His endearment was diminished by Que's suggestion, and her suspicions heightened by Amaria's testimony. Her heartbeat pounded in her ear. Her ear hurt. Her heart was about to leap out of her chest. Her throat swelled from trying to hold back tears. She'd held her breath and waited for him to say he loved her. She held his hand and closed her eyes. An image of the Reverend Doctor in the pulpit in his vestment flashed.

Her expression soured as they started back to the hotel.

Her neck throbbed. Pain racked her body. She bobbled. "I need to go back to my room," she whispered.

"What's wrong?"

She turned so he couldn't see the tears that clouded her vision. "I hurt my shoulder last night. The medical team gave me something for pain earlier, but the pain's returned."

Finus released her hand and stepped back to look at her. "I'm sorry, I should have noticed. You've favored your shoulder all day today, haven't you? Do you want me to get you anything?"

"No, just let me get some rest before dinner."

🍂

During the formal closing dinner Julian Pierce sat in Cassandra's seat. There had been a swirl of whispering about her absence.

Julian nudged him. "Reverend Gates, stand up."

Years of programming kicked in and he stood and was recognized with the rest of the conference conveners. The accolades for a successful conference flew over his shoulders. He clapped with the rest of the crowd and went back to sulking, present in body if not spirit. He absently pushed the food around on his plate and worried about Cassandra.

"Get your head out of the clouds. They're about to announce the election results." Inez tried to joke with him. He shot her a nasty look. His head was in the mayonnaise, the Portuguese expression that he often used with Cassandra.

He stood and accepted the applause when the election results were read. He'd made Assembly history. The youngest man ever elected church examiner.

He looked over at Fred, who shrugged. He had not been successful. Inez tried to cover her glee with a dinner napkin. Over desert Finus pondered all of the moments he'd wasted with Cassandra.

His mind wandered back to the garden at his birthday party, then to a yellow day when they sat in the park and she read to him from a romance novel. Or was it at the Symphonietta, when he first heard her sing. Or when she turned up her nose at him during the rolling revival. No, it can't go back that far. Can it?

He didn't start out with any intention of falling for her. She really wasn't his type, yet there was something about her that kept him wanting to see her again. He'd tried to put his finger on what it was for months now. It was like the pull he experienced when his father preached. But not quite. It was more like the gentle never-ending, soul-moving nudge his mother gave him when she wanted him to do something she knew would be for his own good. It was his mother's influence, not his father's preaching, that had caused him to accept his calling. And he was a better man for it.

"You don't have to stay any longer. I think your obligation has been met."

Inez's nudge couldn't budge him. It was his duty to endure. Cassandra would understand.

Assembly members began to drift among the tables to say their farewells. A parade of women, young and old, walked past the table. The tigers had resumed the hunt.

"Rev. Gates, if you need someone to talk to…"

"Finus, you should meet my daughter…sister… niece…friend…"

"Dr. Gates, if you'd like…"

"Excuse me, Rev. Gates." He sighed and looked up. Who was this in his face now?

"Yes, yes, what is it?" He knew he sounded nasty, but he'd reached his limit.

"I don't mean to disturb you. I'm the nurse that treated Dr. Brownley this morning and I just wanted to ask how she was doing."

His eyes narrowed in recognition. "You're a member at the Cathedral, right?" But he wasn't interested in that, he leaned forward. "Her injury isn't that bad. Is it?"

"Didn't she tell you she has an acromio clavicular joint sprain?"

His head snapped back.

"I'm glad she took my advice and decided to get some rest. She was in some pain this morning, but with that type of injury the pain is progressive. I was able to get more Tylenol 3 for her. Can I ask you to take these to her?"

Finus leaned back in his chair. Any further and he'd hit the floor. *I should have stayed with her. How could I be so selfish?*

The nurse stirred him from his racing thoughts. "Reverend Gates, will you make sure that she gets these and also remind her that she shouldn't lift or carry anything heavy for a few days, like luggage? Although I'm sure with the way you treat her she won't have to lift a finger getting through the airport."

"I'm sorry, Miss…"

"Robbie Xander."

He stood abruptly, rocked forward, and caught himself by grabbing the edge of the table. "Come with me. I'll take you to her room."

❦

It took quite a bit to get Cassandra settled. She was in so much pain; Robbie called in a doctor to give Cassandra a shot of morphine. Finus only left her side long enough to walk the doctor out of Cassandra's suite.

He closed the door and looked back at Robbie. "Thank you. I'll take it from here." He attempted to usher Robbie from the suite.

"With that morphine shot, I don't feel right leaving her alone. I'll stay," she offered.

"I'm not leaving her side." His brow furrowed. "Umm, Robbie, I need to ask…"

She shook her head. "I'm sorry, Rev. Gates, I haven't heard a word you've said in the last few minutes. Take good care of my patient."

After Robbie left, he sat semi-reclined in bed with Cassandra. He held her and they got comfortable. "I should have noticed."

"I should have said something." She snuggled closer.

"Ca-San, going forward let's promise to be honest with each other."

She smiled and yawned.

He kissed her softly until her cell phone rang.

"Baby, can you get that? It's Yogi. Put her on speaker."

He picked up her phone from the nightstand. "She's right here, hold on." Finus said and pushed the speaker feature on her Blackberry.

"Don't tell her we're in the bed," Cassandra whispered loudly.

Yolanda's hoots filled the room.

"Umm, it's not like that, Yolanda," he said.

Cassandra giggled.

"Yolanda, please let your mother know she's all right and that I'll take good care of her. I'll also send a car so you can meet her at the airport tomorrow night. She'll have a note from our doctor detailing the treatment she's received."

"You're not going to pin a note on me like a little girl," Cassandra said. "Yogi, we're in bed, hang up."

He looked down at Cassandra. Her face was full of a loopy grin.

"Goodnight, Yolanda." He switched off the phone. "Are you all right?"

"Where's Amaria?"

He looked at his watch. "By now singing at the post-conference party I'm hosting. Why do you ask?"

"I'm happy you're here with me." She attempted to bring him closer with her free arm.

He kissed the top of her head and gently resisted her urge to recline further. "You know my celibacy is important to me."

"I know that." She placed an index finger on his lip. "But that doesn't mean we can't kiss and tickle or occasionally bump and grind."

"Miss Brownley, is that you or the medication talking?"

"No, Doc it's me. I'm a wolf."

He erupted in laughter. *Good Lord, yes.*

Chapter 23

In September Finus couldn't get home enough to satisfy himself. His responsibilities as a church examiner had come faster and presented more challenges than he'd anticipated. He was assigned to shepherd a one-hundred-year-old mainline Baptist church in Iowa into the Assembly. That task, coupled with the success of his musical investment, kept him on the road. Cassandra pretended not to mind since another school year had started.

He stared out at the skyline as his limo snaked through downtown L.A. toward the Wilshire Theatre. He scowled at his reflection in the glass. He didn't want to go to the one-thousand-dollar-a-plate AIDS benefit tonight. But tonight was business, an offshoot from his investment in Will's music venture. With Amaria's hit song, invitations for benefits, galas, and awards shows had poured in at a steady clip. Will insisted he share the spotlight. Two years ago this would have been his Eden. Now he just wanted to go home.

He drummed on the window. Amaria would probably press him tonight; she didn't care that he was in a relationship. She'd said he had enough to go around. *Not.* His lips twisted. She was certainly up front about what she wanted and wasn't taking no for an answer. He pulled out his BlackBerry and sent a message to

Janet. *Book a seat for me on tonight's red eye and don't make travel arrangement for the Holiday Gospel Fest.* Cassandra declined his invitation to attend the event next weekend in Atlanta. He knew it was because Amaria was scheduled to perform. He didn't need to go, either.

❦

"Cassandra, girl, you've been in bed all day. I know you're hurt, but it's Saturday night. Let's at least take the kids to a movie." Yogi stood by the small bureau in the bedroom they shared growing up. Cassandra rolled her eyes and pulled a pillow over her face.

The immobilizing sling on her shoulder prevented her from rolling over to face the wall, as she'd done when they were girls. All she wanted to do was take another nap. When Finus was home she'd put up a good front so as not to interfere with the precious little time they had together. But a month of battling her shoulder injury had sapped her strength. To get the extra help she needed she spent the weekends at her mother's house.

Cassandra shifted on the bed until she could sit up.

"Hey, Phyllis, I got her to move," Yolanda called out to their mother.

Cassandra opened her mouth to comment, but then closed it and her eyes.

"Now is maybe a good time to tell her."

Phyllis's voice seemed closer. She opened her eyes. Their mother sat at the edge of Yogi's bed twisting a copy of the *Black Pages*.

She drew in a deep breath. "Tell me what?" The walls of the tiny bedroom closed in on her. "What's in the paper, Phyllis?"

"Here, read it for yourself. This week's society column is full of news from L.A. about Finus."

She reached for the papers in her mother's outstretched hand. "Let me see that," she hissed. True enough, in print and pictures, a grinning Finus with Amaria. She threw the papers to the floor. "Finus isn't cheating on me."

"Then they should teach avoiding the appearance of evil in his church," her mother said.

Yolanda walked over to her bed and put an arm around her wounded sister. "Did you know she's shooting her next video here?" Yolanda gave her a one-armed hug. "We wanted to make sure you knew in case…"

"In case what? You both know I'm not going anywhere near the Cathedral or the Assembly looking like this." She paused and glanced down at her bland sweater secured on the sides by Velcro. "And I already know all of this." She lowered herself onto the bed and struggled to face the wall. "One of the teachers at school keeps me well informed."

The warmth of her mother's hand stroked her back. She buried her face deep in the pillow.

🦋

At precisely eight p.m. on Sunday evening, Finus picked up the phone next to his bed. He dialed and waited. No answer, just a mechanical recording of the sweet voice he'd longed to hear all day. *Where is she?* He looked out his bedroom window at the dark gray Chicago skyline. He was stretched out on his bed, glad to be home. The banging and laughing of the video production crew in his living room seeped into his sanctuary. They were too loud as they wrapped up their day-long shoot.

A satisfied smile crept across his face; he was going to appear in a music video. All he'd had to do was sit contemplatively in a wing back chair and look out on the city's skyline. It had taken longer than expected because today he was fidgety. He checked his watch. He shouldn't wait any longer. He dialed her again. She picked up. He smiled. There was a nervous energy across the line. He launched into mindless pleasantries. "I wanted to come earlier, but today was the bishop's call."

"It was a busy day."

Her reply sounded a little frosty. He forged ahead. "Yes, with all the obligations of the day time slipped away. Guess who drew the short straw?"

She didn't reply.

"Fred said it was fitting since I'm a national officer. Then I went to dinner at the house and I stayed talking longer than I planned."

She exhaled loudly. "Honored to be on your list."

The coolness of her response flared his impatience. Something crashed into a wall. He sat up, paused for a moment, and swung his feet onto the floor. "What's gotten into you?"

"You know," she started in a weary voice, "it was a busy day for the pink and green investigative agency. It wasn't even noon when Yolanda got the first call from a sorority sister. I understand Amaria was your *special guest* at the Cathedral today?"

" 'Mari's in town to shoot a video, and as an Assembly member she's required to attend local services."

Her lips smacked.

He stood up. "You know nothing good comes from idle gossip. Do you also believe what they're printing in the *Black Pages* now?"

Her silent response deflated him.

He waited for his question to resonate. His face twitched. The spaces between her silence and the noisy crew were maddening. "Where do you go? Even when you are talking to me. Why can't you let me into that pretty little head of yours? I'm trying so hard to understand you."

She said with annoyance, "Where are you? What's all that noise?"

"That's the camera crew packing up. I just shot a cameo for Amaria's video!"

"How exciting." Her tone was flat, dry, without the sweetness he craved.

"It was. I didn't realize how much went into the filming. You won't believe how long it took to get a few minutes of usable footage on me. The crew's been here all day, setting up the location, adding lights, and rearranging my furniture, which I didn't like. But they are putting everything back where it belongs."

"I really am last on your list."

He closed his eyes. "Don't look at it like that. Time is money, and in a sense I'm paying for this video."

"Do you really want her and me?" Her voice was a tired little air.

He walked towards the bedroom door. "Let me close this door because I'm sure I did not hear what you just said." He slammed the door, adding to the noise from the crew.

"Compared to her I lead a very pedestrian life," she whispered.

He sat down and stared out at the twinkling city lights. He didn't care for her insinuation or tone. "It's good to be home. Fred asked me today when I planned to return to my pedestrian, or as he called it, preordained life."

"I'm talking about my life."

She sounded so tired, so sad, his soul cringed. "I'm determined to always be honest with you. I'll keep praying that you'll soon be able to trust me."

Her silence was not encouraging.

"Talk to me, Cassandra."

"I'm sure you aren't used to families like mine."

He'd counseled people long enough to know a red herring, but if this was the path she needed he'd listen. Collar on.

"My dear, I am a minister in a modern age. Your family is not unlike most. Everyone is living out the consequences of their actions or inaction. We all have disappointments and hurts as the result. Aunt Jo has never married, but she has two children. Grandpa was so disappointed in this he left her nothing. This caused a tremendous rift in our family. He died never having reconciled with Jo." She didn't respond, but he knew she was listening. "And I never told you the reason I object so strongly to Brother Whitney, besides the obvious. I held that out of respect to Cherie. Whitney is the father of her son, and he has never considered doing the right thing." He let this revelation sink in before continuing. "I know it's late, but I'm coming over."

"And what?"

"Remove any doubts you have about us."

He could picture her in her den silently holding the phone. "Cassandra?"

"Only you would say something so beautiful, but that's not possible. I'm at my mother's house."

A smile erupted across his face. A scowl chased it away. "I see... I still want to see you."

"Oooh," she gasped. "I look terrible."

He heard what sounded like the rustle of bed covers. "I'm sure you don't, and I don't care about that. Are you happy with the distance that's growing between us?"

"No. I need to go, Brown's waiting for me."

But she didn't hang up. She held onto their connection, this call. He should just go to her mother's house. The image of Phyllis answering the door in a house dress with a rolling pin danced across his mind.

The thought of a confrontation with Phyllis stilled him.

"Cassandra, you're right about the lateness of the hour."

He looked at his watch. He rocked back and forth on his heels. A burst of laughter erupted from his kitchen. He'd be free to leave if these people weren't in his house. He shouldn't have let Janet go home early. He needed to see her face-to-face to explain why he let Amaria use his apartment for her video. Amaria had been trying to tempt him for months, but he'd realized anew where his heart lay when Amaria sang at the eleven o'clock service. As 'Mari belted out a rousing new modern spiritual, all he heard was Cassandra's voice singing his birthday prayer.

"I only want you," he said.

"I love you." Sweetness returned to her tone.

"I need to see you. Let me come get you."

"No!"

"Your shoulder's bothering you, isn't it?"

"Yes."

He sighed. "Go home and get your rest. I'll call you tomorrow from Iowa. It will be late, and not because your last on my list."

"You're gone again?" She sniffled.

"Hey, you said no for tonight, so we'll talk again tomorrow. I'll be home on Thursday and I'm coming straight to you."

❧

Cassandra opened her front door on Monday morning, expecting to see her brother's truck. Instead she walked straight into Finus's arms.

"I couldn't leave town without seeing you," he said as they rode towards Westmore in his Town Car.

She nestled into the shelter of his arms and held him as tightly as she could.

"I called Gladys last night. She's arranging for some of the ladies in the missionary society to cook for you."

"They don't need to do that."

"Don't protest. It's already done. And I'm also leaving the car and driver at your disposal. I'm sorry, I should have taken better care of you. And you should have let me hit the floor."

"I'd never let you do that."

He smiled. "I've fallen flat on my face many times before and survived." He kissed her hand. "There's something else I need to tell you."

She took in a sharp breath.

"Bishop Morton made his transition last night."

"Oh, I'm so sorry to hear that."

"Thank you. I'll have Janet add your name to my condolences. But this means I won't be home on Thursday. I'm going to Alabama to be with the family."

"I understand." She looked down at their interlocked hands. "Finus, can you ask the driver to pull over for a minute?"

"Why?"

"I can't be caught kissing on school grounds."

Chapter 24

Monday didn't go well. The colony church in Iowa was close to splitting over the requirement that all members accept the twelve tenants of the BMA. He'd spent hours in a contentious meeting explaining over and over the Assembly's creed. Most of the discussion involved splitting hairs over the meanings of scriptures and church doctrine. He'd also been interrupted several times by Amaria. He'd left Chicago before saying goodbye to her, and she wasn't pleased.

On Wednesday evening at Bible study things declined further. Finus left for Alabama on Thursday morning with a splitting headache, feeling like he'd failed. When he arrived he found a grieving family, a divided church family, and Amaria.

Finus was in rare form at eleven p.m. when he called Cassandra. Nothing she said satisfied him.

"You don't sound well."

The concern in her voice annoyed him. How could she know how he felt? "I feel fine, and I've asked you more than once not to assign me feelings, health, or otherwise." He couldn't stand for her to ask about his health. He hated the thought of her thinking of him as less than whole. "I called because I think it's important you know that I do what I say I'm going to do."

"And you always get what you want, too." Her voice was light.

Things between them had changed. She was usually able to affect some small turnaround in his sour moods. But tonight, he was in no mood for small jokes.

"Yes, I do, unless it becomes more trouble than it's worth." Why had he said that? Dread and sorrow washed over him as soon as the comment slipped from his lips.

"Ouch! Was that a personal attack?"

He scrunched up his face. "If you choose to look at it that way."

"Umm. I've had a long day," she said.

"Me, too."

"So let me ask you this. Why is Amaria everywhere you are?"

"I am tired of you questioning my fidelity," he said slowly.

"And I can't stand these calls anymore."

"This really isn't about me, is it? This is about what Gregory did to you."

"That's how it feels," she hissed.

"Don't punish me for another man's mistake." He started to pace. "How can you say you love me and not trust me? Are you even able to trust me? Because if you can't, then there's no basis for anything else." He sat down heavily on the hotel bed. He had switched on the lamp beside the bed, but the room still seemed too dark. He stood up and turned on the lamps on the other side of the room. "How long do I have to play this cat and mouse game with you? I'm growing weary of it."

"I'm not playing any games with you, and if that's what you think, then, well, that's up to you. I think it's best we say goodnight."

His head shot back. He lowered his head and his tone. "I'm going to have what I want."

"You can't have her and me."

His fingers began to drum on the hotel desk. "Do you realize while you're saying 'Get back cat' somebody else is saying, 'Hello kitty'?"

"You know what, Finus Gates? I can deal with your moodiness, but sometimes you can be just mean, and I don't think I want to accept that. Why would you say something like that to me? I am well aware of your many opportunities."

Her words fell on his ears in slow, measured tones. He sat down heavily in an armchair. "It's the meds."

"No, it's not, and you know it," she screeched. "Finus, I have too much respect for you to hang up this phone in your face, so I'm going to say goodnight."

Finus slammed down the phone with finality. A hundred lamps could shed no light on his mood. "She'll call me when she comes to her senses."

Cassandra angrily shook the phone receiver with her right arm. Had he hung up on her? "Oh, no, he didn't!" She hopped up. "See, that's why you hate him."

She walked around her house ranting. "That arrogant, conceited, condescending, boorish bastard. I can't believe he had the nerve to hang up on me after all I've put up with from him. 'Don't touch me. Don't try to start a relationship with me, no, not till I'm ready. We can't talk; I've got a convention to run. Don't you worry about Amaria. Don't, don't, stop, wait…'"

She yelled her way to the kitchen. "Who does he think he is? They may treat him like a prince up at that church of his, but he's just a man, and a crazy one if he thinks I'm going to fall for that mess he's selling. What the hell's he thinking? Classic Madonna-whore complex. What makes him think I'm willing to be his Madonna? I'm supposed to sit quietly at home and pray, while he runs around with that whore Amaria? No, not going to happen. Not again. That negro must be crazy. God, I hate him. I hate the Reverend Doctor Finus Gideon Gates." The refrigerator door shook when she slammed it. Not a single piece of chocolate. So she poured a glass of water.

Her tirade continued as she prepared for bed. She didn't stop yelling until she slid into bed. She shivered between the cold sheets. "Another night, another year alone." There'd be no man to warm her between the covers this winter.

She winced. No Doc to keep her warm and make her laugh. She missed his kindness and gentle manners. Tears formed in her eyes as she thought back on all the time she'd spent with him. She hugged her pillow to stifle her tears. No more cozy rides in his Boxster. No more opportunities to sit close to him in a crowded room. No more warm, lingering kisses on the forehead.

A scripture ran through her mind: *Delight thy self in the Lord and he will give you the desire of your heart.*

"All I want is Doc."

She shot up. "What am I saying? How is it possible for me to love Doc and hate the Reverend Doctor?" She spent half the night crying and pondering her conundrum.

At eight-thirty the next morning she looked up to see Brenda Thomas at the door of her office. "Here with another unsolicited report?"

"I don't know what you mean. I just stopped by to let you know what some of the staff and students are saying behind your back."

"What?"

Brenda stepped closer to her desk. "That you've become judgmental, unyielding, and uncompromising."

Everything she hated about Finus.

She cut her eyes. "Okay, that's enough. Thank you, Brenda. You should go get a cup of coffee or something before your planning period is over. Please close my door on your way out." She waved her good arm to dismiss the teacher.

She covered her face with her hands. Faced with the reality that she was acting very much like the man she hated drained what remained of her resolve this morning. It would be impossible to hide out in her office all day and cry. She walked over to her closet and grabbed her coat and bag. At last she was able to put her finger on what she hated most about Finus. It was the part of herself that she didn't admire. She called the car service to take her home.

❧

Two days passed and he still hadn't called. She sat by her bed and sorted mail while Yolanda cleaned her bedroom. She wanted to be more grateful for the family she had instead of crying for the family that would never exist with Finus.

"Throw that away, too." She pointed to a vase of wilting flowers from Finus.

" 'San?"

She turned towards the bed. The fresh sheet Yolanda was using to make her bed billowed like a sail.

"I'm going to bring the kids over tonight to spend the weekend. Jamal and I have big plans."

Cassandra rolled her eyes up to the ceiling. "No, I'm not up to it." She glanced at her shoulder sling. "And you shouldn't be sleeping with Jamal already. That's not the way to get a man."

She closed her eyes as Yogi argued the case for spending the weekend with the man she'd known for a month. When she glanced over at her sister, she saw a flash of anger in her eyes.

"I don't think I'll take any relationship advice from you. Maybe if you had slept with Finus…"

"That's just an evil thing to say, especially when you're asking me for a favor."

Yolanda pulled the blanket up on the bed. "You're right, I just can't stand the self-righteousness." Yolanda sat down on her freshly made bed. "I can't stand to see you like this. You're just withering away. Cassandra, call Finus and straighten things out or move on with your life."

On Sunday she claimed her shoulder was bothering her too much to leave the house. She moped around the entire day and didn't answer when the bell rang. When the garage door mechanism engaged, she had to get up. She cursed her meddlesome family.

Her mother stood in her kitchen. "Me and the kids brought you a plate."

Cassandra stood in the doorway and glowered.

"Sit down and let me heat up this plate."

"No, I'll do it." Cassandra trudged over to the counter to unwrap her plate.

"Did Yogi do this?"

"Yeah, she fixed your plate before she left with Jamal."

In her haste Yogi hadn't bothered to put the potato salad and sliced tomatoes on a separate plate. The pot licker from the greens ran into the baked chicken. Warmed over in the microwave it would be a mushy mess. Like her life.

Instead of throwing the plate in the trash she warmed it up and pushed the food around her plate while her mother recanted all of the gossip about Finus and Amaria she'd read in the *Black Pages*.

"I'm not trying to be cruel. I just want you to move on."

After her family left, she clicked on the TV and mindlessly searched one hundred and one channels. Hours later she still flipped. At ten p.m. she clicked on the re-airing of Sunday services at the Garden Cathedral. She wished she had the fellowship of a church family to help her through this period of her life. She had decided in August to join the Assembly, but now couldn't.

Cassandra hesitated before she answered the phone. Her heart beat double time.

"Hello, it's me."

"Hello Finus." Her breath caught in her throat.

"I'm calling to apologize. It…it has been brought to my attention that I…well, I was out of line, and for that I apologize."

She held the phone in silence. She could hear a repetitive tap, tap, tap on the other end. It sounded as if he were drumming his fingers on a table, one of his many annoying little quirks.

"I miss you."

He spoke directly to her heart. Her lips parted with an audible smack. "Don't."

"I don't understand what happened between us."

She inhaled.

"Listen." He drew an audible breath.

The phone slipped in her grasp. He had deliberately slowed down the cadence in his voice. It was an old preacher's trick to hold attention. "I know it's a school night. And you're probably getting ready to turn in. Let me call you later in the week, when I return to Chicago for the groundbreaking service."

"Yes, no, oh, I don't know."

"Tell you what. Take a few days to think about it. About you, me, and what I'm sure we can have if you would only give us a chance."

She sighed heavily and grimaced. Half of her heart yearned to tell him how she really felt. The other half seized with hurt. "Okay, goodnight." She held the phone to her chest long after he signed off. Was her agreement only to get him off the phone? Or was she ready to hope that he might change?

Brenda burst into her office first thing Monday morning waving a church bulletin. "Girl, Reverend Gates preached at the Cathedral yesterday and you won't believe this."

Cassandra clutched the sides of her desk. She leaned back and braced herself.

"Here, look at this." Brenda pushed a paper church bulletin under her nose. "He preached a sermon entitled 'Gittin' Ready'. You know the congregation was shocked to see such a country word in our bulletin."

Cassandra looked down at the program.

"Oh, he proudly proclaimed that there was no typo in the program. You know how he gets when he pokes out his chest. He meant to say it like that, 'gittin' ready'. Then he reminded us that his people were from Alabama and he went to college there."

Cassandra held her hand up in gesture to stop. "Brenda, please."

Brenda cruised right through her traffic warning. "I got to tell you this 'cause you probably know him better than most. It seems Rev. Gates has a whoop after all. He just keeps it hidden under all of that prestige and pretentiousness. Girl, he preached until the choir got happy and started singing 'God is Preparing Me.' You know that song."

Cassandra nodded and wondered what or who had so inspired the Reverend Doctor to let Doc preach.

"Then," Brenda continued, "he walked over to the senior choir and testified. How'd he say it?" She paused.

Cassandra cringed.

"Oh yes, he said that God was rearranging him. Then he asked if anyone had ever been to the proving grounds because God was proving and improving him. I thought he was going to break out and sing! I'm telling you, I never thought I'd see that out of him. You know, the invitation was so compelling ten people joined the Assembly. I'll never forget what he said about coming to the Lord unprepared. Him, Mr. Perfect Precision, him who's always so condescending about other people's weakness. He said it was okay to come as you are and that God would prepare you for the work he had laid out for you."

She prayed Brenda was finished.

Brenda flapped her arms up and down. "And he wasn't finished. He went to work on the Assembly members. He told us that we could continue to waste our time talking about him when we needed to be getting ready for what God wanted to do in our own lives. And if we wanted to talk about something, talk about his sermon. He said he was still getting ready because God was still going to bless him. Then he told us that we made a mistake in thinking that he has everything and that God has been dealing with him and getting him ready for the only thing that his money definitely cannot buy. He told us money can buy you some loving, but not real love."

Brenda inhaled swiftly. "Then he waved a finger at us and said, 'Now go run tell dat!'" Brenda shrieked. "Then, poof, he disappeared." The teacher flopped down on Cassandra's office sofa and took several long, deep breaths. "Cat got your tongue, Dr. Brownley? I understand it, because it sure got ours yesterday."

"No, Brenda, I'm thinking I have work to do. Excuse me."

"Cassandra, you've changed."

After dismissing the teacher a stabbing pain shot through her shoulder. She picked up the phone and left a message for Sheila Lawson, the real estate agent at the lake.

Cassandra left school at midday on Friday. She still didn't know how she'd let Sheila convince her to come to this bidder's conference for the Baker house. She had explained to Sheila on Monday that she was prepared to lose her earnest money and walk away. She couldn't buy the house next to Finus. Sheila explained to her that even if she sold the house the next day the difference between the asking price and the value of the property was so great she could resell and make enough profit to buy any other house anywhere she wanted. Sheila pushed realtor's ethics and told her Mrs. Baker was praying that her bid would win out. The other party, who had worked entirely through a series of attorneys, was probably an investor who wouldn't care anything about the neighborhood.

It was really for Jalen and Yasmine that she made this trip. She wanted a nice place for her family to spend the summers. It seemed simple enough. Both bidders had presented their best and final offers. The bids would be opened and the matter would be settled. Then tomorrow she would attend the groundbreaking ceremony for the Gates School and present her resignation letter to Mrs. Herbert.

She tried to focus on the two-hour drive to the lake, but her mind continued to wander to the good times that she had shared with Finus. She changed the radio station to the news and her mind went to the program for the groundbreaking ceremony. For the rest of the drive her brain tortured her. She was a fool for letting the gossip in the *Black Pages* and her experience with Greg destroy their relationship. She prayed Finus would be in a receptive mood tomorrow and they could talk after the groundbreaking service.

Chapter 25

Finus had racked his brain for days trying to figure it out. He'd spent hours over the past week in the garden praying and wrestling with his conclusion. He tried to blame the epilepsy. But that theory had been challenged by all of his friends and family. Even Aunt Jo, who had never met Cassandra, refused to indulge his hypothesis.

"From everything you've said I can't picture her as being that shallow." His aunt's words reverberated in his ear.

"Or did Inez or Lydia say that?"

He was determined to get ready. He realized how much he needed the sweet peace of her presence beside him. She calmed him. She comforted him. She supported him, encouraged him. And he trusted her. He looked out on his mother's now-thriving garden. The climbing rose bush that Cassandra once commented might take over the house had been pruned back into its proper place. Cassandra was right, he needed pruning. Sometimes he was just plain mean, and she wasn't going to let him get away with it.

"And I didn't, either."

"Aw, Mom," he muttered as he closed the garage at his lake house. This was not a time when he wanted to hear his mother's voice. "Now I know it's time to go. I'm talking to myself and hearing voices."

Cassandra arrived early and chatted with Sheila while they waited for the other party. They had a few minutes to talk since the other party had called ahead to say that he was running a little late. The door to the conference room opened and Finus stepped through the threshold.

Cassandra jumped.

"Cassandra!" He spoke first.

"You two know each other?" Sheila Lawson looked around as tension filled the room. "Then this should be easy to resolve."

"No, I don't think so," Cassandra snapped.

He took a few steps into the room and cleared his throat, as he did before he preached. "Ms. Lawson, could you give us a minute alone."

"I don't have anything to say to you." She stood up and walked toward the window, turning her back to Sheila and Finus.

"I'm going to get the paperwork."

She watched the reflection as Sheila backed out of the conference room.

"I'm just as surprised as you are." His rich voice filled the small conference room. "But I'm grateful for this moment."

Her brow furrowed. "Finus, what do you want with the Baker house? You already have a house at the lake. You, you..." She ran out of words.

"I thought I'd buy the Baker house as a wedding gift for my bride. Knowing my future in-laws, I think it would be best," he said glibly.

His words struck her dumb. *Did I hear him say 'wedding gift', 'bride'?* She took a step closer to the office window. *Oh, God, I can't deal with this. Well, he always said when it happened it would be quick. But wasn't it just a few days ago when he wanted me? Oh, God, what have I done?* Her face was hot with tears.

"Cassandra, turn around," he said, his voice closer.

His arms wrapped around her waist and he held her for a moment before turning her around to face him. He held her face gently with his strong hands, then planted a warm, familiar kiss on her forehead. "I want to buy the Baker house for you."

She couldn't move, see, hear, or think.

"Cassandra, I've been praying every day for some time now, for you to be my bride." He kissed her on the forehead again. "Marry me?" His lips pressed against hers and his arms trembled.

The slow shake brought her back from the dark place in her mind where she only heard the words *marry* and *bride*. She wondered if he was having a seizure. "Finus, are you okay?"

"There you are," he said softly. "You scared me. Girl, you're heavy." He shifted her weight off his arms. "Did you hear anything I said?"

She pushed away from him. "No, not after the word wedding. You always said that when it happened for you it would be fast. I just didn't expect it would be so soon after…" Tears flowed down her cheeks.

"Cassandra, I was wrong. It didn't happen like I thought. I always thought I'd fall in love quickly, but I realized that I fell in love gradually. Cassandra, I love you and I just asked you to marry me."

She stood back and locked her knees.

"Oh, no, you aren't going back there again." Finus closed the distance between them and kissed her again. This time she responded with all of the love she had for him.

"Well, excuse me. I didn't think you knew each other that well!" Shelia Lawson stood against the frame of the conference room door.

"Yes, actually," Finus spoke while holding onto her. "Cassandra and I…" He looked at a beaming Cassandra as she nodded her head yes.

He stuck his chest out. "Cassandra's going to be my bride."

"What?" Sheila cried.

Cassandra regained her voice. "It just happened."

"Wow, well, then this shouldn't be hard to resolve."

"Sheila, let us finish this up quickly." The Reverend Doctor Gates took over the conversation.

They all sat down around the conference table. Finus and Cassandra sat next to each other holding hands and giggling as Sheila began to open the bids.

"It really doesn't matter. Whatever those bids say, I'm going to buy that house for my bride. What do I need to sign? Send the remaining paperwork to my attorney."

"Cassandra, that's exactly what he said when he called earlier. You are a very lucky woman, and I hope you'll tell me someday how you two wound up in a bidding war over this house."

Ten minutes later Finus and Cassandra hopped into the Boxster and sped towards his lake house. His phone rang. He turned it off.

"I missed you so much. I can't tell you how miserable I've been. I've been horrible to be around; I've been horrible to you. Fred and Inez are probably at the end of their very long ropes with me. Fred is so displeased with me. He couldn't believe that I let you go. He cheered you for dumping me and then castigated me for getting dumped."

"I didn't dump you. I was selfish. I wanted all of you, so I took a foolish risk and almost lost you."

He reached over and covered her hand with his. "No, my love, you were right. Everyone had it right except me. David laughed at me because after a year of courting, I couldn't come up with the right words to tell you how I felt. If I haven't said it already, Cassandra, I love you. Me, the Reverend Doctor, Finus, and all my other alter egos and I'm so sorry for the ways I've mistreated you."

"All forgiven."

"I have prayed so hard and planned what I would say to you. But when I saw you in that office, I decided not to wait another minute."

"Doc, what are you listening to?" She smiled as heard her own voice on his car stereo.

"Wherever I am, I keep the CD you gave me close. I go to sleep every night listening to you sing my prayer. I prayed God would show me the way to win your heart. That's how I decided to buy you the Baker house."

"You didn't need to find a way to my heart, you were already there."

"And I didn't realize that until I came here Sunday night."

"I heard you disappeared on Sunday." She beamed. "I should have guessed you'd come here."

He laughed. "Then you should have come out here and got me. Yes, this is where we always come. It's my family's secret hideaway. I needed to come here and think after you hung up on me."

They spent the rest of the afternoon making up, making out, and making plans.

Right here is truly where I'm going to be for the rest of my life. Thank you, Jesus! Thank you, Lord!

Hours later the house phone rang. Finus stumbled into the kitchen to answer.

"Hello." He dropped the phone.

"Finus, Finus, are you there?" He heard David Broadnaux's booming voice coming from the floor. He reached down to pick up the receiver.

"Yeah?"

"Doc, are you all right? We've been trying to locate you for hours. We even had the police drive by the lake house. Didn't you get your messages? You got everybody worried sick about you. We've been checking accident reports and ERs for hours. Why haven't you answered? Why did you turn off your phone? It took Fred until just now to find this number."

"David, I'm fine. We weren't thinking. I'm sorry. Tell everyone we're fine. We'll see you all in the morning."

"What's this 'we' stuff? Are you sure you're okay?"

He spied her purse on the kitchen table and grinned. "Yes, fine. Look, I'll fill you all in when we see you in the morning. Tell everyone I'm okay. I'm sorry. Go to bed. We've got a big day tomorrow." As Finus hung up the phone Cassandra walked into the kitchen.

"I heard the phone ring and I realized no one knows we're here."

"Yeah, that was David. They were looking for me, but I assured them all is well."

She wrapped her arms around his waist. "And did you tell them?"

"No. Why'd you let me fall asleep? I woke up and you weren't there. I thought for a minute I had imagined everything."

She smiled and kissed the side of his face. "No, love, this is real, and if it's a dream I don't ever want to wake up." She loosened her hold and took a short step back.

He grinned. "We have a lot more to talk about, Miss Cassandra. What time is it, anyway?" Finus looked over at the stove; eleven twenty-five. "Well, I don't think it would displease God if we prayed now and you slept beside me again tonight."

"Are you sure? I don't ever want to compromise who you are or jeopardize your standing in the church. I was just upstairs, making up the guest room."

"It's not like we haven't done it before." He winked. "Don't worry, I'll behave myself."

After they prayed, they went upstairs to his bedroom. Once they settled, he kissed her goodnight and turned his back. Cassandra rolled over on her side. Her stomach contracted a tiny bit. The first time she got engaged her intended had not turned his back to her in bed.

God did not intend for the honeymoon to begin on the eve of the engagement. She lay there long after she was sure Finus was asleep and prayed she was all he wanted. She didn't want to be just damn good enough. She thought over the events of the day and the ways each of his personas expressed love for her. In the ride from the real estate office Finus drove slowly and kissed her hand at every stop sign. When they went to the yacht club for dinner the Reverend Doctor continually praised the Lord for blessing him with a godly mate. She thought about what she had told her sister about accepting whatever this man offered her if she were lucky enough for him to ask. Then she giggled. Doc had insisted that they sit in the garden after dinner. He had kissed her breathless under the blanket of the stars. *There's no reason to feel insecure.* She prayed another prayer of thanksgiving and focused on the one thing she knew for sure; she loved the Reverend Doctor Finus Gideon 'Doc' Gates with all her heart.

Chapter 26

On a perfect early fall morning, the Reverend Doctor Finus Gideon Gates stood at a makeshift outdoor podium in the garden at the Cathedral. Those who knew could tell he was stalling.

The extra-large white tent set up for the groundbreaking ceremony was overflowing. Assembly members from throughout the district and several national church leaders had come to celebrate the groundbreaking of the Gates School. Finus was making a bigger than necessary 'to do' about who was in attendance. He had already recognized every auxiliary and church administrator present by name. The program was running a little late. Whispers rose among those gathered.

Finus had disappeared last night. The bishop and his family had been frantic to find him. He'd been absent so much in recent months some members were surprised to see him.

When he could stall no longer, he began speaking. "I want to put aside my prepared text and speak this morning about love, sacrifice, and my mother. You all know Corinthians 13." The congregation nodded their agreement while wondering what was going on.

"And where I was puffed up and vain, love was humble and kind. I've been reminded of this lesson my mother tried to teach me. She's been with me in spirit so heavily in the past few months; I feel her presence today. I've spent a lot of time remembering her strength and wisdom. So much so, Bishop Sutton asked me if I were wearing my mourner's robes again, because I've been so sad. I thought I was missing Mother."

He continued speaking of the quiet dignity, strength, and grace of Wilma Gates and the true partnership his parents had shared. "Even after her two-dollar shares of Microsoft grew to over a hundred, she remained a true and humble steward of those blessings that she preserved for the future generations of our family. I know my parents would delight at the prospect of this school. And I'm sure they're in heaven discussing how the school came to be named in her honor instead of Dad's." While the congregation laughed, Cassandra stood in the back, where she thought she was unnoticed, shedding silent tears.

He preached with an uncharacteristic compassion when he spoke of the sacrifice many in the Assembly would make to send their children to the church's private school. "It is the unselfish nature of true love. I've learned a lot about love from your example. Love is not flashy and fast. A real and enduring love is a slow, steady pulse, a constant unwavering care. It's the kind of love that characterizes the families that make up this great Assembly. That is how my mother and father loved each other, and how they loved this church. And how I love you."

His eyes scanned the crowd and he smiled broadly. "Today, along with my family I salute the past and turn towards the future with two beginnings. I asked my Aunt Josephine Gideon to stand with me today and break the ground to honor the past, but Auntie, please allow me to ask others to stand with us today."

"If you have been following your program you'll notice that we skipped over one presentation. Gladys, will you please join me on the podium. Dr. Brownley, I see you trying to escape notice in the back. Please come forward." The aisles cleared and there was considerable rumbling as Cassandra walked up to the dais. "I've spent the better part of a year trying to show you to your proper place. There is a seat for you on the stage."

Finus addressed the two ladies that stood holding hands. "I owe you both a huge debt." Gladys pressed Cassandra's hand and smiled reassuringly at her.

"I'm thankful and grateful to you both." He presented each of them a dozen yellow roses. "Now Gladys, if you will do the honors." He stepped back and placed his arm possessively around Cassandra's waist.

A ripple of whispers whipped through the tent.

"On behalf of the Gates School committee," Gladys began in spite of the rumble that passed through the crowd, "I'm pleased to announce the institution of the Finus Gates and Cassandra Brownley Friendship Fellowship to be awarded annually to two deserving students from the inner city to attend the Gates School."

Cassandra flushed and looked at Finus with happy eyes.

"I will personally fund the endowment and, my dear, if the name of the fellowship doesn't suit you, you may change it at any time," Finus whispered in her ear. She blushed as fresh tears of joy fell from her already swollen eyes.

"Have you told your mother?"

She nodded.

Finus released his hold and stepped back in front of the microphone. He looked back at Cassandra with a wicked little smile, the same smile full of mischief he had flashed the first day they met. "There's one thing that you don't know about me. And that is that I have never been able to keep a secret." He turned back to face the congregation. "I don't see how the Assembly maintains its reputation for secrecy with me as a member." He looked back and winked at her. "Excepting those things a pastor can't tell, you should know I can't hold water and I certainly cannot hold this much longer." He took a breath. "I'm so happy I want to shout from the rooftops. I'm so glad that love gives a chance to reform." He turned to Bishop Sutton and the other assembled church leaders. "If love keeps teaching, maybe one day I'll be fit."

He stepped back and took Cassandra's hand. "Now let me say that the prayers of the righteous availith much, and I'm thankful to all of the righteous people that have prayed for and with me over the past few months. Cassandra…" He squeezed her palm and looked into her glistening eyes. "Thank you, thank you for everything you have done for this project and helping to establish a lasting legacy to my parents. Thank you for showing me that slow, steady pulse that is the greatest kind of love." He turned and faced the congregation. "Let me let you all in on a secret. May I introduce to some and present to many my lady elect, my future wife, my fiancée, Dr. Cassandra Brownley." The tent erupted in applause and Finus stole a quick kiss.

"Now let's break this ground in celebration of the future."

"Wallace, are you pleased with our son's choice?"
"Yes, Wilma. Now can you rest in peace?"

About the Author

Regena Bryant is a training and organizational development specialist, motivational speaker, registered corporate coach, and now a romance writer.

In 2004, she made a pact with her nephew. "If you give me a college degree, I'll write a book." For the next five years she actively worked on crafting *Except on Sunday*, her first novel.

Regena lives in suburban Chicago with her husband, children, and her nephew's college diploma.

Visit her website at <u>www.regenabryant.com</u>.

2011 Mass Market Titles

January

From This Moment
Sean Young
ISBN-13: 978-1-58571-383-7
ISBN-10: 1-58571-383-X
$6.99

Nihon Nights
Trisha/Monica Haddad
ISBN-13: 978-1-58571-382-0
ISBN-10: 1-58571-382-1
$6.99

February

The Davis Years
Nicole Green
ISBN-13: 978-1-58571-390-5
ISBN-10: 1-58571-390-2
$6.99

Allegro
Adora Bennett
ISBN-13: 978-158571-391-2
ISBN-10: 1-58571-391-0
$6.99

March

Lies in Disguise
Bernice Layton
ISBN-13: 978-1-58571-392-9
ISBN-10: 1-58571-392-9
$6.99

Steady
Ruthie Robinson
ISBN-13: 978-1-58571-393-6
ISBN-10: 1-58571-393-7
$6.99

April

The Right Maneuver
LaShell Stratton-Childers
ISBN-13: 978-1-58571-394-3
ISBN-10: 1-58571-394-5
$6.99

Riding the Corporate Ladder
Keith Walker
ISBN-13: 978-1-58571-395-0
ISBN-10: 1-58571-395-3
$6.99

May

Separate Dreams
Joan Early
ISBN-13: 978-1-58571-434-6
ISBN-10: 1-58571-434-8
$6.99

I Take This Woman
Chamein Canton
ISBN-13: 978-1-58571-435-3
ISBN-10: 1-58571-435-6
$6.99

June

Inside Out
Grayson Cole
ISBN-13: 978-1-58571-437-7
ISBN-10: 1-58571-437-2
$6.99

2011 Mass Market Titles (continued)
July

The Other Side of the
  Mountain
Janice Angelique
ISBN-13: 978-1-58571-442-1
ISBN-10: 1-58571-442-9
$6.99

Holding Her Breath
Nicole Green
ISBN-13: 978-1-58571-439-1
ISBN-10: 1-58571-439-9
$6.99

August

The Sea of Aaron
Kymberly Hunt
ISBN-13: 978-1-58571-440-7
ISBN-10: 1-58571-440-2
$6.99

The Finley Sisters' Oath of
  Romance
Keith Thomas Walker
ISBN-13: 978-1-58571-441-4
ISBN-10: 1-58571-441-0
$6.99

September

Except on Sunday
Regena Bryant
ISBN-13: 978-1-58571-443-8
ISBN-10: 1-58571-443-7
$6.99

Light's Out
Ruthie Robinson
ISBN-13: 978-1-58571-445-2
ISBN-10: 1-58571-445-3
$6.99

October

The Heart Knows
Renee Wynn
ISBN-13: 978-1-58571-444-5
ISBN-10: 1-58571-444-5
$6.99

Best Friends; Better Lovers
Celya Bowers
ISBN-13: 978-1-58571-455-1
ISBN-10: 1-58571-455-0
$6.99

November

Caress
Grayson Cole
ISBN-13: 978-1-58571-454-4
ISBN-10: 1-58571-454-2
$6.99

A Love Built to Last
L. S. Childers
ISBN-13: 978-1-58571-448-3
ISBN-10: 1-58571-448-8
$6.99

December

Fractured
Wendy Byrne
ISBN-13: 978-1-58571-449-0
ISBN-10: 1-58571-449-6
$6.99

Everything in Between
Crystal Hubbard
ISBN-13: 978-1-58571-396-7
ISBN-10: 1-58571-396-1
$6.99

Other Genesis Press, Inc. Titles

Other Genesis Press, Inc. Titles (continued)

Other Genesis Press, Inc. Titles (continued)

Other Genesis Press, Inc. Titles (continued)

Other Genesis Press, Inc. Titles (continued)

Other Genesis Press, Inc. Titles (continued)

Path of Thorns	Annetta P. Lee	$9.95
Peace Be Still	Colette Haywood	$12.95
Picture Perfect	Reon Carter	$8.95
Playing for Keeps	Stephanie Salinas	$8.95
Pride & Joi	Gay G. Gunn	$8.95
Promises Made	Bernice Layton	$6.99
Promises of Forever	Celya Bowers	$6.99
Promises to Keep	Alicia Wiggins	$8.95
Quiet Storm	Donna Hill	$10.95
Reckless Surrender	Rochelle Alers	$6.95
Red Polka Dot in a World Full of Plaid	Varian Johnson	$12.95
Red Sky	Renee Alexis	$6.99
Reluctant Captive	Joyce Jackson	$8.95
Rendezvous With Fate	Jeanne Sumerix	$8.95
Revelations	Cheris F. Hodges	$8.95
Reye's Gold	Ruthie Robinson	$6.99
Rivers of the Soul	Leslie Esdaile	$8.95
Rocky Mountain Romance	Kathleen Suzanne	$8.95
Rooms of the Heart	Donna Hill	$8.95
Rough on Rats and Tough on Cats	Chris Parker	$12.95
Save Me	Africa Fine	$6.99
Secret Library Vol. 1	Nina Sheridan	$18.95
Secret Library Vol. 2	Cassandra Colt	$8.95
Secret Thunder	Annetta P. Lee	$9.95
Shades of Brown	Denise Becker	$8.95
Shades of Desire	Monica White	$8.95
Shadows in the Moonlight	Jeanne Sumerix	$8.95
Show Me the Sun	Miriam Shumba	$6.99
Sin	Crystal Rhodes	$8.95
Singing a Song…	Crystal Rhodes	$6.99
Six O'Clock	Katrina Spencer	$6.99
Small Sensations	Crystal V. Rhodes	$6.99
Small Whispers	Annetta P. Lee	$6.99
So Amazing	Sinclair LeBeau	$8.95
Somebody's Someone	Sinclair LeBeau	$8.95
Someone to Love	Alicia Wiggins	$8.95
Song in the Park	Martin Brant	$15.95
Soul Eyes	Wayne L. Wilson	$12.95

Other Genesis Press, Inc. Titles (continued)

Soul to Soul	Donna Hill	$8.95
Southern Comfort	J.M. Jeffries	$8.95
Southern Fried Standards	S.R. Maddox	$6.99
Still the Storm	Sharon Robinson	$8.95
Still Waters Run Deep	Leslie Esdaile	$8.95
Still Waters...	Crystal V. Rhodes	$6.99
Stolen Jewels	Michele Sudler	$6.99
Stolen Memories	Michele Sudler	$6.99
Stories to Excite You	Anna Forrest/Divine	$14.95
Storm	Pamela Leigh Starr	$6.99
Subtle Secrets	Wanda Y. Thomas	$8.95
Suddenly You	Crystal Hubbard	$9.95
Swan	Africa Fine	$6.99
Sweet Repercussions	Kimberley White	$9.95
Sweet Sensations	Gwyneth Bolton	$9.95
Sweet Tomorrows	Kimberly White	$8.95
Taken by You	Dorothy Elizabeth Love	$9.95
Tattooed Tears	T. T. Henderson	$8.95
Tempting Faith	Crystal Hubbard	$6.99
That Which Has Horns	Miriam Shumba	$6.99
The Business of Love	Cheris F. Hodges	$6.99
The Color Line	Lizzette Grayson Carter	$9.95
The Color of Trouble	Dyanne Davis	$8.95
The Disappearance of Allison Jones	Kayla Perrin	$5.95
The Doctor's Wife	Mildred Riley	$6.99
The Fires Within	Beverly Clark	$9.95
The Foursome	Celya Bowers	$6.99
The Honey Dipper's Legacy	Myra Pannell-Allen	$14.95
The Joker's Love Tune	Sidney Rickman	$15.95
The Little Pretender	Barbara Cartland	$10.95
The Love We Had	Natalie Dunbar	$8.95
The Man Who Could Fly	Bob & Milana Beamon	$18.95
The Missing Link	Charlyne Dickerson	$8.95
The Mission	Pamela Leigh Starr	$6.99
The More Things Change	Chamein Canton	$6.99
The Perfect Frame	Beverly Clark	$9.95
The Price of Love	Sinclair LeBeau	$8.95
The Smoking Life	Ilene Barth	$29.95
The Words of the Pitcher	Kei Swanson	$8.95

Other Genesis Press, Inc. Titles (continued)

Things Forbidden	Maryam Diaab	$6.99
This Life Isn't Perfect Holla	Sandra Foy	$6.99
Three Doors Down	Michele Sudler	$6.99
Three Wishes	Seressia Glass	$8.95
Ties That Bind	Kathleen Suzanne	$8.95
Tiger Woods	Libby Hughes	$5.95
Time Is of the Essence	Angie Daniels	$9.95
Timeless Devotion	Bella McFarland	$9.95
Tomorrow's Promise	Leslie Esdaile	$8.95
Truly Inseparable	Wanda Y. Thomas	$8.95
Two Sides to Every Story	Dyanne Davis	$9.95
Unbeweavable	Katrina Spencer	$6.99
Unbreak My Heart	Dar Tomlinson	$8.95
Unclear and Present Danger	Michele Cameron	$6.99
Uncommon Prayer	Kenneth Swanson	$9.95
Unconditional	A.C. Arthur	$9.95
Unconditional Love	Alicia Wiggins	$8.95
Undying Love	Renee Alexis	$6.99
Until Death Do Us Part	Susan Paul	$8.95
Vows of Passion	Bella McFarland	$9.95
Waiting for Mr. Darcy	Chamein Canton	$6.99
Waiting in the Shadows	Michele Sudler	$6.99
Wayward Dreams	Gail McFarland	$6.99
Wedding Gown	Dyanne Davis	$8.95
What's Under Benjamin's Bed	Sandra Schaffer	$8.95
When a Man Loves a Woman	LaConnie Taylor-Jones	$6.99
When Dreams Float	Dorothy Elizabeth Love	$8.95
When I'm With You	LaConnie Taylor-Jones	$6.99
When Lightning Strikes	Michele Cameron	$6.99
Where I Want to Be	Maryam Diaab	$6.99
Whispers in the Night	Dorothy Elizabeth Love	$8.95
Whispers in the Sand	LaFlorya Gauthier	$10.95
Who's That Lady?	Andrea Jackson	$9.95
Wild Ravens	AlTonya Washington	$9.95
Yesterday Is Gone	Beverly Clark	$10.95
Yesterday's Dreams, Tomorrow's Promises	Reon Laudat	$8.95
Your Precious Love	Sinclair LeBeau	$8.95

Order Form

Mail to: Genesis Press, Inc.
P.O. Box 101
Columbus, MS 39703

Name _____
Address _____
City/State _____ Zip _____
Telephone _____

Ship to (if different from above)
Name _____
Address _____
City/State _____ Zip _____
Telephone _____

Credit Card Information
Credit Card # _____
Expiration Date (mm/yy) _____

☐Visa ☐Mastercard
☐AmEx ☐Discover

Qty.	Author	Title	Price	Total

Use this order
form, or call

1-888-INDIGO-1

Total for books _____
Shipping and handling:
$5 first two books,
$1 each additional book
Total S & H _____
Total amount enclosed _____
Mississippi residents add 7% sales tax

Visit www.genesis-press.com for latest releases and excerpts.